MW01139400

A Ponderosa
Romantic Comedy

CAPTAIN
Dreamboat

USA Today Bestselling Author
TAWNA FENSKE

CAPTAIN DREAMBOAT

TAWNA FENSKE

For the volunteers. Whether you're building parks or orphanages or a sticker collection for your kid's teacher, your sacrifice does not go unnoticed. Thank you for making the world a better place.

ABOUT CAPTAIN DREAMBOAT

Jonathan Bracelyn pours his soul into saving the world, and he's still nowhere near cancelling out the sins of dear ol' dad. But when a medical crisis prompts Jon to toss his sister the ultimate lifeline, he's forced to hang up his captain's hat and hit pause on the one thing that makes him…well, *him.*

At least he has Blanka Pavlo's heart-flooding smile to buoy his spirits. A brilliant scientist, she knows things can't last with the do-gooder Bracelyn brother. Not even if he kisses like a dream and boasts biceps as hefty as his heart. Blanka's learned the hard way how lonely life is in the shadow of a saint, so she's giving the hottie hero a wide berth.

Except Jonathan sucks at self-care, so maybe she'll lend a hand (and other tingly parts) to help him out. Soon, they're bonding over awkward bubble baths and a disturbingly homely cat, while struggling to remember it's all temporary. But the harder they brace for goodbye, the louder their hearts declare they're already in too deep.

ALSO IN THE PONDEROSA RESORT ROMANTIC COMEDY SERIES

- Studmuffin Santa
- Chef Sugarlips
- Sergeant Sexypants
- Hottie Lumberjack
- Stiff Suit
- Mancandy Crush (novella)
- Captain Dreamboat
- Snowbound Squeeze (novella)
- Dr. Hot Stuff (coming soon!)

If you dig the Ponderosa Resort books, you might also like my Juniper Ridge Romantic Comedy Series. There's even some crossover with characters featured in both worlds. Check it out here:

- Show Time
- Let It Show (coming March 2021!)
- Show Down (coming soon!)
- Just for Show (coming soon!)

- Show and Tell (coming soon!)
- Show of Hands (coming soon!)

CHAPTER 1

JONATHAN

"*F*or the love of Christ, put that down."

I turn toward James's voice with my arms full of heavy stereo gear, greeting my brother's pained grimace with my cheeriest grin. "You wanted to sing 'Bohemian Rhapsody' on the karaoke machine before we load up?"

James scowls, looking like a cross between a GQ model and a frustrated undertaker in his tuxedo for Bree's wedding. "This is not your job," he says.

My job, at least in my role as James's brother, is to make the stuffy bastard smile. I shift the DJ's controller in my arms and give him an obnoxious wink.

"You're just worried I'll end up with bigger muscles than you," I reply, ignoring big brother's orders to drop the bulky gear. "Then your hot girlfriend will realize you're a pansy and leave you for me."

Lily busts out laughing and hooks an elbow around James's wholly impressive bicep. She's the girlfriend, and so nuts about the guy she wouldn't care if his muscles were grape-sized and covered in feathers.

Her covert ass-squeeze earns a smile from James, and I throw her a mental high-five. Mission accomplished.

"You wish, Sailor Boy." Lily brushes a shock of red hair off her forehead. "Seriously, though, didn't Bree hire like a zillion well-paid college kids to do the wedding cleanup?"

"I'm just helping out the DJ." Okay, this sound board thing is heavy, but I refuse to put it down. "He's got a bad back, so I offered to run this out to his van."

James sighs. "Fine. But then knock it off and go mingle. It's our duty to keep our sister's guests entertained."

My brother's all about duty, but I guess I've got no room to talk. I shift the controller in my arms so I can throw James a mock salute before turning and heading the other way through the reception hall.

I've almost reached the door when my gaze lands on one of Bree's friends. Blanka Pavlo sits at a corner table with her bare legs crossed beneath the floaty hem of a blue sundress that matches her eyes.

Her blond hair is swept into a fancy updo, and I nearly stumble at the sight of her. We met last month at a grade school career day Bree dragged me to, and I haven't stopped thinking about her since. It's the smile, I think. Broad and bright and completely unselfconscious, with an adorable gap between her front teeth.

I don't believe in love at first sight, but I would glue my lips to a hotplate for five seconds of seeing her smile.

She must feel me staring, because she turns and meets my eyes. Her smile falters, and she blinks slowly. Twice, three times, like she's telegraphing secret code. When her gaze shifts again, I realize who's sitting beside her.

Oh.

Lady Isabella Blankenship, aka my brand-new sister. She's white as the half-eaten wedding cake on her plate, and her finishing school posture has gone all wilted daisy.

Blanka cuts her gaze back to me and mouths one word.

Help.

I practically sprint, forgetting the weight of the gear in my arms. When I reach the table, I set down the controller and try to look casual.

"Ladies. Everything okay here?"

Blanka opens her mouth to answer, but Isabella beats her to it.

"I'm great! Everything's fine! I'm having such a lovely time."

There's a faint sheen of sweat on her brow, and her expression's much too cheery to be real.

One look at Blanka tells me it isn't. She studies my sister like she's deciding something, then looks back at me. "Izzy just fainted."

"I most certainly did not!" My sister's forcing that smile for all she's worth. "I merely stumbled, that's all." She tries to throw in a casual hand-flip but ends up clocking Blanka in the chin.

Blanka ducks back and throws me a meaningful look. *See?*

"Oh, my goodness, I'm so sorry." Isabella draws both hands to her mouth, tears glittering in her eyes. "I'm so clumsy sometimes. I apologize."

Blanka puts an arm around my sister's shoulders and rubs her arm. "Not a problem. But I'm worried about you."

"Nonsense, I'm fine."

I survey Isabella's face, doing my best to figure out what's wrong. I'm hardly an expert on her expressions, considering I met her last week. I never knew she existed until a month ago.

"Have you—uh—been enjoying the champagne?" I try.

Isabella stiffens and gives me a prim look. "I don't consume alcohol."

Right. She mentioned that when we met. "Are you still feeling dizzy?"

"I'm not dizzy at all." She smooths down the stiff fabric of her skirt. "Just a touch of jetlag, nothing to worry about."

"I feel ya on the jetlag." And I know damn well it doesn't look like this. The flight from Isabella's homeland in southern Europe is similar to travel times from here to the launch point for rescue missions I captain in the Mediterranean. Jetlag can suck the wind from your sails, but this is different. "You look pretty pale."

I glance at Blanka, whose expression suggests she's not buying the jetlag story, either. Damn, she's beautiful. There's something familiar about her, too. Like maybe we've crossed paths somewhere before we met in Central Oregon. It's on the tip of my brain, but I can't quite touch it.

My sister lurches to her feet. "I need to use the powder room." Bracing herself on the wall, she starts to move.

"I'll join you." Blanka jumps up and offers Isabella a hand.

My sister gives her a feeble smile and waves her off. "I'm fine, really. I won't be gone more than a few minutes."

Blanka bites her lip. "I think it might be best if—"

"Please." Isabella shoots her a pleading look. "I just need a bit of privacy."

Hesitating, Blanka looks at me. I shrug, unsure how much to push.

"All right," Blanka relents. "Just promise you'll come right back here?"

"I swear," Isabella says. "I'll be five minutes, that's all."

"Okay." Blanka watches her move down the hall on shaky legs. Isabella's dark hair is pinned back in a twist, and her skin is pale against the pink and white of her dress.

The second she turns a corner, Blanka's blue eyes swing back to me. "I saw her sitting alone and came to see if she was okay." She's whispering, and I lean close so I don't miss anything. "Something seemed off. She's acting dazed and a little slow."

"I noticed the same thing." And I'm trying *not* to notice how good Blanka smells. Something flowery, maybe lupine. The candy-sweet fragrance reminds me of the Alaska shores where I spent my Coast Guard years.

4

"She keeps saying she doesn't want to be a burden," Blanka continues. "That she doesn't want to ruin Bree's big day."

"That sounds like her. When I picked her up at the airport, she wouldn't stop apologizing for her flight being five minutes late. Wouldn't let me carry her bag and got all red and flustered when I tried to address her as 'your ladyship.'"

"That's her official title?"

"Yeah, but she doesn't want us to use it. Says she doesn't want to cause trouble. That she just wants to blend in."

Blanka frowns. "My father's like that. Had a full-blown heart attack last year without telling a soul."

"Your father," I repeat, wondering why that's pinging bells in my head. "What's his—"

"Can I help with this?" Blanka interrupts, patting the side of the DJ's controller.

Right. I'd forgotten about it. "I just need to run it out to the van. Won't be more than two minutes."

"Let me help." Not waiting for an answer, she hoists up one end like it's a sack of cotton balls.

"Damn, you're strong." I blurt the words before I remember that's not a compliment women usually love, but Blanka just beams.

"I can bench one-eighty-nine," she says. "Come on."

I grab the other end, weirdly turned on by the flex of her forearms and the fact that she truly does not give a fuck what I think. She charges toward the door, pulling me with her as we head out into the sunlit parking lot. A gentle wind ripples off the mountains, smelling of snow and pinesap, and my heart curls into a purring ball as the breeze ruffles the fine blonde hairs around Blanka's ears.

God, her ears. They're like perfect pink seashells, with little pearl studs on the lobes.

It occurs to me I've lost my marbles if I'm turned on by a woman's ears. Maybe I've spent too long at sea.

"I don't want to leave Izzy alone long, so let's hurry," Blanka says as we approach the van emblazoned with the DJ's logo.

"You call her Izzy?"

"She asked me to." Blanka grabs the van's door handle and shoves it open. "What do you call her?"

"Mostly 'hey, you,'" I admit as we shove the equipment into the back of the van and close the door. "She suggested Izzy, but that feels too informal, so—"

"Gotcha." Blanka smiles. "Bracelyn family avoidance."

"Hey."

Okay, she's not wrong. Blanka's a hydrology researcher at the US Geological Survey's satellite lab where Lily works, so I'm betting James's girlfriend has offered an earful about my brother's closed-off nature. We're polar opposites in most ways, but James and I do have that in common.

"Come on." I start to walk briskly to the lodge, but Blanka kicks into a full-on jog. Impressive, considering her strappy heeled sandals. Man, those legs.

We're both breathing heavy by the time we hit the doors, and I wonder if anyone thinks we slipped out for a quickie.

I like that thought way more than I should.

But the instant my gaze lands on Isabella sitting pale-faced in the corner, I throw a glass of ice on my libido. She looks worse than before.

"Damn." Blanka grabs a bottle of fizzy water out of the tub next to the bar and makes a beeline for my sister.

I hurry after her, noticing how Isabella's hands shake as she tries to lift her cake fork. She sees us approaching and forces the corners of her mouth into a smile.

"Hello," she says with forced cheer. "You just missed the bouquet toss. Doesn't Bree look beautiful?"

"Here." Blanka shoves the water into my sister's shaky palm. "How are you feeling?"

"Fantastic." Isabella tries for a wide grin, but the paleness of her face lends it more of a Jack-o-lantern effect than an actual joy. She makes a valiant effort to unscrew the cap on the bottle before giving up. Blanka eases it from her grip and twists the top off.

"Thanks." My sister takes the bottle back. "It's such an honor to be invited to a family event like this. I know you all just met me, but—"

"How many fingers am I holding up?" I shove my hand into the space between us, earning a quirked brow from Blanka.

"Three, of course." Isabella takes a sip of water, then wipes the cold bottle over her forehead.

Blanka drops the arched brow, then turns back to Izzy. "Are you feeling fatigued or confused or queasy or anything?"

She takes another sip of water and straightens in her seat. "Of course," she says. "I'm still getting over jetlag. My ankles are swelling like crazy."

She lifts the hem of her pink and white dress to show the tops of her ankles. Whoa, she's not kidding. Those are some serious cankles.

I stop myself from blurting that aloud and comb my brain for some other test of mental faculties. Some way to figure out what's going on with my sister.

Back in my Coast Guard days, my buddies would hammer each other with absurd questions to figure out who was most lucid after a night at the bar. Mostly we'd end up calling cabs, which may be what my sister needs.

"Why do 'fat chance' and 'slim chance' mean the same thing?" I try again.

Izzy blinks. "I beg your pardon?"

Blanka furrows her brow. "I've wondered the same thing. English is such a bizarre language."

"That's right, you speak seven languages." Not that I memorized every detail about her during her career day presentation.

"Eight," Blanka corrects, glancing back at my sister. "English colloquialisms are a challenge, though."

Isabella's eyes are jumping between Blanka and me, so maybe this is a good thing. A chance to watch how she tracks a conversation, if she's clearheaded enough to participate.

"You mean like buttering someone up?" I offer, sifting through my brain for more idioms. "Or rubbing someone the wrong way?"

Hell. I had to pick two filthy-sounding phrases.

But Blanka doesn't recoil, so she must've missed the perv factor. "Actually, I've researched both of those at length," she says. "The butter one has its origins in ancient India, where devoutly religious citizens would throw butter at statues of their gods to seek favor."

"No kidding?" Damn, I learn something new every day.

"And the rubbing one," she continues as I force myself not to think about rubbing any part of Blanka's body. "That traces back to colonial America where wealthy homeowners would chastise servants for cleaning the floors incorrectly and leaving streaks."

"I had no idea." What I *did* know is that super-smart women are my catnip, which is making it hard to stay focused.

I glance back at Isabella, who's making a valiant effort to follow along. Or to look like someone who's following along.

"That's—fascinating." She offers a weak smile.

Blanka watches her warily, then glances at me. Once again, I swear she uses some sort of telepathy voodoo magic.

Should we keep going? Is this helping?

I nod once. Blanka bites her lip and continues.

"Okay," she says. "Another one that gets me—why is it 'a penny for your thoughts,' but you 'put your two cents in'? What happened to the other penny?"

"That's a damn good question." I rifle around in my brain to find something intelligent to contribute to the conversation. "I do know the 'penny for your thoughts' line traces back to Sir

Thomas More's *Four Last Things* from the early 1500s," I offer, hoping Blanka's at least a little impressed by the fact that I've pulled this historical tidbit out of thin air. "'*In such wise that, not without some note and reproach of such vagrant mind, other folk suddenly say to them, 'A penny for your thought.'*'"

That came out dorkier than I meant it to, and I probably sound like a prep school snob.

But Blanka smiles, and damned if those blue eyes don't send waves of happy heat sloshing through my chest.

*Focu*s.

I glance back at Isabella. She's tracking the conversation in a listless sort of way with glazed eyes. Is it my imagination, or is there an odd yellowish tint around the whites?

She catches me looking at her and takes another sip of water. "Fascinating."

The word comes out forced, and I don't know if she's talking about the seltzer or the conversation. Either way, I'm thinking we should keep going a little longer.

"Ever wondered why fingers have fingertips, but toes don't have toe tips?" I throw out. "But 'tiptoe' is a verb, while 'tipfinger' isn't?"

Laughing, Blanka shakes her head. "Don't get me started. Take the word shit."

"Take it where?"

"No, I mean think of all the meanings—'you ain't shit' is an insult," she says, warming to the topic. "But 'you are not shit' is a reassurance."

"And 'you're the shit,' is a compliment," I add. "That *is* weird." I glance at Izzy, who looks more than a little baked. But her eyes are ping-ponging between us, doing a decent job of following along. Maybe we should keep going.

"Have you ever wondered why it's called 'tuna fish,'" I ask, "but no one ever says 'chicken bird'?"

"Or 'pork pig,'" Blanka says. "That *is* weird."

9

"Porky Pig?" Izzy looks from Blanka to me, eyes glazed. "I'm sorry, I have no idea what we're talking about."

Fuck. This isn't good. We really need a medical opinion. I've got basic first aid training, but that won't get us far. I wish my mother were here. She's a retired nurse, and she'd know what to do.

But even my untrained eye can see my sister's taking a turn for the worse.

Wait. "Is the expression 'turn for the worse' or 'turn for the worst'?" I look from Blanka to Izzy, genuinely unsure.

Probably a good indication I shouldn't be the one assessing anyone's mental health, but Blanka rallies anyway.

"Worse is a comparative word, just like better," she offers. "The expression is 'take a turn for the worse,' though it's far simpler to say 'worsen.'"

"Good point." I glance back at my sister, who's swaying a little in her seat.

Sensing my eyes on her, Izzy bolts to her feet again.

"Excuse me." She starts to sway, and I jump up to catch her before she falls. She overcorrects and tips the other way, but Blanka's there sliding under her arm.

"We've got you," she soothes. "Look, maybe you need to get checked out. A doctor or something—"

"No!" Izzy winces and clutches her low back. "I'm fine. I don't want to make a scene. Please. Just let me go back to my room and rest."

I catch Blanka's eye, and she's thinking the same thing I am. No way in hell we're putting my sister to bed alone. Whatever's going on here is more serious than that.

Blanka breaks eye contact and starts scanning the room. "Bradley Parker is a doctor," she says. "He was at the wedding, right?"

"Right." Thank God one of us is thinking clearly. I survey the crowd, looking for the guy I've played poker with a couple times.

I spot him in a corner chatting with Sean, my famous chef brother. Sean's wife, Amber, catches me staring and gives us a curious look.

"Please." Isabella's voice is faint. "Let's try not to make a scene."

Sean says something to Bradley that makes him laugh, and the two guys do some kind of shoulder slap ritual. The doc is having a good time, and I hate to ruin it.

But I've got a bad feeling about Isabella.

"Wait here." I ease my sister back into the chair and look at Blanka, who nods in silent agreement. "We'll be discreet," I assure her. "I promise. But if he thinks you should go to the hospital, you're going to the hospital."

Isabella grimaces, lips pressed together in a thin line. The fact that she's stopped arguing tells me plenty.

I turn and sprint toward Bradley Parker, mentally chanting a prayer for my sister. A sister I've known a week and already love as fiercely as all my other siblings.

"Hurry," Blanka calls behind me.

I move faster, my body responding by instinct to her command, to the urgency in her voice.

It's the moment I know I'd do anything she asked of me. Anything.

Almost.

CHAPTER 2

BLANKA

"We're less inclined to suspect membranous nephropathy and leaning toward a possible diagnosis of Pauci-immune glomerulonephritis."

I blink a few times, trying to wrap my brain around Dr. Bradley Parker's pronouncement. I've got a master's degree in biology and a PhD in hydrology, and most of that was Greek to me.

I should mention I'm fluent in Greek.

"I'm sorry, could you repeat that?" Jonathan Bracelyn has the same relaxed, open expression he's worn every time I've seen him, but the worry lines notched in his forehead show what's behind the sailor's practiced ease. "In English, maybe."

Bradley puts his hands in his lab coat pockets and nods. "In simple terms, it's an acute, sudden loss of kidney function. And it's not good."

"Clearly." I order myself to breathe, not to think about what could have happened if we'd failed to get Izzy here quickly.

We're standing in a painfully bright hallway between the ER and the ICU, the air around us humming with beeps and buzzes of medical equipment. A harried-looking nurse rushes past on my right, while to my left, tropical fish bob among the bubbles in an oblong tank. I stare at the aquarium, cataloguing the occupants in my head.

Pearl gourami. Corydoras catfish. Zebra danios. The soothing swirl of trivia calms my brain like it always does.

"We can start dialysis immediately," Bradley continues. "But ultimately she's going to need a kidney transplant."

Oh, no.

I close my eyes as dread washes through me. For a second, I'm back in the hospital the day I found out my dad had a heart attack. Two of them, without saying a word to anyone. It was only when the third required surgery that he finally told us.

But Izzy's not my father. I open my eyes again and look at Bradley. "Kidney transplant," I repeat, hoping I've heard wrong. "Aren't waiting lists miles long? I've heard of people waiting five or six years for kidneys."

"Or longer." Bradley's voice is grim, and when I open my eyes, his expression's just as somber. "Sorry, I know this isn't the best news. She asked me to come out and tell you right away. She also wanted me to ask you to please not worry."

The way he says it, he knows that's not going to happen. What an awful thing for the Bracelyns to face on the day of Bree's wedding.

Beside me, Jonathan clears his throat. "She can have one of mine."

We stare at him. Bradley and I both stand watching that handsome face and waiting for the punchline.

There's no punchline. He's dead serious.

"A kidney," Bradley says, just in case there's been a misunderstanding. "You're offering to donate a kidney."

"Right." A slow smile melts the worry on Jonathan's face, and my stomach flips over. "Her birthday's coming up, and I wasn't sure what to get her. Do you guys giftwrap?"

Bradley starts to laugh, thinking it's a joke. But I can see in Jon's eyes that he's not kidding. Not about this.

Bradley tugs at the stethoscope around his neck and shifts back into doctor mode. "It's a little more complicated than that," he says. "You'd have to be a match, not to mention an entire battery of tests. Chest x-ray, blood and urine analysis, electrocardiogram, intravenous pyelogram, renal arteriogram, not to mention all kinds of psychological tests for—"

"I know," Jonathan interrupts. "I went through it when they thought my stepdad might need a kidney."

"You—really?" Bradley blinks, regrouping. "Was that recent?"

"Couple years ago." He shrugs. "I wasn't a match, and he ended up recovering without a transplant. But I added my name to the live donor registry."

I watch the wheels turning in Bradley's head as he shifts from "what the hell?" to "this could happen."

I'm still struggling to catch up, to wrap my brain around the fact that the handsomest man I've ever met just offered an organ to a woman he's known a week. Who does that?

Jonathan Bracelyn, that's who.

"Wow." Bradley looks shaken, too. "Okay, well, we'd obviously have to determine if you're a match for Ms.—for Izzy."

His eye twitches when he says that, like he's not used to calling patients by nicknames. I don't blame him, but I know how Izzy insisted I drop the formalities and treat her like a regular person.

I wonder if Jon can do the same if this kidney thing happens.

"Let's get the ball rolling." Jonathan claps his hands together, and I glimpse the man he must be at the controls of a ship. There's a commanding force behind all that good cheer, and I'm surprised to feel my body responding.

Alpha males aren't my thing, or any guy intent on taking charge. I've got my life under control just fine by myself, thank you.

But Jonathan Bracelyn isn't the chest-thumping, knuckle-dragging sort of alpha. Maybe that's why it's hot.

"What do we need to do?" he asks.

Bradley's still regrouping. "I'll see what I can pull up in the database. I'll need access to your records."

"The procedure would be done in Portland?" I'm not sure how I know this, but probably from endless hours spent browsing the internet to keep my brain busy. "That's where the closest transplant centers are, right?"

"That's right," Bradley says. "Both OHSU and Legacy can handle kidney transplants. Izzy would be in great hands at either facility."

Something flickers behind his doctorly composure, a spark of emotion that's outside the zone of regular compassion for a patient. I know him socially, since he spent several months as Lily's friend with benefits. That's before he broke things off citing desires for a real relationship, something Lily avoided like the plague.

Days later, she fell for James. Life's funny that way.

"Can I go talk to her?" Jonathan asks. "Isabella, I mean. I told my family I'd give them a report. It's the only reason they're not here breathing down your neck."

Bradley shakes his head. "I thought we were going to have to hold your brothers back with pepper spray when we left with her."

"They only stayed because Izzy didn't want to make a fuss," I point out. "Or to ruin Bree's big day with something that might have just been jetlag."

But this definitely isn't jetlag. And we're all reeling with what it means.

"Izzy's resting now," Bradley says. "She agreed to let me brief you on her condition, but she'd prefer to keep it quiet from the rest of the family for the time being. How did she put it? 'I don't want to be—'"

"'—a burden,'" Jonathan finishes, nodding grimly. "Yeah, I've heard it."

I raise my hand, not wanting to interrupt. Jonathan quirks an eyebrow at me. "Yes?"

"I don't mean to intrude, but if Izzy thought a ride to the hospital was too much to accept, do you really think she's going to take one of your kidneys?"

Bradley nods. "She's got a point."

Jonathan shrugs, surprisingly calm for a guy who's just offered a body part to someone he barely knows. "She's my sister. We're family. She needs help, and I may be able to provide that. It's simple."

I look into his green eyes, and there's not a flicker of uncertainty there. To Jonathan Bracelyn, it really is that simple. I know from career day that he's devoted his life to humanitarian work, but I realize now it runs deeper than that. His need to save others, it must come from somewhere.

Part of me wants to know everything. Every bit of history that makes this man who he is.

Part of me—the part intent on avoiding any sort of romantic entanglement—knows I need to keep my distance from this man.

Bradley takes a step back, tugging his stethoscope. "I'll go see what I can pull up from your records, and I'll order a new battery of tests. In the meantime, think it over. Make sure you're certain before we broach the subject with Isabella."

Jonathan nods. "I'm certain."

His voice, his posture—everything about him tells me this is true. Jonathan's not backing down.

This is the same guy who's saved thousands of lives. Literally, *thousands.* He was modest at career day, but Bree cut him off and explained how Jon rescues refugees fleeing dangerous conditions in northern Africa to seek amnesty in Europe. Most don't make it across the rough seas on flimsy rafts more suited for lake paddling than a treacherous ocean. They risk it anyway, knowing death is better than what they're facing back home.

And Jonathan's out there braving those same rough seas, rescuing as many souls as he can. I can't even imagine.

As Bradley walks away, I let my gaze slip back to Jonathan's. He's watching me with steady interest and no hint of fear at all.

"You're going to be a match," I murmur. "Aren't you?"

There's no way he can know that—no way either of us could know. But he nods anyway. "Yeah," he says. "I think so, too. Sometimes you're just sure of things."

A strange electric current ripples up my spine, and I'm not sure we're talking about transplants. There's an intensity in his stare, a heat in those green eyes that has nothing to do with organs.

Not kidneys, anyway.

"How are you doing?" I ask. "This is a lot all at once. Your sister sick, the idea of a major operation."

"I'm great." He leans against the wall beside the aquarium, unknotting his bowtie. "I'm glad you're here. I would never have noticed anything was wrong with Izzy."

He's using her nickname, and I wonder if he knows it. If he's consciously made the shift to less formality.

"I feel horrible for her," I say. "I hope she pulls out."

Jonathan cocks his head to the side. "Pulls out?"

I replay the words in my head, running them through the English-Ukrainian translator in the back of my brain. Colloquial phrases are my weakness, but I'm not sure where I bungled that one.

"Pulls—through?"

He laughs and nods. "It's okay; I knew what you meant."

I drag the toe of my sparkly sandal over a mark on the floor, wishing I'd had time to go home and change. It feels weird to be dressed for a wedding as a guy shuffles past us in a hospital gown dragging an IV pole. The patient offers a weak smile, and I smile back, trying not to stare at the space where his left arm should be. Sympathy surges through me, sharp and painful.

I pull my eyes off the man and look back at Jonathan. "Have you ever noticed how many illness-related colloquial phrases exist in English?"

God, here I go. Sprinkle me with a gram of emotional discomfort and watch me fizz trivia like a shaken seltzer.

But Jon just stares at my mouth, then shakes his head. "Can't say I have."

"There's 'sick as a dog,' for starters," I point out. "What does that even mean? Dogs don't get any sicker than cats or guinea pigs or goats, do they?"

He smiles, eyes still on my mouth. Do I have something in my teeth? I run my tongue across them just in case.

"I've never had a dog or a cat or a guinea pig or a goat," he says. "So I guess I don't know."

"Or 'under the weather,' I continue, aware that I might sound like a crazy person. "I know it's an idiom for feeling sick, but what does it actually mean?"

His green eyes spark with interest, and I wonder if he's going to tell me to go Google it. I probably should instead of yammering at him like this. But he answers before I can move. "I actually know that one," he says. "It's a nautical term. It has to do with how bad weather causes a ship to toss and roll, which results in seasickness."

"Oh. That makes sense." I should write that down in the notebook I keep of English phrases. I've lived half my life in the U.S., but I'm constantly learning something new.

I should stop talking anyway. Jonathan has a lot to process, and maybe he needs space. Maybe he's scared. Or conflicted. Or worried. Or—

"Is it weird that I want to kiss you right now?"

I blink, pretty sure I've heard wrong. "Is that another idiom?"

He laughs and shoves his hands in his tuxedo pockets. "No. I was just standing here thinking how much I want to kiss you," he says. "I don't know, maybe it's the prospect of life-altering surgery or something."

My heart thuds in my ears. I'm not having surgery, but I want to kiss him, too. What's that about? My pulse flutters, libido lunging on the end of its tether like an excited dog.

But my inner science geek grabs the leash and wrestles it to the ground. "Dopamine," I tell him, licking my lips. "It's the brain's pleasure chemical, and it can be triggered by things like danger or the prospect of death."

"Really?" His gaze flicks over my mouth again. "I think I'm getting hits of dopamine every time you turn on the professor talk."

Heat creeps into my cheeks, and I know I should back away. Most guys get turned off when I morph into a human encyclopedia, so I don't understand what's happening here.

"Maybe Autassassinophilia," I hear myself blurt.

"Say what?"

"Autassassinophilia," I repeat, wishing I could make myself shut up. "That's when someone's sexually aroused by a fear of death."

Stop talking, Blanka. Stop talking.

But of course, I don't. "Autassassinophilia can overlap with other fetishes like being turned on by the thought of drowning or choking," I continue, wondering if there's some medical intervention I could get to stitch my lips together.

Jonathan laughs again, but he's not laughing at me. And the heat in his eyes isn't vanishing. If anything, it's blazed from a smolder to a full-on flame. "Maybe I just want to kiss you because I'm insanely attracted to you." His voice is a low rumble I feel deep in my belly. "What's the scientific term for that?"

My palms go clammy, and my heart is doing jumping jacks in my chest. I'm not sure I remember how to breathe.

But I somehow remember the textbook explanation of human

male arousal. "I suppose it depends on whether you're talking about the mental component—the cortical responsiveness to sensory stimulation—or the physical component involving penile sensitivity, neural response to stimuli—"

By some miracle, I stop myself before blathering on about impending orgasm. The urge to slap duct tape over my mouth is overwhelming.

Jonathan has a better idea.

He steps forward, so close our bodies nearly touch. He lifts a hand, and I think he's going to touch my face. I want him to; I want it so badly that I hear myself gasp. My pulse is jumping, and I'm positive he sees my pupils are dilated, how my breath is coming faster, how the textbook definition of arousal is playing out in full-color 3D.

He tucks a strand of hair behind my ear, and I blast through the entire sexual response cycle right there in the hospital hallway.

"Okay. Kiss me," I whisper.

He doesn't need to be asked. He lowers his face to mine, tilting so our mouths connect. I go up on tiptoe to meet him, pressing my lips to his.

Then we're kissing, slow at first, like we're both afraid this might be a joke.

But no one's laughing as his tongue grazes mine. All uncertainty melts away as he pulls me to him, and we dissolve into each other.

I'm the one who deepens the kiss, lacing my fingers into the feathery hair at his nape. There's no awkwardness like there sometimes is with first kisses. Just softness and heat and so much desire I can scarcely keep standing.

Maybe he senses this, because he backs me up against the wall and braces us between the elevator buttons and a portable defibrillator. It's the least erotic spot imaginable, so why does my whole body turn to liquified lust?

Each stroke of his tongue, the glide of our mouths together, feels like we're made to fit together. His hand nestles in the small of my back, and I arch into him like a key sliding into a lock. A soft moan ripples between us, and I'm not sure if it's me or him.

"Blanka," he murmurs, kissing me again. "This is crazy," he breathes. "I want you so m—"

"Okay, I found you in the living donor database and—oh, I'm sorry."

Bradley's voice bursts the hot balloon between us, and Jon and I spring apart. I smooth my dress down with sweaty palms, conscious of the fact that my updo is now updone. Undone? Heat floods my face, but no one's looking at me.

Jon's looking at Bradley, and Bradley's looking at a clipboard in his hand and shaking his head in wonder. When he meets Jonathan's eye, I know. I know what he's going to say.

"You're a match."

Jonathan takes a deep breath. "A match."

"With Isabella. For kidney donation." Bradley looks from Jon to me, then back again. "It's only preliminary, and there are lots of other steps, but we might be able to fast-track this if you're serious. If you're really ready."

Jonathan nods slowly, his eyes glazed and glittery. His hair is spikey where I ran my hands through it, and I wonder what's going through his mind.

When he looks at me, my heart takes off sprinting.

"I'm serious," he says. "And I'm ready."

A shiver rakes down my spine, and I can't tell if it's the good kind or the scary kind.

CHAPTER 3

JONATHAN

"You're going to do great, baby." My mother kisses me on the cheek, and I breathe in the scent of the face lotion she's used for as long as I remember. Sweet cream and something earthy like oak leaves, and I float back to bedtime tuck-ins as a little boy.

"We're proud of you, Sea Dog." My stepdad leans in and ruffles my hair, his childhood nickname for me as soothing as my mother's hug.

Tears glitter at the edges of his eyes, which gets me choked up, too. Chuck's a big guy, six-five and a retired Admiral in the U.S. Coast Guard. It may have been my biological father who took me on a boat the first time, but Chuck's the one who taught me to read the sea.

And to be a good man, which is the better lesson anyway.

"Come on, guys." I pull it together enough to scoff. "You heard the doctor. It's a simple procedure. They do these all the time."

"A mom can still worry about her baby," my mom points out. "It's in the rule book."

"And you've had weeks to worry," I remind her. "You should have it out of your system by now."

"Never." She sits back in the guest chair beside my hospital bed, Chuck's hand cupped around her shoulder. There's moisture glinting in her eyes, though she's trying to hide it. "I might be a nurse, but I'm a mom first. And moms are allowed to be emotional for their babies."

She's not the only teary-eyed female who's been in my room these last few weeks. The moment Bree learned what went down at her reception, she slugged James in the gut for not telling her sooner. Then she herded everyone to the hospital before loading the whole family on a private jet so we could meet the transplant team together. My stubborn, very pregnant sister has refused to leave for her honeymoon until she knows we're on the road to recovery.

Summoned by the power of my thoughts, Bree's voice echoes in the hallway. "He can't have any cupcakes until after the surgery. You heard what the doctor said."

"I know." Mark's voice is a low rumble, overlaying the sound of rustling cardboard. "That's why I'm eating them out here."

My mom smiles and stands up with Chuck right behind her. He starts for the door, his posture military straight even though he retired a month ago. My mother watches him go, hesitating.

"Everything okay, Mom?"

She turns back to me and smooths her expression. "Everything's great, baby. Did I mention we're proud of you?"

"Maybe once or twice."

I know I'm not imagining things. Something's bothering my mom, and it's not the fact that I'm lying on a hospital gurney with a bunch of tubes attached to my body. "Is Chuck's health okay?"

"He's fine, sweetie. Everything's fine."

"So tell me what—"

"You need to rest." She leans down and kisses me on the temple. "Just think about *you* right now. About staying strong and healthy and getting through this operation."

My siblings' voices get louder in the hallway, and my mom's

smile almost reaches her eyes. She squeezes my hand, then turns and walks out the door.

Seconds later, Bree sweeps in with Mark, James, and Sean behind her. Sean's sandy hair is rumpled like he's been running his hands through it, though I suspect it's Amber who did the rumpling. The newlywed vibe is strong with those two.

James is all business, yanking at his tie like he does when he's on edge. "I confirmed with Doctors Prescott and Warren that the success rate with laparoscopic procedures is quite good, and Legacy actually performed the first one ever done in Oregon," he says. "They're the only Oregon transplant center to be a member of the Alliance for Paired Donation and—"

"Give it a rest, Iceman." Bree steps in front of him and bends to give me a hug. Tries to, anyway. She's still not used to the baby bump adding girth to her middle, and we end up doing an awkward one-armed squeeze thing. "We were just in Izzy's room. She says to tell you it's okay if you want to back out. That she understands if you change your mind."

"Got it." I'm not changing my mind. I've told Iz that three thousand times, but what's one more? "Tell her I'm still in."

"That's what we told her," Sean says. "That your crippling empathy wouldn't allow you to back out even if you wanted to."

Bree rolls her eyes. "Leave it to a *guy* to make his nicest trait sound like a disease."

"I thought my nicest trait was my ass." Gotta lighten the mood somehow.

"Yeah, well, the hospital's not doing ass transplants this week," Mark replies. "So thanks for hooking Izzy up with the kidney."

"No sweat," I tell them. "Any of you would do the same."

I don't know for sure that's true, but I think it is. We're spared from discussing it when a nurse rolls in with Izzy in a wheelchair. "I told you, I just need to check with him one last time."

"Ma'am." The nurse looks pained. "You're not supposed to leave your room this close to the procedure."

Izzy's green eyes fill with gratitude, and she turns them from the nurse to me. "I know," she says. "Thank you for filling my last request."

Mark frowns. "Don't say it like that. It's fucking grim."

"Only because you went there." Sean shakes his head. "Shut up and let her talk."

They all shuffle back as the nurse wheels Izzy to my bedside. Her ladyship is pale and drawn but still manages to look regal. "Jon." She takes my hand, the one not hooked up to an IV. "You're sure about this? Because if you have any doubts at all—"

"I'm sure, Iz."

Weeks of blood tests and shared medical appointments have taken us from formality to single syllable monikers. Talk about progress.

Izzy's eyes fill with tears. "I just don't know how I'll ever repay you."

"I think I saw corn nuts in the vending machine," I tell her. "Buy me a pack and we're good."

She sniffs and smiles. "You can't eat anything until afterward. Not even Jell-O. Isn't that barbaric?"

"Barbaric," I agree. "Next thing you know, they'll be harvesting our organs."

That gets a smile from the nurse pushing Izzy's chair. "All right," she says. "We really need to take you back. Say your goodbyes."

"*Not* goodbye," Mark insists. "Don't fucking jinx things."

James sighs. "Can we try not swearing at medical personnel?"

The nurse smiles. "Under the circumstances, I think cursing is okay."

"Damn straight," Sean agrees. "Especially when someone's about to manhandle your siblings' guts."

"That is the clinical term for it." I squeeze Izzy's hand. "Gut manhandling. It says so right on the chart."

For some reason, this makes Bree tear up. She bends down to

hug me again, and again, the bump gets in her way. "You need to get through this fast and come home," she sniffles in my ear. "Someone's gotta keep us laughing."

Home.

The word hits me with a gut-punch of emotion I can't identify. I've spent the last decade jumping from one humanitarian mission to another. Somalia. Guatemala. Post-Katrina New Orleans. Anyplace they need someone with two good hands and the urge to be useful. The boating background helps, though it's my stepdad's lessons about service that drive it home for me.

I'll never forget the pride in Chuck's eyes when I announced I was joining the Coast Guard. Then later, the day I declined my father's request to join his yacht racing team and signed on instead with a tsunami relief organization. I was home on break, and Chuck helped with the paperwork at the kitchen table. Later, I heard the words he murmured to my mother in the kitchen.

"Always knew he'd grow up to do great things in the world."

My heart nearly exploded with pride. Maybe I grew up spending summers with another father, attending fancy prep schools paid for by Cortisones Bracelyn's billions. But Mom and Chuck never let me feel less loved than the kids they had together. They never cared that I had a different last name, a different tangle of DNA wrapped around me like an itchy scarf.

James pulls out his phone and holds it up next to my hospital bed. "They found your replacement. You were worried about leaving your crew high and dry, so I asked them to keep me apprised of the situation."

"Which means one less thing for you to worry about," Bree adds. "Sea-Watch will be okay without you for now."

My heart twists at the mention of the humanitarian group I've volunteered with for the last few years. It's good they found another captain. Good that they'll be able to continue the missions without me.

"You'll be back out there in no time." Sean gives a firm nod. "If that's what you want."

"It is." Of course it is.

My brain flashes to Blanka, to that kiss in the hospital hallway. I push the thought aside and focus on my siblings. On these final moments before I'm wheeled back to surgery.

"I love you." Izzy swipes a hand at her eyes, then leans close to give me a hug. "I'm glad I met you. And I'm so lucky you're my brother."

"Don't mention it." I pat her on the back, conscious of the thinness of her frame and the dull ache in my core. "Go on," I tell her. "Get back to your room before they find you missing and start ripping out someone else's kidney by accident."

"Okay." She sniffs and sits back in the wheelchair. "Thank you."

"Welcome," I tell her. "I love you, too."

The nurse pivots and wheels her away, while the rest of my siblings start shuffling to their feet.

"We should go, too," Bree says. "You're going to do great."

Mark grunts and swipes the back of his hand across his brow. "Fuckin' A."

James slides his phone back in his pocket and clamps a hand around my shoulder. "We're proud of you," he says. "I hope you know that."

"I do." All this sappiness is making my throat hurt. "Just don't go expecting me to give the rest of you any body parts."

Sean laughs and bumps my knuckles with his. "Nah, but I will expect your collection of remote-controlled boats if you die. *What?*" he says when Mark punches him in the shoulder.

Mark's brow furrows. "Not funny."

"It was pretty funny," I say.

Bree sniffs and leans down to give me one more hug. "Hurry and get healed," she says. "This family needs its jester."

Another twist of emotion pinches my throat as I hug my sister back. "Aye-aye, captain."

There's another round of hugging before everyone shuffles out. Bree glances one last time over her shoulder and blows me a kiss. I pretend to catch it, stuffing it in the breast pocket of my hospital gown right above my heart.

I can still feel it as their footsteps fade down the hall.

And then I'm alone. I glance at the clock, wondering how long I have until the doctors come wheel me away.

I look down at my abdomen. Its covered by my hospital gown and a layer of bland bedding, but somewhere underneath it lies my kidney. It's an organ I've rarely given much thought to, and I'm about to say goodbye to it.

"Hey, kidney." I say the words out loud, needing to make the most of these last moments. "We've had a good run together," I continue. "You've done your job, even when I put you through that string of bachelor parties in our twenties."

I'm probably imagining the small twitch in my low back, in the space just to the left of my spine. Until recently, I couldn't have pointed to my kidneys or told anyone what they do. Now I'm having full conversations with mine.

"Anyway," I continue, "I want you to take care of Isabella. She'll give you a really great home. Eats clean, doesn't drink alcohol. She'll be way nicer to you than I've been."

I picture my kidney sitting cross-legged on a barstool, absorbing my words. A pensive little pinto bean.

"Isabella's great," I continue. "Smart and kind and funny." A lump forms in my throat, but I push on. "You'll be really happy with her."

"Who are you talking to?"

I glance up to see Blanka in the doorway. Joy spurts through my veins, and I break into a big, dopey grin.

"I was giving my kidney a pep talk," I explain.

She lifts one eyebrow. "I can come back."

"Nah, come in." I pat the bed beside me. "We'd just about finished our conversation."

She smiles as she steps into the room wearing rolled up jeans and a loose white top with the front tucked behind a wide leather belt. I can't tell if she's wearing makeup, but I don't think so. Maybe just the lip gloss that tastes like peppermint. As I stare at her mouth, that tiny gap between her teeth makes my guts twist in a spot that's nowhere near my kidney.

Settling onto the chair beside my bed, she folds her hands in her lap. "Did your kidney have any parting words?"

"It's a lousy conversationalist, actually. Keeps interrupting, rarely makes eye contact."

"Good thing you're getting rid of it." She smiles again, and I go melty all over again at the sight of that gap. "Oh! Here, I almost forgot."

She fishes into a small leather purse and pulls out a bag of cough drops. "I've been reading a lot about kidney transplants," she says. "Your throat will be sore afterward from the intubation, but coughing can be painful, so—" she shrugs and sets the bag on the bedside table. "I thought this might help."

"Thank you." I'm touched by the gesture. That she'd go out of her way to think of it. "Thanks for being here so much these last few weeks. We've all really appreciated it."

"No problem. I had tons of vacation time, and my boss practically ordered me to take it."

"Your boss has a vested interest in kidneys?"

She shrugs and tucks a loose bit of blond hair behind one ear. "At my last performance review, she pointed out that I had nearly a year's worth of unused PTO. This has been a good use for it."

"I've loved having you here."

"I've loved being able to be here for Izzy and—" she hesitates, meeting my eyes shyly before her gaze skitters away. "And you."

We haven't talked about the kiss. Not once in the whirlwind weeks since Bree's wedding. It's partly that we're never alone, surrounded by a steady flow of friends and family and doctors cycling between my room and Izzy's.

It's partly that I'm a big chicken. That I know damn well I can't start anything with Blanka. My life is on the sea, or on any landmass with a population in need. There's no sense getting attached.

That doesn't mean I'm not thinking about that kiss. I haven't *stopped* thinking about it. As Blanka's gaze drops to my mouth, and her cheeks go pink, I get a feeling I might not be alone.

But we are. For the first time in weeks, just the two of us.

I open my mouth to ask. To find out if she's thinking the same thing I am.

But that isn't the question I blurt.

"You grew up in Ukraine, right?" I ask.

Her hands go rigid on her knees, like she's bracing herself for something. "That's right."

"Your last name—Pavlo. Is it your real name?"

"Of course." Her voice is tight, guarded. "Why?"

"I've been trying to figure it out," I tell her. "For weeks, I thought I knew you from somewhere. Thought you looked familiar, but I couldn't place you. I think I've got it."

She says nothing. Just watches me, waiting. Like she knows what's coming and isn't sure she likes it.

But I have to know. It's been bugging me for weeks. "Your father," I say. "He's Thomas Kushnir Kramer, isn't he?"

She blinks slowly, expression revealing nothing.

Then she closes her eyes and takes a long, deep breath.

CHAPTER 4

BLANKA

*J*onathan mistakes my silence for something else. An uncertainty who Thomas Kushnir Kramer is, though I've spent my whole life hearing that name murmured with the same reverence strangers use for sports heroes and movie stars.

"Thomas Kushnir Kramer," he repeats, and I open my eyes to see him studying me with naked curiosity. "Internationally renowned humanitarian regarded for his work to end human trafficking. Established more than two dozen orphanages around the globe. Two-time winner of the Nobel Peace Prize. Otherwise known as the Male Mother Teresa."

"That's right." I nod sharply, aware that my words are coming out clipped and tight. "He's also a finalist for the Robert F. Kennedy Human Rights Award. They're announcing it soon."

"Your dad is a legend."

"Yes," I agree. "He's built dozens of schools in Ecuador with his bare hands. He brokered an international peace treaty between two warring tribes in the Middle East. He spends his free time digging wells in Kenya."

And he always puts his shopping cart back in the rack instead of leaving it in the parking lot. In summary, my father is the world's most selfless man.

Jonathan's still watching me, puzzlement growing in those green eyes. When he reaches out and slips his hand over mine, I'm too distracted to find it surprising.

Or maybe it's just how natural it feels, Jon's fingers lacing through mine. He's watching me with concern in those deep green eyes. "Do you not get along or something?"

"We get along great," I say brightly. "He's very busy." I clear my throat, hunting for something more meaningful to say. "He and my mother decided I'd have her last name instead of his. It had to do with feminist principles and the importance of honoring the maternal bloodline."

In case there was any doubt about my father's self-sacrifice.

Jon's still watching me, and I look down to see I'm gripping his hand too hard. I try to release his fingers, but he holds on. "Is he not a nice guy?"

"He's an amazing guy," I tell him, throwing a hearty dose of enthusiasm behind the words. "The best in the world. You've read the headlines."

"Then what?" His brow creases. "Was he abusive or—"

"No!" I need to stop this line of questioning fast. "Nothing like that. He just—he's perfect."

"I see." The look on his face tells me he absolutely doesn't.

I don't know why I care to make him understand, but I hear myself trying anyway. "It can be difficult to live in the shadow of someone whose every atom is poured into saving the world."

He nods, but I can't tell from his face how those words strike him. If there are any familiar echoes there. "How do you mean?"

I uncross and re-cross my legs, aware that I'm treading on crackly ice by discussing this with a guy who has more in common with my father than I do. "My father's an incredible human," I say carefully. "Last year when he flew out here to visit, he brought ten thousand dollars in supplies for the local home-less shelter."

I don't add that he spent his entire visit helping them build a new cafeteria from the ground up. That the pierogi I made grew cold on the table as I watched the clock and wondered if he'd notice I'd used my grandma's recipe. I even made the deep-fried straw potatoes and the stuffed cabbage rolls he loves.

I ate leftovers for a week, trying not to notice the bitterness of the cabbage or the fact that my father never joined me for a meal.

"You see him often?" Jon asks.

"As often as I can," I chirp, hating the sound of my own voice. "It's a long way between Oregon and…well, wherever he's working."

Which is wherever the charity work takes him. For years, my mother tried to have a career of her own. A talented painter, she had her own small gallery in Kharkiv when they met.

But it was too hard to maintain while following my father around the globe on his life-saving missions. Eventually, she gave up the gallery.

Then, slowly, year by year, she gave up painting.

I watch Jon's mouth, braced for the next question. Braced to deflect.

Instead, I get distracted by his mouth. For weeks, I haven't stopped thinking about that kiss. How tender he was, how I could swear sparks actually flew when his lips touched mine.

But no, we're talking about fathers. Which means kissing is pretty much the last thing that should be on my mind.

"Your father," I say, struggling to recall what I know about him. "Izzy showed me a photo. You kind of look like him."

Jon's face darkens. It's like yanking the chain on a naked bulb and watching the light vanish. "Yeah. I get that a lot."

"He was very handsome," I offer, struggling to walk backward out of the hornet's nest. "Izzy said she never got to meet him?"

"Right. She was raised by the Grand Duke of Dovlano. She

never even knew about my dad—*our* dad—until recently." He clears his throat, eyes brightening as he sees a way out of our conversational downturn. "I got lucky like that, too. My stepdad, Chuck. He's the one who really raised me."

"I met him in the cafeteria." I picture him in my head, tall and imposing with kind eyes and a big laugh. "Your mother's great, too."

"They taught me everything I know about love and kindness and relationships."

Some of the puzzle pieces begin clicking together, and I think back to how his parents held hands at the lunch table last week. "They're very sweet together."

He laughs and shakes his head. "Sweet is one word for it. They're always hugging and kissing and playing grab-ass when they think no one's looking."

I can't imagine that. My own childhood couldn't be more different if I'd been raised by polar bears on Saturn. "I can't decide if that would be nice or weird."

"It's nice." He strokes my thumb with his, sending goose-bumps rippling up my arms. "Chuck's a great guy. Makes my mother way happier than she was with—than she was before."

He doesn't need to explain. I'm not sure how old he was when his parents split, but the emotion in his eyes reveals wounds that aren't fully healed.

"He's very proud of you," I murmur. "Chuck, I mean. He must have told six people in the cafeteria about your kidney donation."

There's that light in Jon's eyes again, thank God. "He's a total badass," Jon says. "Rescued a whole shipload of sailors from a sinking vessel off the coast of Tampa last year. He earned the Distinguished Service Medal."

Not hard to guess how Jon became a hero in his own right. He does see that, doesn't he?

What he's seeing right now is my mouth, if his gaze is any indication. He's not even pretending not to stare, not bothering to hide the heat in his eyes. I recognize the feral, hungry look from the first time we kissed.

His gaze lifts to mine, and he smiles. "We should probably kiss again."

It's a matter-of-fact statement, like suggesting we watch goat videos on YouTube before they wheel him back for surgery.

"What? Why?"

He grins, unfazed by my awkward reply. Or by the way I just licked my lips, which I'm positive he recognizes as a sign I'm not exactly opposed to the idea. "Yep," he says. "Definitely, we should kiss."

"Kiss," I repeat, like it's an unfamiliar word. Like I'm not sitting here dying to pounce on a man in a hospital gown.

"Consider it like a science experiment."

I laugh, conscious of my fingers still twined through his. Of the fact that an electric current hums at every spot where my skin touches his. I order myself not to smile but fail before the thought fully forms. "This is your idea of sweet talk?"

His shrug makes his pecs flex, and my stomach flips over. "I figure we should test that dopey thing you talked about."

"Dopamine?"

"Yeah, dopamine." His grin tells me he already knew that. "I read something about dopamine helping with recovery rates."

"You're making this up, aren't you?"

"Maybe. Is it working?"

It is. "No."

He winks, well aware I'm lying. "You know, it's possible I won't survive this surgery. It would sure be great to kiss you one last time before I kick the bucket."

"Isn't that emotional blackmail?" I don't care what it is. My body's shifting closer to his, already halfway to tearing off his hospital gown and giving him a sponge bath with my tongue.

God, I'm glad I didn't say that out loud.

"What if I ask nicely?" Jon presses.

He doesn't have to ask. I'm already leaning into him, lips moving to brush his. He lets go of my hand and threads his fingers into my hair, pulling me down.

I slide willingly from my chair, drawing my whole body up against his. There must be some hospital rule about making out on gurneys, but I can't bring myself to care. His bare arms are delicious wrapped around me, his chest warm and solid beneath the thin fabric of his hospital gown.

He deepens the kiss, and I arch closer, forgetting my reservations and everything but how it feels to have his hand sliding up my side, skimming the edge of my bra's underwire. I shift so my breast falls into his palm, making us both groan. As his thumb skims my nipple through my shirt, I try to remember why we shouldn't do this. Why I shouldn't *ever* do this with a guy so equipped to make me lose myself completely.

But I can't seem to focus on anything but how good this feels, how soft his lips are, how I'm pretty sure that's not his IV pole I just grazed with my hip.

"Aaaaand, we're ready to—oh, I'm sorry."

We break apart as a pretty, dark-haired physician sails through the door. It's the second time we've been cockblocked by a doctor and a good indication I should reevaluate my life choices.

The doctor smiles at us and gives a knowing wink. "I see you've got the physical exam covered."

Jonathan laughs, releasing me so I slide boneless back into the chair. "She has excellent bedside manner."

I would die of embarrassment if I didn't feel so damn good. I focus on fixing my hair. "The patient is in perfect health," I manage.

Jonathan folds his hands over his abdomen and grins. "All organs functioning well."

The doctor laughs and jots something on a clipboard. "As

much as I hate to break this up, we're ready for you now. Shall we do this?"

I dare a glance at Jon, not sure what I'll see. His expression is calm, almost serene. There's a flush in his cheeks, a tiny smudge of tinted lip gloss at the corner of his mouth.

But there's something new in his eyes. A tiny flicker of fear.

Or maybe I'm imagining it, because he throws me a wink. Then he nods at the doctor. "Let's do this."

* * *

SEVERAL HOURS LATER, Jonathan comes to.

I know this because I'm keeping watch at his bedside. The Bracelyn siblings are down the hall being briefed by Izzy's doctors on some minor complications. She's fine—*I hope*—but with Jon's parents racing across campus to make it back here, they asked me to fill in so he doesn't wake up alone.

Jon gives a peaceful snore and smiles in his sleep, but his eyelids don't flutter. I busy myself arranging the flowers beside his bed. He's got five vases full, bright and cheery and bursting with color. As I fiddle with a vase of tulips, a memory hits like a club to the sternum.

I'm eight years old, watching my mother pace excitedly by the front door. "It's our tenth wedding anniversary." She smiles and adjusts the string of glassy blue beads at her throat. "I probably shouldn't have splurged on this dress, but we're going out to dinner."

"You look pretty, Mama."

She does look pretty, with her makeup and hair fixed special and an excited flush in her cheeks. "Your father's taking me to Kanapa," she says. "It's where we had our first date."

As if on cue, my dad's car swoops into the driveway. He bounds up the walkway with a spring in his step and a big vase of flowers in his hand.

My mother practically levitates.

"Oh, Tom," she says as he bursts through the door. "Those are lovely."

She reaches out to take the flowers, but my father doesn't notice. Not her outstretched arms or her dress or the fact that I'm hovering behind the dining room table.

"Galyna," he says, planting a perfunctory kiss at her temple as he rushes past with the flowers just out of reach. "Sorry I have to run. That cancer patient we've been raising money for—he just got transferred. I'm on my way to visit the family."

"Oh." My mother blinks and takes a step back. "But our dinner reservation is at seven."

"Dinner?" My father looks puzzled. "Now's not really a good time. If we forge ahead with next week's hunger strike, I should really be scaling back on caloric intake."

My mother is too stunned to reply, but I see the tears in her eyes.

My father does not.

He just rushes past, murmuring something about a trip to India in August.

By the time he leaves, my mother is in their bedroom with the door closed. She's careful to muffle her sobs in a pillow, but I hear them anyway.

I still do, more than twenty years later. It's why I'm single, why I'm determined to stay that way forever. Marriage as I've seen it is about sacrifice. It's giving up your dreams to stand in someone else's shadow, and I'm not willing to do that.

"Oh, good, you're here." Jonathan's mom, Wendy, bustles in, jarring me from the memory.

I paste on a smile as she slips into the seat beside me and glances at her watch. "I can't believe he's done so early," she says. "Is that a good sign or bad?"

"Good, I think." I hope, anyway.

"Any movement?"

I shake my head, wondering if I should leave. There's no need for me now that his mother is here. I start to get up, but Wendy puts a hand on my arm.

"Please stay." The smile she gives me is so much like Jonathan's, and I find myself sinking back into the chair. "You've been such a comfort to him through all this. I know he'd want you here."

"Okay." I glance back at Jon, who's still sleeping soundly. "Is Chuck on his way?"

"He's donating blood." Wendy fiddles with her wedding ring. "The transplant team didn't expect Jon out of surgery for another hour, and Chuck saw a blood drive across campus, so—" she shrugs, pride visible in her eyes. "That's just how these guys are."

These guys. Jonathan and Chuck, she means. "Kindhearted?"

Wendy smiles, gesturing to Jon. "Case in point."

I seize the opportunity she's given me, the chance to study him in sleep. He's so peaceful lying there, lashes fanned against his cheeks and his mouth open just a little. I wish he'd drool or snore. Anything to make my heart stop twerking like a drunk soccer mom at the sight of all that masculine perfection.

"The doctors said it'll be any minute now," I say to Wendy.

Maybe our voices rouse him, or maybe the anesthesia's just wearing off. His lashes flutter and stay open. Green eyes land first on his mother, and he gives a small, wobbly smile.

Then his gaze shifts to mine. In an instant, the smile goes nuclear. "Hey," he croaks, lashes fluttering like it's an effort to hold his eyes open. "I lost count. I think I was on twelve?"

His mother tilts her head to the side. "What were you counting?"

Confusion creases his brow, and I can see he's already lost his train of thought. "Gumdrops?"

"Oh," I say, realization dawning. "They probably had him start counting when they were putting him under?"

Both of them smile at me, and Jonathan reaches for my hand. "You're so smart," he says. "This is why I married you."

"I—what?"

His mother touches my elbow and responds before I have a chance. "Anesthesia's always had a funny effect on you." She smooths his hair back from his forehead, turning her smile on me. "When he got his tonsils out at ten, he came to and immediately looked between his legs."

"What? Why?" I shouldn't be talking with Jon's mother about what's between his legs, but I have to know the story.

"The neighbor's dog got neutered the week before," she explains. "Jon was confused about what sort of surgery he'd had. The more we tried to explain it, the more agitated he got, until we finally let him go ahead and inspect things."

"And then he was happy."

"Yes." She smiles, pleased I'm getting it. "It's sometimes best to just go with what the patient wants."

Jonathan is unfazed by our conversation. He's still holding my hand, still operating under the assumption we're a happily married couple.

"Best day of my life," he says, squeezing my hand. "Our wedding day. So many flowers."

I glance at his mother for guidance.

She takes it all in stride. "You always did love the flowers." She glances at the monitor over his bed, and I remember Jon telling me she used to be a nurse. "Remember how you'd ride your bike through that big field of daisies?"

"Zinnias," he says, slurring the word so it comes out sounding like a German curse word. "I grow them, you know."

"You grow zinnias?" I glance at Wendy, who doesn't bat an eyelash.

"What kind?" she asks.

"Oh, all kinds," he slurs, still holding my hand. "Pink and purple and chartreuse and turkey and soap."

I should probably say something. "That sounds…nice."

Jonathan beams. "They are! I won a blue ribbon for them at the Deschutes County Fair last Febree-rary."

"Congratulations." Never mind that the fair happened in August, and I know for a fact he was here at the hospital for pre-surgical testing. "I'm sure they were beautiful."

"Yeah," he agrees. "Not as beautiful as my wife, though."

The look he gives me is so sincere, so heartfelt, that my stomach plummets into my pelvis. Good God, I've never had anyone look at me like this.

I'm saved from responding when a nurse bustles into the room. "Look who's up and around." She hurries over to check a monitor. "Good morning, sleepyhead. How are you feeling?"

Jonathan grins. "Meretricious."

The nurse frowns, but I've got this. "Meretricious," I repeat. "Whorish, superficially appealing, or pretentious. I looked it up last month when I saw it in a word puzzle."

His mother and the nurse respond with perplexed nods, but Jon just grins. "That's my girl," he says. "Smartest babe around."

Everyone smiles, and I'm not sure if the nurse has a clue she's dealing with a guy who is not playing with a full dick.

Deck.

Good lord, I'm glad I didn't say that out loud. My command of English is better than most native speakers, but being around Jon seems to scramble my brain.

"Your vitals look good," the nurse says, jotting something on a clipboard. "Are you experiencing any pain?"

He shakes his head, still gripping my hand in his. "Nope. No siree. I'm always happy when I've got my wife by my side."

"That's so sweet." The nurse smiles as she makes another note on the clipboard. "How long have you two been married?"

"Oh," I say, wondering if I need to set things straight for the medical record. "He's actually not m—"

"Blanka's been just wonderful for him," says Jon's mom,

flashing me a conspiratorial smile. While she didn't answer the nurse's question, she did answer mine. "Seems like they've been together forever."

"Right," I agree, rubbing the pad of my thumb over Jon's knuckles. "And we're still madly in love."

Was that too much?

Jon flashes a smile, and I decide to run with it. Just because marriage scares the hell out of me in real life doesn't mean I can't play along with the fantasy.

I keep going. "Being married to Jonathan has been a dream come true." My heart's pounding in my ears, and I wonder if I should stop while I'm ahead. "Being with a guy who treats me like I hung the moon and stars and all the constellations—what woman wouldn't want that?"

Me. I've never wanted that. I'm fiercely independent, dammit. I own my own home, I have a fulfilling career, and not once have I wished I had a man around to snuff out my light so his can shine brighter.

Everyone's looking at me—the nurse, Wendy, Jonathan. I clamp my mouth shut and order myself to stop talking.

The nurse turns back to Jonathan. "Any nausea?"

His head lolls as he shakes his head, but he's still grinning. Probably the pain meds, but I like to think I'm helping. "Nope." He turns and looks at me. "You know what's great, though?"

"What's great?" I ask, genuinely curious.

"Your homemade bread." He turns to the nurse with a reverence that's almost holy. "She makes this cinnamon-raisin that's just outstanding. The kids love it for cinnamon toast."

The nurse smiles and adjusts the IV bag. "How old are your children?"

Children? Good lord, we're still going. The nurse stops fiddling with the bag and regards me like I'm really a bread-baking wife and mother instead of an awkward hydrology researcher who makes out with strange men in hospitals.

Okay, just one man. And he's not that strange.

"Um, the kids," I try. "They're—"

"Eloise is four and Sinbad is six," Jonathan says proudly. "Want to see pictures?"

"Of course." The nurse looks to me again, but Jonathan reaches under the covers, then frowns. "Hey. Where are my pants?"

His mother reaches over and readjusts the covers. "We'll find them later," she says. "For now, you should probably rest."

He yawns, then looks at me a little morosely. "I never sleep well without Blanka in bed beside me."

Funny that he remembers my name, but not the fact that we've never shared a bed. Or a life or children or—

"Did you remember to feed the cat?" Jon's eyes are closed, so it takes me a second to realize he's talking to me.

Now we have an imaginary cat? "Um—yes," I assure him. "Yes, I did."

"Good. That's good."

He falls silent, drifting off for good this time.

Or not. His eyes fly wide like he's just remembered where he filed the cure for cancer. "Hey!"

"Hey, what?" I ask.

"I need to know about sex." He looks from the nurse to his mom to me.

No one else answers, so I take the reins again. "Um—" I fumble through my brain for a clinical explanation, conscious how warm his hand feels glued to mine. "When two people care about each other very much...or maybe two strangers meet on Tinder, they—"

"I know how sex works." He laughs, shaking his head. "I just need to know when we can have it."

Heat floods my face, and I can't bring myself to look at Wendy. The nurse, bless her, comes to my rescue.

"Dr. Warren will go over all these details with you when you discuss discharge information." She makes another mark on her clipboard, smiling to herself.

But Jonathan is insistent. "Right, but I really need to know. *Now*, I mean." He tries to pat my knee but ends up thumping the corner of the clipboard. "Our sex life—it's like—out-of-this-world phenomenal."

"Is it now?" The nurse is flat out grinning, not meeting my eyes.

Jon nods, undeterred. "Like cheesecake and sunset sailing and blowjob fantastic all folded into one, fat, juicy jellyroll."

Wendy explodes with laughter, dabbing at her eyes. "That's very poetic, son."

The nurse can't hold back her laughter, either. My face flames as she struggles to keep it together, giving Jon the sternest look she can muster. "The doctor will discuss this with you in detail," she says. "Generally speaking, it's a little quicker for kidney donors than it is for the recipients."

"How long?" Jon's not letting this go, and I can't decide if I'm flattered or mortified.

I also can't help wanting the answer.

"A few weeks," the nurse says at last. "But again, it's up to the doctor to—"

"*Weeks?*" Jon's voice is incredulous. "That's too long. What about oral? Can I at least satisfy my wife in other ways?"

Oh my God.

"Why don't we leave that to the doctor to go over with you?" The nurse throws me a sympathetic smile, then nods at Jonathan's mother. "Your wife might not feel like talking about this in front of her mother-in-law."

"Good point, good point." This time when Jon's eyes flutter shut, they don't reopen right away.

The nurse makes a few more notes, then shuffles out of the room with a comment about the doctor coming by soon.

I'm too embarrassed to look at Wendy, so I'm startled when

her hand closes over mine, "Thank you for playing along," she whispers. "Working as a nurse, I learned it's sometimes best to just go with it. To not upset the patient by correcting them or interjecting too much reality."

"Of course."

Jonathan murmurs something softly in his sleep, and I realize he's out again. I should be relieved. I should get up and find coffee or maybe check on Izzy.

But I'm glued to my seat, frozen inside the make-believe world spinning in the space between us. The marriage. The children. I picture waves of zinnias ruffling in the breeze and taste cinnamon and raisins on the back of my tongue.

I'd never admit this out loud, not to Jon or Wendy or even myself. But right now, with Jon's fingers laced through mine and the rhythmic whoosh of his breath tickling the hairs on my forearms, I am already missing a life I've never had.

A life I never in a million years thought I'd want.

CHAPTER 5

JONATHAN

ive days after surgery, I'm cleared to go home. They could have done it sooner, but the icy mountain pass separating the transplant center from Central Oregon had the docs erring on the side of caution. Besides, Izzy's still here.

I swing by her room on my way out. She's sitting up in bed wearing a pink T-shirt with her dark hair damp and loose around her shoulders. Bree's in a chair beside her with one hand on her baby belly and the other clutching a fistful of playing cards.

"Uno!"

I hesitate in the doorway, not wanting to interrupt any sisterly bonding. Bree spent her whole life as the only Bracelyn daughter, and it's cool how easily she scooched aside to make room for one more.

Izzy shifts in her hospital bed and lays down a card of her own. "I'm so sorry, but please draw four."

Bree just laughs, then seems to sense me behind her. Turning around, she waves me inside with one hand cupped around her belly. "You just missed it. He's been kicking like crazy all morning." She slides her hand to the side, brow furrowing in concentration. "There!"

I hustle over, not wanting to miss my nephew's tap dance performance. Bree grabs my hand and sticks it on a spot just below her ribs. "There it is again. Feel that?"

Whoa. "That's amazing." I drop into the adjacent chair as her belly ripples under my palm.

Izzy smiles and shuffles her cards into a neat pile on her lap. "I still can't believe it. You're incubating an entire person in there."

Bree sucks in a breath as the little dude kicks again. "I can't believe your mom did this seven times," she says to me as she lets go of my hand. "Did your sisters kick like crazy?"

Izzy's face scrunches in confusion and it dawns on me she's not fully up to speed on our twisted family tree. We went from "hi, nice to meet you" to "let's slice you open and yank out an organ," missing a few steps in between.

"My mom remarried after she and Dad split up," I explain for Iz's benefit. "She and my stepdad have six daughters together. And yeah, they kicked like hell. Sometimes I could see elbows or knees moving around in there."

Izzy's eyes widen. "You have *eight* sisters?"

I pretend to count my fingers quickly, then nod to Izzy. "Don't tell anyone, but you're my favorite."

Before Bree can slug me or wiggle away, I grab her in a tight, one-armed hug. "Don't tell anyone," I murmur loud enough for Iz to hear. "But you're my favorite."

Bree swats me anyway as I settle back into my chair. She's careful to aim for the shoulder instead of anywhere near my incisions. "In that case, where's my body part?" she asks. "To keep it all even and stuff."

I consider my options. "Would you prefer tonsils or an appendix? I think I can live without either of those."

"Bladder, please." She winces and puts a hand on her belly again. "He's determined to kick mine into oblivion."

"I'll have it giftwrapped and ready for the next major holiday.

Fall equinox?"

Bree pretends to consider that. "Beyoncé's birthday is September 4. I'll take it then."

"Deal."

I glance at Izzy, who's smiling at our exchange. She's got better color than she did a few days ago, and she told me yesterday the transplant team said she's showing no sign of rejecting the new kidney. "You're feeling okay?"

"I feel amazing." She sets her playing cards on the bedside table and reaches for a glass of water. "Did you know there are studies showing people take on traits of their organ donors?"

"God help us." Bree jerks a thumb at me. "One of him is plenty."

I grab Bree's thumb and pretend to take a bite out of it as I address Izzy. "We promise to let you know if you start growing facial hair."

"Or developing Jon's terrible taste in music," Bree adds, yanking her hand away from me.

Izzy smiles, but there's solemnity in her eyes. "If I get even a tiny sliver of your kindness and generosity, I'll be thrilled."

"I'm just glad you're feeling better." I glance at my watch. "I should get out of here. I'm trying to make it back before lunch."

Izzy frowns. "You're not driving all the way back to the resort, are you?"

"Definitely not," Bree says. "I ordered a car for him. He's not supposed to drive on pain meds—"

"Which I'm done taking," I point out. "Only Tylenol now."

"And he can't fly," Bree continues, ever the overprotective sister. "Because of blood clots. It says right on the printout with all the discharge instructions."

"I'm going to regret giving you a copy of that," I mutter.

"Everybody's got one," she says, lifting her chin a little. "Even Blanka. So don't try getting away with anything."

A ripple of heat moves up my arms at the mention of Blanka's name. She had to go back to Bend for work, and I'm surprised how much I've missed seeing her every day.

"I'll be careful," I assure both sisters. "I'm cutting my ab workouts back to six hours a day, and I'm only shooting heroin on weekdays now."

That earns me another swat from Bree, which I manage to dodge because I'm already out of my chair. I dispense another round of hugs before beelining it down to the parking lot where the town car is waiting.

I know I pretend to be annoyed by Bree's overprotective caution, but honestly, I'm grateful. It's nice to settle into the back of this plush car and breathe deeply in silence. I'd almost forgotten what solitude felt like. For weeks, I've been surrounded by doctors and nurses and family.

So much family.

Which I love, absolutely and completely. But sometimes a guy needs alone time.

Which lasts approximately seven minutes before I feel guilty for ignoring the driver like some rich asshole who's too stuck up to make conversation with the help.

So, I chat with Gary. Turns out he raises pygmy goats on a small farm near Madras, and he's got four grandkids under the age of ten. He hands me his wallet so I can admire pictures.

"That's Adelaide right there," he says, eyes on the road as he taps the first photo in a sleeve. "And the little towhead with the dump truck is Jason."

"They're adorable," I say as I flip to the next picture. "How old is the baby?"

"Six months in October. You got kids?"

"No." I struggle to think of what else to add. "My lifestyle doesn't really lend itself to that."

"Huh." Gary draws his wallet back and grins in the rearview mirror. "Maybe you need a new lifestyle."

I laugh and glance out the window. "Not really an option."

He doesn't ask why, and I don't elaborate. The conversation shifts to farm life and goat rearing. We're an hour out of Portland when my phone rings. Apologizing to Gary, I slip it out of my pocket to see my mother's number.

"Hey, Mom."

"Sweetheart! Are you all checked out at the hospital?"

I shift in my seat, conscious of the tight pinch in my abdomen. The pain has been minimal so far, but my body delivers periodic reminders I've been sliced open and had my guts stirred around. "I'm in the car headed home now."

Home.

Funny how the word slips out. It's been years since I stayed in one place long enough to call anyplace home.

My mom doesn't answer right away, and I wonder if she noticed. "You're not driving, right?"

"Nope," I assure her. "Just sitting here like a big, lazy loser."

My mother snorts. "'Lazy' and 'loser' are literally the last two adjectives in the English language to ever describe my son."

The pride in her voice is better than any combination of opiates I've been dosed with this week. I know at some point I should stop caring this much about making my parents proud.

But one glance in the car's side mirror reminds me I'm still a walking, talking, spitting image of Cort Bracelyn. My desperate quest for respect won't end anytime soon.

I need a subject change. "Did Jessie hear back from the Peace Corps?"

"Yes! It's great news." The oldest of Mom and Chuck's girls is my sister with the thirst for humanitarian work, and my mom is practically vibrating with pride. "I was going to tell you, they asked for letters of reference. When you're feeling up to it, maybe you could put something together for her."

"Of course. I'll do it right away. I can email something tonight."

"Don't rush," she says. "Oh, and Casey asked if you'd come

speak to her leadership class at the high school when you're back on your feet."

"Absolutely." With this many sisters, I'll never run out of ways to earn my keep. I add both things to my mental to-do list, conscious of how stir-crazy I've gotten cooped up in the hospital. "So how are things with you?"

"Good," my mother says. "Wonderful."

There's an odd quiver in her voice. It's a strained note I've noticed several times lately, though she's good at hiding it.

The urge to help slams me with the force of a rogue wave, so I try again. "You know, if you ever want to talk about anything…"

I trail off, waiting for her to insist she's fine. That everything's okay. When the silence drags out, I know something's very wrong. "Mom?"

"It's nothing, sweetie," she says. "It really isn't."

"Then what?"

Another long pause, then a sigh. "It's just—things have been strained with Chuck lately."

She must be kidding. "You two were just in my room yesterday teasing and laughing. He had his arm around you the whole time."

"It's fine, honey. I don't want to burden you with this."

"Mom." I wince as the car hits a bump and a twinge of pain bites at the incision site. "You know you can talk to me about anything. Come on, what's up?"

She sighs. "Ever since he retired, something's just been…off."

"Have you talked to him about it?"

"Of course! We talk all the time."

"What does he say?"

She hesitates. "He says it's nothing." She clears her throat. "So it's nothing."

Her voice tilts up at the end, like she's asking a question. I'm afraid to say the words out loud, but someone needs to. "You're not worried it's another woman, are you? Because Chuck would never—"

"No!" She sucks in a quick breath. "He wouldn't."

There's that question in her voice again. "Of course not," I assure her.

"I swore I'd never stay with another man who cheated."

My father. She's talking about Cort fucking Bracelyn. Not just the fact that he cheated, but that she knew he was a cheater when they met, and she married him anyway.

It's her deepest regret.

"Chuck wouldn't do that," she insists.

"He definitely wouldn't." I'm sure of it. Positive.

"He knows that would be a deal breaker."

"He'd be an idiot to screw around on you," I tell her. "Chuck's no idiot."

"You're right, of course." She gives a stilted little laugh. "I guess I'll keep trying to talk to him."

"Put those kickass communication skills to work," I tell her. "I've always admired what you guys have."

"We'll figure it out." She's projecting a brightness she doesn't feel, and I wrack my brain for some way to help. To make her feel better.

"What if you planned a romantic getaway?" I suggest.

"I've tried." She sighs. "He says he spent his whole Coast Guard career traveling around. He doesn't feel like running off to Hawaii or Tahiti or wherever."

"Maybe something closer," I suggest. "A romantic weekend at Ponderosa Luxury Ranch Resort." I enunciate it the same way the announcer does in all our ads, and my mother laughs.

"Tempting."

"Come on, you know it's beautiful," I point out. "And not that far from you guys."

"Maybe." There's a fresh twinge of hope in her voice, but she moves on quickly. "Enough about me. How are *you* doing? Are you really okay?"

"I'm great," I assure her, not quite ready to let this go. My mother's hurting, and the urge to help is overwhelming. "I could book you one of the honeymoon suites. They just added three of them to the lodge. Jacuzzi, mountain views, champagne—"

"All right, *all right*, I'll bring it up with Chuck." She's laughing in earnest now, and I'm grateful I've given her that. "Did the doctors say anything else about you going back to work?"

"Eight weeks," I mutter, hating how useless I feel. "That's until I can travel again or do physical labor. There are other ways to volunteer, though."

There's a long pause, and I can tell my mom is carefully considering her words. "Do you ever think about settling down? Maybe taking a break from all the humanitarian work and getting married? Starting a family?"

A bright flash of memory lights up a corner of my brain. Flowers and fresh-baked bread, though I have no idea what it means. For some reason my mind injects a picture of Blanka, and it takes me a second to catch my breath.

"Someday," I say carefully, not wanting to get my mother's hopes up. "There's just so much work to do. So many people who need help."

"I'm proud of you, baby," she says. "You know I am. I just want grandbabies someday."

"Someday." That's nice and vague.

"I just want to see you happy."

"I *am* happy." The words sound dull, so I try again. "I have the most fulfilling work on the planet. I've got great friends and obviously an amazing family."

"Obviously." My mom sounds upbeat, though I'm not sure she's buying what I'm selling.

I'm not sure I am.

Static crackles on the line, and I'm saved by the climbing

elevation. "We're getting into a dead zone, so I'm going to lose you. Take care, okay?"

"You, too, sweetie."

I pause, not ready to hang up yet. Mountains march past the car window, craggy and snowcapped and so different from the oceanic landscapes I'm used to. "Say the word, and I'll set you up at the resort," I tell her. "Maybe a romantic dinner at one of these guest chef things Sean's always doing."

"I'll think about it," she says. "Now go rest."

"Will do. I love you."

"I love you, too."

I switch off the phone and lean back against the seats. I know I should pick up my conversation with Gary. It has to be boring driving rich assholes around the way he does.

But I end up getting lost in my own thoughts.

My father had the same limo driver for eight years. Jimmy would drive me from the airport when I visited, and he'd slip me peppermint candies and stories about playing in a jazz band.

Once, I repeated one to my dad. Something about a lost trombone and a guy in the front row with a hearing aid that screeched. My father got the weirdest look on his face.

"Jimmy? Who the fuck is Jimmy?"

At the front of the town car, Gary adjusts the rearview mirror. "You comfortable back there? Need more air conditioning or anything?"

"I'm good, thanks," I tell him. "And thank you for driving. Really, I appreciate it."

"No problem, Mr. Bracelyn."

"Jonathan's fine," I tell him. "Or Jon."

He nods and says nothing, so I let my mind wander again.

By the time Ponderosa Resort rolls into view, I've worked out a plan in my mind. I'll follow the recovery protocol to a tee, maybe see about moving my next checkup a few days earlier. Once I'm cleared to start exercising again, I'll get back into shape and return to the Mediterranean. Sea-Watch still needs me, or maybe there are more opportunities. Hurricane relief in the Bahamas or Puerto Rico. Wherever I can do the most good.

As Gary pulls the car up to the bank of family cabins, a wave of unexpected emotion swirls around my abdomen. Probably a side-effect of all the meds they pumped into me at the hospital, but it gets stronger when I glance at Mark's cabin. There's the tandem bike he bought last month with his wife, Chelsea. And beside that is the little pink bike that belongs to his stepdaughter, Libby. He was so damn proud last month when he took off the training wheels and showed her how to coast down the driveway without them. Who'd have thought my gruff, lumberjack brother would be the ultimate family man?

Unclipping my seatbelt, I ease out of the car. I'm moving around to grab my bag from the back when Gary leaps in front of me. "Please, Mr. Bracelyn," he says. "Let me get your things."

"No need, Gary." And what's with the Mr. Bracelyn thing? "I've only got the one bag."

"Please, sir." He looks pained. "Ms. Bracelyn—um, Mrs. Bracelyn-Dugan," he corrects himself. "She said you're not supposed to lift anything weighing more than ten pounds."

Shit. She's right.

Still, I hesitate. The bag isn't that heavy, and Gary told me earlier he had back surgery last year.

"Sir," he pleads again. "If you don't let me help, Mrs. Bracelyn-Dugan will be angry."

He's got me there. The last thing I want to do is get the poor guy in trouble. "Okay."

I let him take the bag, then trudge ahead feeling like a useless appendage. I pull out the keys and unlock the door, swinging it wide. "You can just throw it on the floor over there."

"I'd rather take it to your room." He looks sheepish. "She asked me to unpack it for you."

For the love of—

"That's fine," I tell him. "Straight down the hall."

I leave the front door open, savoring the feel of crisp autumn air filtering through my living room. The place is stuffy after being closed up for a couple weeks. I rummage in my pocket for tip money, though Bree made it clear she pre-paid everything.

All I've got is a hundred-dollar bill.

I'm hardly hurting for cash, so I hand it over as soon as Gary comes back out. "Thank you," I tell him. "I appreciate the help."

His eyes widen, but he nods and pockets the money. "Thank you, S—Jonathan."

"Thank *you*. It's been a pleasure talking with you, Gary. Say hi to the family."

"Sir." He nods and hustles out the open door, pausing like he's unsure whether to close it.

"Go ahead and leave it," I tell him. "I need the fresh air."

"Of course."

And then he's gone.

My stomach growls, and I realize it's been hours since I ate. Longer than that since I had anything but hospital food. I should reheat one of the gourmet meals Sean stocked in my freezer before I left for the hospital. Or maybe make a sandwich.

Instead, I move to the living room windows and prop those open. It's warm for September, and the fresh air feels nice. From the wide bank of windows at the back of the cabin, I smell the water from the nearby creek, and beyond that, the pond where I used to float toy boats as a kid.

"Here, son. Try this one." The memory of my father's voice drifts back to me, along with the specter of Cort Bracelyn holding a remote-controlled boat the size of a small country. "None of those pansy-ass vessels. You want a real yacht."

"But, Dad." I remember looking down at the little yellow and white sailboat in my hands. A gift from Mom and Chuck, though my father didn't know that. "I like this one, and besides—the pond's small."

"Ah, but the world is large, my boy." My father clapped me on the back, making me drop the yellow sailboat on the muddy bank. The mast snapped in two, but my dad didn't notice. "Glad you're taking after me. A real sailor, just like your old man."

Sailor. Only my father would think of racing a two-million-dollar, 75-foot monohull yacht as *sailing.*

"Brrrrow."

I jerk myself from the memory to see the rattiest cat I've ever laid eyes on just strolling into my living room.

At least I think it's a cat.

Its fur is the dingy hue of muddy pond water, though it might be white under all that filth. A chunk of one ear is missing, and there's a deep, healed scar across one cheek. The cat's stump of a tail ends in a weird knot suggesting an accident of some kind, or maybe a fondness for eating paint chips. As the animal squints at me with one eye closed, I notice a severe underbite that gives it the look of a vampire with one fang.

"Holy shit." I start toward it, but the cat skitters under an end table and hisses. I hold up my hands. "Right, okay. Are you hurt or hungry or—?"

The cat ignores me and starts cleaning itself. He leans up against my end table, plump belly rippling with each tongue stroke. Okay, so he's not starving. But he looks like hell. I step closer to survey him for more damage, but the cat gives a low growl, and I back off.

Wait. What's wrong with its paws? They're like big catchers' mitts, with an extra two or three toes on each one. How many toes do cats have?

"Did you grow up next to a nuclear power plant or something?"

The cat ignores me and keeps grooming. The scar on his face, the ripped ear, the funky tail—these all look like old injuries, and I don't see any fresh blood. His ribs aren't sticking out, and his belly is round and soft-looking.

I tiptoe closer, ready to try again.

The cat growls.

"Food," I decide. "You must need food."

I hurry to the kitchen and locate a can of chicken and a can opener. Cracking it open, I scoop half the contents onto a saucer.

"Here you go." I hustle back into the living room holding out the plate like I'm a waiter in a cat restaurant. "Don't eat too fast or you'll get sick."

I have no idea if that's true, and neither does the cat. He stops cleaning himself and stares at me with deep suspicion.

"It's organic and low sodium," I tell him. "My brother went nuts stocking healthy food for me."

A twinge in my side feels a little like homesickness, though I couldn't say for sure what or who I'm missing. Maybe the kidney.

The cat glares as I set the saucer on the floor and back away. Watching me for a few more seconds, he sniffs the air, then walks over and inspects the plate. When he looks up at me, the eye I thought was missing squints back through a half-slit lid.

"You do have both eyes." I don't know why I keep talking to him like he can understand me. "Can I take a look and see if—"

"Brrrrow!"

He's insistent this time, and while I don't speak cat, I'm guessing that's "stay the fuck away from me." Or from the food, which he's sniffing with mild interest. He looks up and licks his chops but doesn't go for the chicken.

"You're a dark meat guy instead of breast?" I guess. "I hear ya. I'm a leg man myself, so—"

"Hello?"

I look up to see Blanka standing in my still-open doorway. A warm rush floods my system, like sunshine bursting through clouds after a rainstorm. Her hair is swept back in a ponytail, and she's wearing jeans and a pink and green flannel button-down knotted at the waist. There's a hint of pink lace scooped low where the top buttons meet, and I order myself not to stare. I drop my eyes to the dish she's holding, an oblong thing covered with foil. It looks heavy, and I hurry forward to take it from her.

"No, you don't." She pivots away, using her body to shield the pan. "You're not supposed to lift anything, remember?"

"Over ten pounds," I point out as she moves toward my kitchen. "That can't weigh more than a couple."

"You've never had my vareniki. It's very dense."

"I would very much love to have your vareniki." I have no idea what vareniki is, but I definitely want hers. "Is that for me?"

No, dumbass. She brought food to wave under your nose and throw the trash.

I follow her straight to the dining room, curious how she knows the way. This place belonged to my cousin, Brandon, before he moved next door with his reindeer ranching fiancée. It's mostly been a guest cabin since then, but it's mine when I visit.

"I make it with lots of potatoes and mushrooms and onions," Blanka says as I trail after her like a kid following a bright red balloon. "It's very filling. And I already checked the list and confirmed with your doctor that it's okay for you to have it."

"Thank you."

God, she's beautiful. Her shirt looks unbearably soft, and so does everything underneath. There's the pink lace again, peeking out between the buttons as she sets the dish down. I drop my eyes to her feet, admiring bare shins and white canvas flats. Beautiful ankles. Is there anything about her that's not lovely?

"This is very kind of you," I tell her, returning my attention to her face. "Can I ask what vareniki is?"

Blanka peels back the foil and my stomach growls loudly.

"They're a little like pierogi," she says proudly. "Hand-filled dumplings made with unleavened dough wrapped around savory filling."

"Delicious." I'm not sure if I mean her or the dumplings, but both are making my mouth water.

I focus on the dumplings so I don't make an ass of myself. Row upon endless row of lovely, steamed dough, plump with filling. They smell like heaven, and my stomach growls again.

"I brought sour cream to go with them," she says.

"I think I love you."

I'm only half joking, but she laughs like I've said something hilarious. "Where are your plates?"

"I'll get them."

"Sit!" She commands it with such authority that I can't help obeying.

"That cupboard on the end." I point it out, along with the drawer that holds forks. "You're seriously a lifesaver. I'm starving."

"Hmm," she says, nudging the half-empty can of chicken on my counter. "You must be if you're eating this straight from the can."

"What? Oh, that." I glance around for the cat. He's lurking under the end table, eyeing us with deep suspicion. There's a telltale hunk of chicken stuck to one side of his face, so at least I know he's eaten. "The cat needed food, and I didn't have kibble."

"You have a cat?"

I nod toward the bedraggled creature in the corner. "Pretty sure it's a cat. It sort of wandered in."

Blanka stoops down to peer at it. A low rumble echoes under the end table, and it takes me a second to realize it's purring. "It wandered into your house, and you fed it?"

"I thought it might be hungry."

We both stare at the cat, whose plump belly nearly covers its oversized hind feet. He looks like hell, but the thing must weigh twenty pounds.

"Seems pretty well-fed to me," Blanka observes.

"I thought if I bribed him with food, I'd have a better shot at catching him so I can take him to the vet."

Blanka draws her eyes off the cat and studies me for a

moment. I'm not sure what she's thinking, but I can't help feeling judged. I straighten in my chair, wincing at the twinge beneath the surgical site.

"When's the last time you took your pain medicine?" she asks.

Damn. She doesn't miss anything.

"A few hours," I admit. "I'm supposed to take it with food."

My stomach gives a loud growl. From under the end table, the cat growls back.

"Let's get you fed," Blanka says.

She gets to work setting up plates and napkins and forks, quick and confident in her movements. I want to help, but I suspect she'd body-slam me back into the chair if I tried to get up.

"Man, that smells good. Thank you."

"Here you go." She scoops a giant pile of pillowy dumplings onto a plate and hands it to me. "My grandmother used to make these. It's an old family recipe."

"These look amazing."

"They are," she says as she slides into the chair beside me. "Hurry up and eat before you faint or something."

I do what she says, spearing a fat dumpling with the tines of my fork. Steam billows out, along with a dribble of cheese and smooshed potato. I shove the whole thing in my mouth, not caring if I burn my tongue. That's how hungry I am.

"Holy cow." I groan around a mouthful of dumpling. "This is insanely good. Seriously, the best thing I've ever tasted."

She lifts an eyebrow. "You have a brother who's a Michelin starred chef."

"Don't tell him," I say as I spear another— "What did you call these things again?"

I should quit talking with my mouth full, but I can't stop eating. Can't stop looking at Blanka, either, but only one of those things is rude. I think.

"Vareniki." She says it with the faintest hint of an accent, which is sexy as hell. So is the way she eats with gusto, loving the meal as much as I do.

She finishes chewing, then points her fork toward the cat. "Are you planning to keep him?"

I shake my head and stab another dumpling. "I won't be around long enough to have a pet. But I'll get him fixed up and find him a good home."

"Hmm." There's that sound again, and I'll be damned if I know what it means. It's like she's assessing me or something, which might just be the scientist in her. "The cat appears to be polydactyl."

"Poly what—Oh, you mean his paws?" I fork up another bite of dumpling. "I noticed that. He must have two or three extra toes on each foot."

"Also called a Hemingway cat," she says thoughtfully. "Or a Hemingway polydactyl."

"As in Ernest?"

"Yes." She cuts into a particularly plump dumpling, spearing half of it onto the tines of her fork. "They were originally bred to live on ships. The larger paws give them superior balance and hunting abilities."

"No kidding?" I glance back at the cat. "We have something in common. Except I don't eat mice."

I might have if Blanka hadn't shown up with food. God, this is good. I should probably grab a glass of water so I don't choke. But first—

"The cat needs water." I start to stand, but Blanka puts a hand on my shoulder.

"I'll get it." She moves to my kitchen like she owns the place, locating a bowl on her first try at opening cupboards. She fills it from the tap, then returns to the living room and sets it beside the plate. The cat gives her an adoring look before starting to drink.

"I should get him to a vet." I glance at my watch. "I wonder if I could find one that's still open."

Blanka turns back to me and frowns. "You should eat your damn lunch."

Her vehemence surprises me. And turns me on a little, if I'm being honest.

"Yes, ma'am." I throw her a mock salute, then pick up my fork. I'm down to my last three dumplings, but I definitely saw more in that dish. Would it be rude to ask for seconds?

Blanka's quiet a long time, studying the cat. I glance back at him. He's actually kind of cute in a homely way.

"May I share an observation?" Blanka asks suddenly.

I nod and swallow. "About the cat?"

"About *you*."

I reach for the water glass that's magically appeared beside my plate. When did she grab that? I take a big gulp and nod. "Go right ahead."

"You were starving," she says. "You said so yourself. Yet you fed the cat—a stray cat you don't know—before taking care of your own needs."

I set the glass down and shrug. "It's not like I was ready to drop dead or anything."

She rolls her eyes at me. "You just had major surgery. You need to take care of yourself."

I spear the last Vareniki onto my fork and grin. "And I am. Thank you."

She shakes her head and scoops another big helping of dumplings onto my plate. I could kiss her.

Before I can embarrass myself by attempting it, she gets up and disappears down the hall. Moments later, she reappears with a handful of pill bottles that Gary must have stashed in the bathroom.

"I wasn't sure which one you needed, so I brought them all."

"Thank you." I grab what I need and swallow it down with water.

"My observation is about you," she says, picking up where she left off. "You've been on airplanes, of course."

Huh? "Of course," I agree, not sure where this is going.

"There's that line in the announcements—a statement about putting on your own oxygen mask before helping others. You know what I'm talking about?"

"Sure," I say, wary. "It's about putting masks on children."

She gives me a pointed look, blue eyes piercing through me. "It's about taking care of yourself," she says slowly. "Making sure your needs are met so you're able to be useful to other people."

Huh. I never considered that.

"That is my goal in life," I admit.

"To be useful to other people?"

"To be of service," I say. "To help others."

"Why?"

"Why?" It occurs to me that no one's ever asked that. "Because I grew up wealthy," I say slowly. "The privilege I had, I don't take that for granted."

"I see," she says, and I wonder if she does. If she knows that's not the whole story.

"I want to give back," I continue. "It's the right thing to do."

She's watching my face, hands folded on the table. I'm exposed and vulnerable, stripped to a threadbare hospital gown even though I'm in jeans and a sweatshirt.

"It's admirable, what you do," she says at last.

"Thank you."

Blanka gets up and refills my water glass without being asked. "You don't have to do that," I call.

She doesn't respond. Just sits back down and looks at me. "Do you practice self-care?"

"Self-care?" I watch her face, wondering if this is some kind of dirty joke. "What do you mean?"

"Surely you've heard of self-care?" She takes a sip from her own water glass, eyes never leaving my face.

"You're talking about getting manicures or something?"

She sighs and sets down her glass. "That's an oversimplification of the term, but yes. That would be one form of self-care. It's really anything that gives you pleasure."

I can think of several things off the top of my head that would give me pleasure, but I'm not saying any of them aloud.

Blanka hears me anyway. "Yes, even *that*. Sex can be a form of self-care. Or masturbation."

Holy shit. Are we having this conversation?

"Don't look so scandalized," she says. "These are basic, biological functions. I'm a scientist."

"A hydrology researcher," I point out like an idiot. "I wasn't braced for you to go from manicures to jackin' the beanstalk."

"I'll consider more foreplay next time." She spears another dumpling. "Sexual gratification aside, I'm talking about other things. Napping. Meditation. Reading a good book. Taking a bath. Going for a walk. There are all kinds of things you can do to treat yourself. To practice self-care and make sure your body and mind are rested and restored."

"Huh." Gotta admit, she has a point. "What if helping others is what revs me up?"

"I'm not talking about revving you up," she says. "I'm talking about winding down. You need both." She stares at me for a long, long time. "Don't you ever do something just for *you*?"

My brain flashes on our first kiss. How selfish it was to pull her to me, to kiss her without any thought to what Isabella was going through or what other patients might think.

To kiss her because I desperately, urgently wanted to.

Blanka watches my face, blue eyes fixed on mine. I swear she's looking right through me, seeing the pictures flashing in my brain like naughty centerfolds.

There's a flicker of heat in her eyes, and I realize she's

thinking the same thing. About the kiss in the hallway. Or the second one in my hospital room. I'm not imagining this, right?

She licks her lips, eyes still fixed on me. "A bath," she says.

I blink. "What?"

"A bath." She looks deep into my eyes. "That's self-care. It sounds nice, doesn't it?"

I stare at her, afraid to say the wrong thing. "It does." I hesitate. "Maybe after I take the cat to the vet and finish a reference letter for my sister and—"

"No, now." She smiles again, eyes still filled with heat. "If I join you, will you agree to take a bath? To relax."

There is nothing at all relaxing about the thought of being naked in a tub with Blanka. My body responds to the huskiness of her voice, the suggestion in her eyes. If there was any question about kidney donation affecting a guy's ability to rise to the occasion, my libido is shouting a firm answer.

"Yes," I manage to croak. "A bath sounds good." I clear my throat, hoping I haven't heard wrong. "Together."

"Perfect." She stands up and gives me a smile that's full of promise. "Let's do it."

She reaches between her breasts and unfastens a button. Then another. And another. And another.

My jaw drops as she parts the flannel shirt to reveal a fitted pink spaghetti-strap top with a lacy fringe around the neckline. I don't know if it's lingerie or just a tank top, but it is now my favorite garment in the history of clothing.

I'm still gawking like a moron, still sitting there with my mouth hanging open when she shrugs the button-down off her shoulders and hands it to me.

"I'll start the water."

Then she turns and walks down the hall.

CHAPTER 6

BLANKA

I can't believe I did that.

The striptease, the suggestive offer...none of that is my standard operating procedure.

Neither is standing fully clothed in ankle-deep water with my bare toes inches from those of a shirtless ship captain.

Jonathan watches me through rising steam with a look one could most accurately describe as *befuddled.*

Then he smiles, and my stomach rolls in a big, sloshy somersault. "This is quite possibly the weirdest thing I've ever done."

"Do you need help rolling your jeans a little higher?"

He quirks one eyebrow. "That will make it less weird?"

"No, but it'll make your jeans less damp."

He doesn't have a response for that, but his bemused look leaves me smiling, too.

Or maybe that's the sight of all that bare skin. Jon had his shirt off before he reached the bathroom, and I certainly wasn't going to suggest he put it back on. To insist that my self-care bath idea was purely innocent.

Mostly.

I let my eyes travel the broad expanse of his chest, the solid ridges of his abdomen. Four small incisions mark the spots where the transplant team inserted laparoscopic tools and cameras. There's a bigger scar below that where they extracted the kidney. That's another thing I never knew; that donors have the kidney extracted from the front. I've learned a lot these past few weeks.

I bite my lip and meet his eyes. "Does it hurt?"

He looks down like he's seeing the incisions for the first time. Like he's forgotten they're there, or never noticed he has the world's most perfect torso.

With a shrug, he meets my eyes again. "Not really. It mostly feels like I did a thousand crunches at the gym."

His abs are a testament to that, but I bite my tongue. "The paperwork said there'd be a lot of swelling. I'm not seeing it."

"Oh, there's plenty of swelling." He laughs and shakes his head. "Okay, I didn't mean that to sound dirty."

I hadn't heard it like that, which is surprising since my brain has been steeping in sex from the moment I walked through his door. "I don't see swelling at the incision sites," I point out, determined to keep this as clinical as possible. "I don't even see stitches."

"The stitches are mostly internal. They used some kind of surgical glue on the outside. I get to peel that off ten days post-op."

I want to feel it. Want to run my fingers over those smooth ridges of abdominal muscle. Never in my life have I had a greater urge to touch another human. A male human. Very, *very* male, and quite possibly *not* human.

How can anyone look this good with his shirt off?

"Are you grossed out?" he asks.

"What?"

"By the scars. It's a little weird seeing them."

"Oh. No. Not at all." *Jesus.* "You look good to me." I shove my hands in the pockets of my jeans to keep from reaching for him.

Jon grins like he knows what I'm thinking. Then he leans down to adjust the taps, adding more heat to our bathtub mix. His face is turned away, but I see him wince.

"Let me get it," I tell him.

"I'm okay." He straightens and looks around his bathroom. "So this is a self-care bubble bath."

"Maybe not a normal one," I admit. "The paperwork says you're not supposed to submerge the incisions. I thought we could just sit on the edge and soak our feet."

He laughs and scratches the back of his neck, making his abdominal muscles ripple. I curl my fingers deeper into my pockets and order myself to keep breathing.

"Blame Bree," he says. "She's the one who picked out the vintage clawfoot tub with no edges for sitting."

"Maybe I could find a bench or something." I glance around the bathroom, but there's nothing the right height. "Sorry, this isn't how I pictured it when I suggested this."

Slowly, he reaches out and catches my left wrist in his palm. Then the other, peeling my hands out of my pockets. Lacing his fingers through mine, he smiles into my eyes. "This is perfect. I'm more relaxed already."

"Really?"

"Really."

He might be humoring me. I'm not sure. So much nuance can be lost in translation.

The water's still rising, climbing the backs of our calves. It feels scandalous to stand here in my jeans and this thin little cami top. At least the light is muted, flickering with a half-dozen little battery-powered candles I found on a shelf outside the bathroom. Bree's touch, I'm sure.

The crackling fire is all mine, procured from a YouTube video playing on my iPad beside the sink. I tried to think of everything.

"It's all about ambiance," I explain. "To help get you into a positive frame of mind."

He stares at the scoop-front of my cami top and nods. "Nailed it."

"Thank you."

Lifting his gaze to mine, he gives a sheepish grin. "I'm probably not supposed to address my compliments directly to your breasts."

"I think that ceased being true when I took off my top to coax you in here."

"Good point." He grins. "I'd climb onto the roof and follow you off the edge for the opportunity to admire your cleavage for five seconds."

That is possibly the best compliment I've ever received. Also, not medically advisable for a guy recovering from major surgery.

"It's just a camisole." I tug at the lacy neckline, still shocked I did that. "I wear them under button-up shirts for modesty."

He laughs and lets his eyes linger over my breasts. "If this is modesty, I'd love to see your version of immodest."

I'd love for him to see it, too. I'd love to rip off my top and press his face into my breasts and—

"Oh, I almost forgot." My cheeks are hot as I stretch out to grab two champagne flutes off the counter. I found them in the hallway minibar, along with an unopened pint of half-and-half. "Sorry it's not champagne," I tell him. "It says on page three you're not supposed to have alcohol right away."

He smiles and takes a sip of half-and-half. "Did you really read all the discharge instructions?"

"Didn't you?"

"I skimmed."

I sip my own glass of half-and-half and wonder if I should have gone with tap water. I thought this would be more decadent, but it might be adding to the weird element. "I think the alcohol restriction is more about contraindications for pain medicine."

"Which I'm pretty much done with," he says. "I've been doing fine with Tylenol since day three."

"Impressive." I'm looking at his abs again, which are even more impressive. I order myself to meet his eyes, then I wish I hadn't. The dark green irises are filled with heat, and my mouth goes dry again.

I take another sip from my glass.

"We forgot to toast." He holds his glass up, and I stop drinking to clink my glass with his. "To dish soap bubble baths."

I laugh and swish my toes through the bubbles. "It's all I could find. Hopefully, this won't dry out our skin."

"Nah, it's moisturizing Palmolive," he says. "The smell of it is giving me the urge to scrub pots."

"Let's not act on that urge."

It sounds flirty when it comes out of my mouth, and I wonder if he hears that. He gives a knowing smile but doesn't comment. How many of my urges are written all over my face? Does he know I've thought about undressing him at least twelve times since we set foot in this bathroom?

Conscious of my flaming face, I lean down to turn off the water.

"Mood music." Jon's voice echoes overhead, and I straighten to see him setting his champagne glass on a shelf beside the shampoo bottles. "We need mood music."

"Oh. I should have thought of that."

"I've got it." He slides his phone from the back pocket of his jeans and taps the screen a couple times. "Maybe Pandora has a station for fully-clothed bubble baths?"

Before he can scroll, the phone blasts the chorus of a Jimmy Buffet song. I'm not sure of the title, but Jimmy is enthusiastic about getting drunk and screwing.

"Crap." Jon taps hard on the screen to halt Jimmy's plans. "Sorry about that. I'm kind of a Parrothead. Bree teases me about it all the time."

"Parrothead?" I thumb through my mental dictionary and come up empty. "Is that like a pothead?"

He laughs. "Nah, that's what they call Jimmy Buffet fans. My father took me to a concert when I was ten. We had front row VIP tickets and a clear view of the remote-controlled shark flying over the crowd."

It takes me a second to realize he's talking about his biological father, not the kindhearted stepdad I met at the hospital.

"Cort Bracelyn," I say, pulling the name from the musty trunk in my memory. "Were you close before he passed?"

Jon doesn't look up from his phone. "No."

I recall our conversation at the hospital. The darkening in his eyes when I pointed out how much he resembled that photo of his father. I open my mouth to change the subject, but Jon speaks first.

"I've been compared to him my whole life." He looks up and speaks the words like a confession, like admitting he kicks babies or snorts baking soda. "Eyes, hair, cheekbones—even the damn chin. I'm his spitting image, so everyone assumes we're alike."

"And you're not?"

"I sure as hell hope not." He shakes his head, and I try to recall what I've heard about his father.

"He was an entrepreneur." I think that's the right way to say "richer than God."

"He was a jerk." Jon's jaw is tight, his words clipped. "He lied and cheated his way through life. Death, too," he adds, though I'm not sure what that means. "I've made it my mission to be his opposite, if that makes sense."

It does, I think. "I admire my mother more than anyone in the world, but I try to be her opposite, too."

"How do you mean?"

I shrug, part of me wishing I'd never brought this up. "She gave up everything to marry my father. Left her hometown to follow him around the globe. Gave up her career as an artist."

"Your mom's an artist?"

"Was." I hesitate, then slip my phone out of my pocket and toggle to the folder of images. "These are some of her paintings."

I hand the phone over, then watch Jon's face as he scrolls. "Wow. These are incredible. She's not painting anymore?"

"Not really." Not as the owner of her own gallery anymore. Not for anything other than charity auctions to benefit my father's causes.

"She's incredibly talented." Jon scrolls to the end, then holds the phone out. "Thanks for sharing these."

"Of course." I take the phone back and slip it into my pocket, feeling the warmth of his hand. "Anyway, we were talking about your father. About how you try not to be like him."

His eyes darken again, and I wonder if I shouldn't have circled back. It's obviously a sensitive subject. "I do my best not to be a dick," he says. "That's pretty much it. Treating women with respect, making a positive impact on the world. That sort of thing."

"From where I stand, you're doing a great job."

He grins and sloshes a hunk of bubbles up my bare shin. "You're standing in a tub of Palmolive, so I'll take that with a grain of salt."

I consider sharing the origins of that phrase, which I researched just last month. It traces back to Pliny the Elder and salt as an antidote to poison, but I decide to hold my tongue. There's a good chance Jon thinks I'm nuts already, so no sense adding to that.

Instead, I lift my glass of half-and-half. "Cheers to your mother and stepfather," I say. "You said they're the ones who raised you?"

"Yeah." A troubled look passes over his face, but it's gone in an instant. "Now *that's* a kickass marriage. Kinda the opposite of how my father spent his life."

"I enjoyed watching them together." There's a twist of envy in my voice, and I wonder if he notices. "At the hospital. They seem so in tune with one another."

I have no plans to marry, ever. But if I did, I'd want a marriage like Wendy and Chuck have. One filled with kindness and love and mutual respect.

Why the hell am I thinking about marriage?

"We should all be so lucky." Jon clinks his glass against mine. "Cheers to Chuck and Wendy." He takes a sip, and when he lowers the glass, there's the tiniest hint of milk mustache on his upper lip. I want to lick it. I want to cover his mouth with mine and press my body up against—

"Music," he says. "I almost forgot." He sets the glass down. "Hey, Alexa—play sexy music."

Sexy music?

I must look surprised, because Jon shrugs and gives a funny little half-smile. "Seems like that would give us a mellow, self-care sorta vibe."

A rounded orb on the counter flickers blue light, then follows with a female voice. "Here's a playlist you might like," Alexa says. "Playing X-rated R&B jams from Amazon music."

Before we can react, bass rumbles from the speakers. There's some electronic thumping, then a growly voice.

I want to fuck you in the—

"Alexa, stop!" Jon's laughing, but he looks horrified. "Not the mood I had in mind."

I'm laughing, too, since it seems better than the alternative. Better than pointing out the X-rated things I'd like to do with the man sharing this bathtub with me.

I need to get a grip.

"Um, maybe suggest love songs?" I offer. "That should be more mellow."

"Good thinking." Jon directs his voice toward the device. "Alexa, play romantic music."

Another flicker of light. "Playing 'Under the Covers Country,'" she announces.

There's a twangy flare of steel guitar, followed by some banjo. Then a male voice begins crooning about his pickup truck.

Jon looks at me. "Maybe no music."

"Silence is good."

I half expect Alexa to deliver Simon and Garfunkel's "Sound of Silence," but no. Jon gives the command and Alexa's work is done.

He's smiling again, too. All good things.

"Speaking of fathers," he says, "how's yours doing?"

And just like that, I'm not smiling. Oh, I'm faking it well enough. But inside, I'm wishing we could talk about anything else. Mass shootings. Genocide. Various forms of torture.

"He's doing well, thanks," I say. "He's giving a talk at Columbia University next month."

"I know. I saw it in his newsletter."

Which just made this weirder. I take another sip of creamer.

"Hey," he says softly. "Look at me."

I do it. Look right into his eyes instead of at his abs. It should make this easier, but it doesn't. Lord, the man has lovely eyes.

"I'm getting the sense that you like talking about your father almost as much as I like talking about mine," he says. "True?"

"True." I clutch my glass, wondering how much he'll push.

"So what do you say we start fresh with something more self-care oriented."

"Deal," I say as relief floods through me. "Like what?"

He thinks about it a moment. "Is it a bad sign that I can't think of anything?"

Probably, but I hold onto that thought. "How about that song— From the *Sound of Music*? She has all kinds of suggestions in there."

Jonathan frowns, and I wonder if maybe he's never seen it.

"Raindrops on roses…" I prompt.

"Ah," he says, light dawning. "And whiskers on kittens."

Summoned by Jon's words, the feline from the living room lumbers into the bathroom and looks around. The cat stares at us for a few beats like he's never seen two fully clothed humans standing in a sudsy bathtub.

He's never seen a bathtub, judging from the filth-matted fur. He puts his oversized lobster claw paws on the edge and peers at the water.

"Hey, kitty," Jonathan says. "How was lunch?"

The cat's whiskers twitch, but he doesn't respond. Just looks at the water like he's thinking about getting in. "You're welcome to join us," Jon says in a voice so soothing I'm ready to purr. "We could get you clean before I take you to the vet and then find your owners. Or find you a home."

The cat gives a low rumble that could either be a growl or a purr.

"I didn't see it in the hospital paperwork," I tell him. "But I'm pretty sure bathing a feral cat that may have rabies is not on your list of approved activities."

The cat drops its paws to the ground and saunters off.

Jon shrugs. "Probably not. You know what I was surprised to see on there?"

"What?"

"Jogging," he says. "I'm allowed to start running right away."

"You're a runner?"

"Not really. But I should start, since most other things are forbidden for a couple weeks. Weightlifting and contact sports and anything that involves my abdominals, like rowing. And international travel. That's off-limits for eight weeks."

"Did you know that going in?"

"Yeah," he says. "I did."

Which makes his gift to Isabella that much more meaningful. He knew he'd be giving up many of the things that make him who he is, but he did it anyway.

My urge to touch him is yielding to a different urge. A deeper one, a desire to kiss and connect and bury my face in his chest. None of those things are prohibited on the paperwork, but I don't think I should mention that.

"What are you thinking?" he asks.

"Why?"

"Because whatever's making you smile like that seems like something I should know about."

I'm that transparent?

I decide to be honest, since there's no way I'll come up with a convincing fib fast enough. "I was thinking about kissing you," I admit.

"I see."

The bemusement in his voice is back, though I can't bring myself to look at him. I look down into the bathwater, steeling myself.

"The first two times, you started it," I remind him. "You asked to kiss me."

"Are you asking now?"

I nod slowly, not trusting myself to speak. I know this is a bad idea. Jon Bracelyn has already penetrated my armor in a thousand tender spots, and that's the last thing I need right now.

But I find myself stepping forward anyway, bringing us face to face. So close I can feel his breath in my hair.

Water swirls around my shins, splashing the cuffs of my jeans. I don't care about that. All I care about is touching him, pressing my lips to his again. My hands rise like they're controlled by puppet strings, coming to rest on either side of his chest.

His skin is hot and smooth, and he makes a strangled noise that's somewhere between a hiss and a groan. I start to pull back, afraid I've bumped one of the incisions.

But Jon grabs my wrists and pins my hands in place. The look in his eyes is frantic, hungry. "Don't stop. Please."

The desperation in his voice matches what's thrumming

through my veins. A primal need, an urgency I've never felt before. Flattening my palms, I let my fingertips graze his nipples.

He closes his eyes and groans for real this time. "God, Blanka."

I close my eyes, too, breathing him in. Absorbing him through my senses. He smells like sunshine and saltwater, though I know he's been trapped in a hospital for days.

But Jon Bracelyn was born with the ocean in his veins, and I can feel it pulling me under. Washing through me in warm, gentle waves.

When I open my eyes, he's watching me. "Do you have any idea how beautiful you are?"

It's a strange quirk of the English language. One of those questions I'm not supposed to answer. But English isn't my native language, and there's no hiding what he does to me.

"Yes," I answer honestly. "You make me feel beautiful."

Surprise flashes in his eyes, and I worry I've misspoken. That something got lost in translation. But a slow smile spreads over his face instead. "Where have you been all my life?"

I don't know how to answer that, so I don't try. Not with words, anyway. I stretch up on the balls of my feet, palms flat on his chest. I'm trying to be careful, to kiss gently in case he's sore.

But all that flies out the window the instant our lips touch. He lets go of my wrists and pulls me against him, lips crushing mine as his hands slide around to cup my ass. I fight my urge to press against him, to arch my body into his tender abdomen. I need to be careful.

Not just with his incisions. With my heart, since I feel it tripping out of a slow trot and into a frantic gallop. I could lose myself in these kisses, in the simmering heat of his touch.

His kisses are rough and hungry, like a man who's been starved. I feel it too, this strange current of desperation. The craving for more, more, *more*.

One hand abandons its post on my ass and slides up my side, skimming my waist, my ribs through the thin cotton camisole.

When he gets to my breast, he hesitates with his hand just at the tender edge.

"I want to touch you," he murmurs. "Please."

I'm not sure if it's a question, but I nod anyway. My consent flips a switch, and his big hand closes around me. He's gentle at first, testing the weight of me. It feels way too good, and I groan and press into his palm.

"Blanka." He says my name on a groan, shooting a thousand tiny lust rockets through my body. I slide my hand around him, finding my way to the front of his jeans. "I want you so much."

"We can't," I gasp, even as I'm stroking the thick length of him through rough denim. "With the surgery you're not supposed to—"

"Page six," he gasps, kissing his way down my throat. "Third paragraph down. 'Kidney donor may engage in sexual activity when he or she feels well enough to do so.'"

"You memorized it?"

He nods, lips moving down over my collar bones. "I thought it might be important."

I clutch the back of his head, thinking nothing's more important than this. This moment, right here.

"I don't think they expect you to get busy in a bathtub the day you get home from the hospital," I murmur.

"Bedroom's down the hall," he says between kisses.

I can't believe we're talking about this. I can't believe I'm considering it.

His mouth finds my nipple through the thin cotton of my cami, and I lose all sense of logic. I'm still stroking him through his jeans, still wondering what the hell has gotten into me.

"We can't," I groan as he licks my nipple through the fabric. My resistance has nothing to do with medical concerns, and everything to do with keeping a tight leash on my heart. "We shouldn't." Even I hear the weakness of my protest as my fingers clench around him. "Please don't stop."

Talk about mixed messages.

He responds by flicking the strap off my shoulder, baring the tops of my breasts. I've still got a bra, but the lacy cups offer up the contents like they're on a platter. Jonathan gives a low moan and hooks a finger in the lace, tugging it down.

Then he feasts on my breasts, one at a time, and it's all I can do to stay upright. This is insane. He just had a major organ removed, and we barely know each other.

"*Ty moe povitria.*" The words slip through my lips before I have the chance to stop them, and I clutch the back of his head to hold him in place. To keep his mouth right there on that spot beneath my left breast.

He does it again, and I shudder.

"Mmm," he says, shifting to my right breast. "So the underside of your left breast makes you speak in tongues."

I laugh, still gripping his hair. "Not tongues." I groan as he moves back to my left breast, and unplanned words slip out again.

"*Ty naykrashhyy muzhcyna.*"

"What does that mean?" He's addressing the words to my breasts again, and I'm grateful this time. It means he can't see the flush in my cheeks.

"Nothing," I murmur. "Just nonsense words."

I expect him to push. To demand an answer.

Instead, he strokes me with his tongue. I groan again and tug at the button on his jeans. We shouldn't do this, I know. But I'm working his zipper anyway, tugging it down and stroking him as he—

"Jon! Hey, Jonathan."

We jerk back as his brother's voice calls from the other end of the house. Water sloshes our calves as we spring apart and James's footsteps draw closer. He's muttering something I can't make out, but I hear the words "fucking lunatic" and figure this can't be good.

Another voice joins the mix—Lily. "He wouldn't just leave his front door open."

Oh, shit.

"You're sure that's Blanka's car?" James is muttering.

"Positive."

I struggle to loop my bra strap over my shoulder as Jonathan tugs down the hem of my top. The footsteps get closer.

And then they're in the doorway.

James blinks into the dimness of the bathroom, taking it all in. The sudsy water, the flickering candles, Jonathan's rumpled hair.

It's Lily who speaks first.

"Whoa, girl." She laughs so hard she has to clutch James's arm for support. "I don't know what's happening here, but I approve."

James is frowning, but it's more confusion than dismay. "Why are you standing in the bathtub?" he asks. "With your clothes on. And champagne flutes full of—you know what, never mind."

He yanks at his tie and flicks a hand back toward the living room. "Your front door is wide open. Wild animals could get in."

Lily gives her trademark Cheshire cat grin. "Looks like they already did."

It's then the mangy cat makes his appearance known. He gives a low growl from his perch in the corner, surveying the newcomers with distaste. "Brrrrow."

James stares. "What the hell is that?"

"A cat," Jonathan offers. "I think."

His brother regards the animal with mild alarm. "You've been home from the hospital an hour and you've had time to eat lunch, adopt a cat, and grope some poor girl in the bathtub?"

Jonathan shrugs and gives an unapologetic grin. "The literature said organ donation makes you a superhero."

Lily shoots a pointed look at Jonathan before turning back to James. "You can probably skip the sympathy for the poor girl," she says. "I don't think Blanka's experiencing great hardship. Not the bad kind of hardship, anyway."

That's when I glance down and see Jon's fly is half unzipped. Hardship is on full display, so to speak.

"Everything's fine here." I step in front of Jonathan to give him some privacy.

He rests a hand on my hip. "We're following post-op instructions to a tee."

James sighs. "We were concerned Jonathan had fallen," he says. "Or gone crazy."

Jon grins and squeezes my hip. "I wouldn't it out."

I glance down and see wet smudges on the front of my tank top. The imprint of his mouth is everywhere, even the places not dotted with damp kisses.

What the hell am I doing?

"I should get going." I scan the bathroom for my shirt, belatedly remembering it's back in the living room. "I—um—I should leave you to your recovery."

Or regain my dignity somehow. The latter seems unlikely.

I'm out of the tub and sloshing water on the floor before anyone can stop me. There's a fluffy purple towel on a hook by the door, and I snatch it on my way out. Draping it shawl-like over my breasts, I sprint for the living room.

"Don't feel bad," Lily calls after me. "We've been busted tons of times."

"Not at risk of bodily injury," James mutters.

But I'm already around the corner and out of sight. Did we really forget to cover the food? I wrap the foil over the top and hurry to the fridge, counting on it to cool my flaming face. Shoving the food inside, I turn to see James, Lily, and Jon watching me from the living room.

"You don't need to go." Lily grabs James by the arm and tugs him toward the door. "Now that we know everything's okay, we'll get out of here."

Jon's watching me with concern etched into his brow. "Everything's okay. Right?"

I nod, shrugging into my shirt. "Of course. Everything's great."

But everything's not okay. My fleeting thoughts about relationships, my accidental Ukrainian utterances—none of that is normal for me. My brain has been scrambled, and I need to find a way to shove the mental eggs back in their shells.

"I'll call you," I say brightly to Jonathan. "To see if you need anything. Food. Or books. Or—anything."

Not sex. Definitely not that. Not a relationship, either. That's the furthest thing from my mind.

James and Lily stand silent by the door, possibly still questioning my sanity. Grabbing my car keys, I move past them with as much dignity as I can muster. "It was good seeing you," I call. "Glad you're doing well."

And like a bank robber fleeing a crime, I turn and run through the door.

CHAPTER 7

JONATHAN

A couple weeks later, my mom and Chuck come to stay.

But it's not the romantic getaway I'd envisioned. For starters, all the honeymoon suites are booked up. The standard lodge rooms are nice, but not ideal for a married couple and their twenty-something daughter.

Which is the other thing making this romantic getaway not very romantic. My second-oldest sister, Gretchen, is along for the trip. A research scientist working on her PhD, she's interviewing for a Masters-level teaching gig at OSU Cascades. Her trip out here was planned way before I lured my parents with the prospect of a romantic getaway, and it was Mom's idea to make it a family thing.

"Kinda defeating the purpose, Mom," I told her on the phone when she explained the change in plans.

"I know, sweetie. But we don't get to see Gretchen that often and Chuck and I are so proud of her and—"

"At least let me loan you my cabin," I insisted. "I can move in with James and Lily for now so you and Chuck can have your own room."

With a king-sized bed. And a door that locks. And—okay, I don't need this mental picture about my mom and stepdad.

"Absolutely not," my mother huffed. "You're still recovering. I'm not kicking you out of your own home."

"I could clear out the guest room for Gretchen, then." Dammit, I knew it was a bad idea to invite Mark and Chelsea to store furniture here while they repaint bedrooms. "Or check with Izzy about the extra room in her cabin."

Iz is staying at Bree's old place, though now that I think about it, my twin cousins might be visiting. Dammit, how can a zillion-dollar resort with gobs of rooms be this low on options for a last-minute romantic getaway?

"We'll manage, honey. Besides, it's a good chance for us to spend time with you kids."

Which is what I'm doing now, I guess.

My mom and Gretchen went into town to shop, so Chuck and I are fishing in the pond. It's relentlessly sunny for late-September, and the autumn breeze ripples oaky and crisp across the water's surface.

"It's damn beautiful here." Chuck casts his line out and eases back against the stone bench we're sharing.

"Sure is." The memory of that broken toy sailboat is on the edge of my brain, but I don't share it. No need to spotlight my father's pettiness.

Instead, I nod toward an aspen at the water's edge. "See that tree over there?"

Chuck looks up and squints at the bark. "The one with the initials in it?"

"Sean paid an arborist to do that," I tell him. "It was a surprise for Amber, before they got married. Sort of a romantic gesture."

"Huh."

Chuck adjusts his line with no further comment about romantic gestures. So much for subtlety.

I study the tree, conscious of the faint tightening of strings around my heart. I'm not jealous of my brother's happiness. I'm thrilled my siblings have found their soulmates. Sean, Bree, Mark, even Iceman himself, James.

What is it about being back here that has me picturing it for myself? Entertaining the idea of settling down. I know my lifestyle doesn't lend itself to the family thing, but maybe with the right woman…

No. I can't afford to think that way. My place is out there in the world helping others less fortunate. It's service and duty and all the qualities Chuck taught me.

I force my attention back to my stepdad, pushing away thoughts of Blanka. I need to figure out what's wrong between my parents.

"What's new with you?" I try. "Things going okay?"

"Things are terrific." He reels in his line, adjusts something, then casts again.

"Retirement going well?"

"Retirement's great." Chuck takes a sip of his beer. "Can't complain."

He never has, about anything. Not the pressures of a career in the Coast Guard or the struggles of raising six daughters and his wife's son from another marriage. It's one of the things I love about him.

Since my mom loves him, too, I keep pushing. "Everything okay healthwise?"

"Fit as a fiddle." Another sip of his beer. "What did you think of the Seahawks' starting lineup last week?"

Hell. And it's not like he's blowing me off. Chuck's never liked the spotlight, never wanted to be the focus of attention.

"It was a good game," I manage. I didn't watch, actually, but I read the recap in the paper.

"Yeah." He adjusts his line, then leans back against the bench. "If they can get it together on defense, they'll have a shot at the playoffs this year."

"Got that right." Okay, I need to steer this conversation back on track. "You know, Mom really likes the Seahawks. Maybe you guys could drive to Seattle sometime, catch a game up there."

He tugs his line, mulling that over. "Not a bad idea."

A warm pulse of hope throbs through me. But it's short-lived.

"She and Gretchen could make it a girls' trip," he says. "Did you know they offered her a position at U-dub, too?"

"I—yeah, she mentioned it."

Chuck beams, so proud of his daughter he's nearly glowing. He's always been proud of his kids, even me. The one not biologically related to him.

"Yeah, she's sure got a good head on her shoulders." Chuck claps me on the back. "That's a great idea, Sea Dog. I'll surprise her and your mom with Seahawks tickets and maybe a night in one of those fancy hotels near the stadium."

And that's pretty much the end of that. I go back to fishing quietly, mind still swimming in a sea of doubt. There has to be a way to get my mom and Chuck reconnecting. To help fix whatever's off between them.

It's not until later that evening that I take a break. I'm sitting on my front porch in an Adirondack chair, watching the sun sink slowly toward the mountains as I plug weird search terms into my laptop. Things like "midlife marriage trouble" and "empty nest marital discord." Hardly normal web searches for a single guy in his early thirties.

"Brrrrow."

I peer over my laptop to see the cat ambling toward me in his snaggle-toothed glory. He narrows his eyes and passes by, flicking his mangled tail with disinterest.

"Good to see you, too," I mutter.

"Brrrrow." He throws that one over his shoulder like a curse word, which it probably is.

Or maybe he's judging me. I should probably close this article on ten tips for spicing up your marriage. It's not like I'm going to forward it to my mother, inviting her to buy bondage tape and talk dirty in the bedroom.

Christ, I need to stop.

But instead of closing the laptop, I toggle to the business plan James sent this morning. It's for Dreamland Tours, a company owned by my cousin Val's fiancé. Josh plans to sell, and since Ponderosa has first dibs on buying, James asked me to take a look at the business plan.

"They specialize in boat trips," he said gruffly when he explained it at our last family meeting. "Rafting, canoeing, kayaking, that sort of thing."

"Sounds fun," I replied, wishing desperately for a chance to do any of that. As soon as my doc clears it, I'll be back out on the water. I'm aching to feel the rocking swell, to watch the rainbow ripples of current swirling around me.

"You know boating," James continued. "Tell me if we're missing anything. Hot new trends in kayaks or inflatable swans or whatever the hell people are floating on these days."

I scroll through the document there on my front porch, jotting notes about watercraft maintenance budgets and the possibility of acquiring some of those new standup boards that act like a treadmill on water.

An idea niggles at the back of my brain, a way to combine boating with charity. I scribble more notes, losing myself in the familiar flow of service. Of making myself useful.

"Brrrrow."

The cat's back again, still keeping his distance. He parades in front of me like a runway model, keeping his ratty body just out of reach. Pausing at the welcome mat, he digs his monster paws into the sisal.

"Anything else you'd like to use as your own personal scratching post?" I ask him.

The cat ignores me. A low rumble emanates from his direction, a gravel-filled purr I've grown to appreciate.

Still.

"I'm not talking to you," I tell him. "I tried taking you to the vet, and you hid in Mark's woodpile, hissing."

I swear to God, the cat shoots me a smug smile. Then he twines himself around my ankles, catching me by surprise. It's the closest he's come to letting me touch him, though technically, he's touching me.

"You are filthy." More purring, like he's proud of it. "And kind of a mess."

But less damaged than I first assumed. The mangled tail, the torn ear, the scar on his face—they're all well-healed, like long ago battle scars. He doesn't seem bothered, but I'd still like to get him checked out.

The crunch of gravel pulls my attention to the driveway. My heart jams into my throat as I spot Blanka's car moving toward me. We haven't spoken since the bathtub incident, and I'm trying to play it cool.

I wreck that to hell as soon as she gets out of her car. Leaping from my chair like a gameshow contestant, I wave at her as she steps out onto the driveway.

"Hey, Blanka."

"Jonathan." She's wearing jeans and a pink T-shirt, unfathomably beautiful with her hair caught back in a loose ponytail. Spotting me, she draws a stack of books to her chest like she thinks I might steal them.

"How's it going?" I fight to keep my voice casual, even sitting back down in the chair like it's no big deal to see her. Like my heart isn't slamming against my ribs at the sight of those cool blue eyes.

Blanka bites her lip. "Is Izzy home?"

Izzy, of course. She's here to see my sister. "She and Bree went to Portland this morning," I tell her. "The doctors wanted some follow-up testing."

Her brow furrows. "Is she okay?"

"Yep. It's just routine stuff. Are those for her?" I point at the books she's still clutching against her breasts.

Breasts that are permanently burned into my brain, the tight nipples, the soft, round fullness, the taste of—

"Yeah, just some books I offered to loan Izzy." She glances at the cabin where my sister's been staying. "I should have called first."

"I can hang on to them for her if you want."

Her cheeks pinken a little as she hesitates. "I'd rather hand them off directly, if that's okay."

"Suit yourself." Okay, now I'm curious. "You afraid I'll forget or something?"

"No. I just—I'd rather give them to Izzy."

Now I'm *really* curious. "You can leave them on her porch if you want. They'll be back tomorrow around lunch."

She glances toward the porch of the tidy cedar cabin that once belonged to Bree. It's got charming little flower boxes and a pretty paver path, but the porch is open to the elements. No overhang at all to protect Blanka's precious armload of reading materials.

"There's a thunderstorm coming tonight," Blanka says, reading my thoughts.

"Is there a reason you don't want me getting my hands on those?" Dammit, I'm staring at her chest again. Not her chest, but the books pressed against it. "You afraid I'm a book thief or something?"

Her eyes flash with something I can't read. She studies me a moment, assessing. "No," she says tightly. "I don't want to have to listen to you make fun of my reading choices or make cracks about Fabio or ripped bodices or—"

"Whoa, whoa, whoa," I say, not sure where we got off track. "What are you talking about?"

"Romance novels." As her chin tilts up, she slowly lowers the stack so I can see the cover on top.

Suzanne Brockman, *Force of Nature.*

"I happen to like them," Blanka says. "And so does Izzy, so I'm loaning her some of my favorites."

It's all I can do to keep a straight face. I should be irritated she'd assume I'm a judgmental prick, but mostly I'm amused. "What kind of romance novels?"

"Romantic suspense." She straightens her spine, squaring her shoulders. "A few are *New York Times* bestsellers, and some are this year's RITA Award finalists." She bites her lip. "The RITAs are—"

"Kinda like the Academy Awards of romance novels, I know." I hold her gaze as her jaw falls open. "So, you've got some Tonya Burrows in there, maybe Katee Robert. Elizabeth Dyer won that category this year, right?"

Blanka stares at me. Just stares. "How do you know that?"

"I've got a lot of time alone in my berth to read," I tell her. "Hemingway and Vonnegut get old after a while. Don't look so shocked. I'm a romantic kinda guy."

I shouldn't be enjoying this as much as I am. This stunned awe on her face, the bright pink tint to her cheeks.

Her throat moves as she swallows. She's regrouping, recalibrating the image she had of me in her mind. I hope she likes this one better.

"I see." Fanning out the stack of books across her arms, she proves me right. There's Elizabeth Dyer's *Fearless* and Tonya Burrows's *Reckless Honor* and yep, even Katee Robert's *The Bastard's Bargain.* I spot a couple more I haven't read and add them to my TBR list as Blanka stares at me like I've grown horns.

Slowly, she piles the books back together, then makes her way up the path to my porch. She lowers herself into the seat beside me without saying a word. When she turns to look at me, her expression is sheepish.

"Sorry I misjudged you," she says.

It takes all my self-control not to bust out grinning. "I'm used to it."

It usually takes the form of folks assuming I'm just like my father, so this seems better somehow.

"And I'm sorry I ran out of here so fast after the bath thing."

That I didn't expect. "If you want, we can pick back up where we left off."

She smiles, and it's like a ray of sun coming out. "I don't really think that's a good idea," she says. "Do you?"

I think it's a fucking fantastic idea, but I settle for shrugging. "I don't see why not. We like each other. You're single. Wait." I frown, realizing we haven't actually had this conversation. "You are single, right?"

"Yes, and I'm planning to stay that way." She bites her lip, tracing a thumbnail over the arm of the chair. "I like my alone time," she says softly. "And I'm not looking for anything serious."

I watch the side of her face, fighting the urge to smile. "And I seem serious to you?"

She looks up, startled. "That's not what I meant. I wasn't suggesting you want to get married and make babies, or even that you're interested in me like that."

"Oh, I am. Interested, I mean. But I'm hardly in a position to start something serious, right? My whole life is sort of in limbo right now."

She considers that, then nods. "I suppose that's true."

I decide to leave it at that. No sense in pushing. It's enough to know neither of us is looking to start a relationship. A fling, on the other hand...

"How are you doing with self-care?" she asks.

"Um, good?"

"What are you doing?"

I glance at the laptop, wondering if I can pretend to be googling yoga techniques or deep breathing. A popup flickers on the screen.

"Don't go! Still want our article on ten tips for a healthy marriage?"

I slam the laptop shut and look at Blanka. "All right, I suck at self-care."

She quirks an eyebrow at me. "You were working?"

"Studying articles," I admit. "Reviewing a business plan."

"I see." She glances toward the other end of the porch. "And the cat's still here. You're still feeding it."

It isn't a question, so I don't bother denying it. I couldn't anyway. She's right, I've been feeding the cat every day. He's not staying—*I'm* not staying—but I can at least make sure he's well-fed while I'm around.

The cat opens one eye and looks at me, then closes it again. "I'm still trying to get him to the vet," I say. "He won't let me pick him up to get him in the carrier."

"Jade at the reindeer ranch is a licensed vet," she says. "She and Amber do spay and neuter clinics a couple times a year."

"Brandon's wife Jade?" Mentally, I connect the dots from my cousin to his wife, then from Sean to *his* wife. "Got it. I see Amber all the time, but I've only met Jade once."

"Jade's more hands-on with the ranch, so she doesn't break away as often."

"Plus, Amber lives here at the resort."

"Right," she says. "They're pretty committed to caring for the cats that get dumped in the country. If you want, I can see if Jade can come take a look at—" she frowns at the pile of fur purring softly between us. "Does the cat have a name?"

"I'm not naming him," I tell her. "That would mean he's staying."

That *I'm* staying. Which I definitely can't do.

"Right." Blanka nods and stares out at the setting sun, a fiery orange cotton ball drifting slowly toward the mountains. Juniper-scented breeze ruffles the loose blonde hairs around her ears, and the sunlight on her face makes my breath stall in my chest.

"But if I were naming him," I continue, embarrassed to admit I've thought of this. "I'd name him Popeye."

The cat rolls onto his back, his preferred position for cleaning his plump belly. He's licking his chest, using one catcher's mitt paw to move the fur around. Damn, that's adorable.

"Popeye, huh?" Blanka studies the cat as though assessing the suitability of the name.

"It's from this kids' cartoon about a sailor who eats spinach and—"

"I know about Popeye," she says, nodding at the cat's exposed underbelly. "I'm just thinking Olive Oyl would be more fitting."

"What? How do you—oh."

I take a closer look at the cat, realizing I have no idea how to distinguish one set of cat genitals from another. "You can really pick out a cat schlong in all the fur?"

She laughs and shakes her head. "No. It's the distended nipples." She says this with perfect clinical indifference, no trace of self-consciousness at all. "She's had babies before. Must have been sometime before she got spayed."

"She's spayed?"

Blanka points at the cat's head. "That's what the tipped ear means. They do that at the feral cat spay and neuter clinics to let people know the animal has been altered."

"Damn." I pause. "Is there anything you don't know?"

"Plenty of things." Blanka smiles and leans back in her chair. "I've never been on a big ship like the kind you drive. Steer. Whatever the verb is."

"Pilot," I say, charmed all over again. "Or helm could work. Depending on the kind of boat, you could also say sail."

She smiles. "Canoeing is more my speed. I have my own. I take it up to the high lakes all the time."

"No kidding? Canoes are heavy as hell."

She shrugs. "I watched YouTube videos on how to move one by yourself. It's all about center of gravity."

And fierce independence, I imagine. Either way, Blanka's kickass strong.

I stretch my legs out in front of me, picturing myself in a canoe. It's been ages since I found myself on a watercraft that wasn't eighty feet long. "I'm dying to get back on the water," I admit.

Crossing her legs, Blanka fiddles with the frayed denim on one knee. "When does your doctor say it'll be okay?"

"I'll find out at my next appointment. She told me last time it could be soon. Light paddling, nothing too strenuous."

"Fingers crossed."

"Thanks." I glance back at the cat, who is still cleaning his—er *her*—belly. "Jessica."

Blanka blinks at me. "What?"

"That's what I'd name the cat," I say. "If I were going to name her. Which I'm not."

She frowns. "Jessica? Is that—a girlfriend?"

The furrow in her brow could almost lead me to think she's jealous. But no, she's just looking for information. "You think I'd have kissed you if I had a girlfriend?"

Shrugging, she glances away. "I don't know you all that well. Plenty of guys have a loose grasp on the concept of fidelity."

Something hot flares unwelcome in my chest. There's a ringing in my ears, the sound of my mother's voice and the clang of the spaghetti pot cracking the wall above my father's head.

"Goddammit, Cort—you have zero concept of fidelity."

That was so long ago, but the smell of tomato sauce burns my nostrils. I look down to see my hands clenched into fists. "I'd never do that," I tell Blanka, forcing my fingers to uncurl. "Never."

She studies my face, assessing me. "It wasn't an accusation. Plenty of people have open relationships. Or she could be an ex-girlfriend or—"

"No." I shake my head, still trying to rid myself of the

memory. "Jessica Watson was the youngest person to sail solo around the world without assistance. This cat—she seems pretty independent."

Blanka nods and glances back at the snaggle-toothed feline. "Jessica," she says, trying it out.

The cat looks up and narrows her eyes in irritation. She doesn't appear to approve of the name. Which is *not* her name, because I'm not naming this cat.

"She likes it," Blanka says. "Or she likes you."

"Yeah, I can tell by how she's glaring at me."

"That's not a glare. Cats narrow their eyes to express comfort with people or other cats or situations. It's a sign of trust."

"Really?" I glance back at the cat and practice narrowing my eyes at her. She does it back to me. "We're blowing kisses at each other."

"Pretty much." Blanka's smile lights up my whole front porch. "So how's the recovery going?"

"Good," I tell her. "I took Bree and Austin's dog for a walk this morning. Helped Izzy pack up some souvenirs to ship to her family in Dovlano. Took Libby to volunteer at the Ronald McDonald House."

"Libby—that's Chelsea's daughter?"

"Mark's stepdaughter," I say, nodding. "She met a bunch of pediatric cancer patients in Portland. I promised her when we got home, we'd find a place here to cheer up sick kids."

"That's really sweet of you. How about relaxation?"

"Like I said—I sorta suck at self-care."

She shakes her head, her expression somewhere between pity and admiration. "If you did half as good a job taking care of yourself as you do other people, you'd be the healthiest guy on the planet."

"I'm healthy." I lift the hem of my shirt to show my healing incisions. "Fit as a fiddle."

Her gaze locks on my abs and holds, pupils flaring. Her lips part slightly, and she makes a strangled sound in her throat. I order myself not to gloat. Not to feel smug she's checking me out.

But I can't help loving that she digs my body. It's only fair, since I'm nuts about hers.

I take my time dropping the hem of my shirt. "I guess I don't know where to start," I admit. "With the self-care thing. Besides the bubble bath."

She smiles, cheeks flushing at the shared memory. "That was just a practice run."

"I tried again," I admit. "It wasn't as fun without dish soap and milk in a champagne flute."

And you. You're what made it fun.

Blanka laughs and flicks her hand toward the laptop. "You've got a computer right there. Google 'self-care ideas.' Let's see if we can come up with more options."

It's dumb that I haven't thought of doing this already. Figuring out ways to take care of my own damn self.

But I've been busy, and I guess it never crossed my mind. "Right."

I flip the laptop open to wake it, toggling quick to escape the marriage popup. I open a Google search window and plug in the words. The computer whirs, then offers a zillion headlines for articles about self-care. There's stuff about classes and meditation and yoga and—

"There." Blanka points at the screen. "Try that one. *Thirty-seven tips for self-care.* There must be something in that."

I click and start to scroll, skimming past the author's long narration about his yoga vacation to Costa Rica and a family history of depression.

When I get to the bolded subheads, I start to read aloud. "*Inhale an upbeat smell.*" I look at Blanka. "What is an upbeat smell?"

"Bacon," she says without hesitation. "Fabric softener. Fresh grass. Peaches. Gravel driveways after a rainstorm. Puppy breath."

Wow. "That is impressively specific."

She looks pleased. "Thanks." Her smile makes my heart catch in my chest. A faint breeze lifts the scent of lupines from her hair to my nostrils, and my heart stutters again.

You. You're an upbeat smell.

I'm glad I don't say that out loud because it sounds creepy.

"What are your upbeat smells?" she asks.

I hesitate, buying myself some time "Salty sea air. My brother's homemade chicken sausage with sage. Juniper. Chocolate chip cookies. My mother's face cream."

She cocks her head. "What brand is it?"

"The face cream?" It never occurred to me to wonder. "I'm not sure."

"My mother always wore one that smelled like roses," Blanka says, smiling faintly. "Every time I'm in a rose garden, it's like I'm back in my childhood bedroom with my mom singing Ukrainian folk songs as I fall asleep."

"Same." I can't believe we share this same memory. "Not roses or the folk songs, but whatever my mother's face cream is. There's something crazy-soothing about the scent of it."

She smiles again, and I turn my attention back to the laptop screen so I don't reach for her. "Oh." I scan the article, surprised to see there's an actual description. "According to this, upbeat smells are things like lavender and peppermint."

Blanka shrugs and tucks her blonde hair behind one ear. "I like ours better."

So do I.

I also like the idea of there being an *ours* or a *we* or anything that links the two of us together.

I keep skimming, desperate to keep myself from going too far down that path. "*Meditation*," I read. "*Stroke a pet*."

We both look down at Jessica, who stares back at us with wide green eyes and her snaggletooth on full display. One ear twitches, but she doesn't blink.

"Can I pet you?" I jab a finger toward the screen. "It says right here I'm supposed to."

The cat stands up and moves to the edge of the porch out of reach. I shift the laptop to my other thigh and lean out to stroke the back of her head, determined not to give up so easily.

"Brrrrow!" She gives a low growl and takes a swipe at my hand.

"Maybe not." I center the laptop back across my knees and keep scrolling. "*Cloud watching*," I read off.

That one gives me pause. I tip my head back to survey a pair of wispy pink clouds drifting slowly across the horizon. Blanka does the same, leaning her head back so the end of her ponytail brushes my arm.

"Damn," I murmur. "That's really pretty."

I might not be talking about the sky.

Blanka smiles and points at one oddly-shaped cloud. "Is it just me or does that look like a giraffe?"

"I don't see it," I admit. "All I see are big, fluffy balls of pink cotton candy."

"And do you find that soothing?"

"Maybe a little." Mostly it gives me a craving for something sweet.

Blanka shifts again, and my lungs fill with her sweetness. Not just her fragrance, but all of her. I release an accidental sigh of pleasure, and Blanka laughs.

"See? It's working already."

An oblong ball of cotton candy cloud inches past the tip of South Sister, then seems to snag on Middle Sister. "Looks like that one may not make it all the way to North Sister."

Blanka throws me a curious look. "You've memorized the mountains?"

"Sure, I've been coming here since I was a kid."

"I still get them mixed up all the time."

I start pointing them out from south to north. "Mt. Bachelor, Broken Top, South Sister, Middle Sister, North Sister, Mt. Washington, Three Fingered Jack, and Mt. Jefferson." I squint at the horizon. "I can sometimes see Mt. Hood on a clear day."

She pretends to applaud. "Very impressive."

I give a mock bow, delighted by her reaction. "A good mariner knows his landmarks." That's something Chuck used to say to me, and the words pinch tight coming up my throat. "Especially the ones that lead the way home."

Home.

There's that word again, slipping out before I've thought things through. I wonder if Blanka notices.

"What else?" she asks. "Does the article have any other self-care suggestions?"

I turn my attention back to the screen. *"Breathing exercises."* I make a note of that one, reminding myself to learn some. *"Do a beauty scavenger hunt.* What the hell is that?"

Blanka peers over my shoulder and starts to read. *"Post pictures online of your favorite nail polish, lipstick, foundation, etc., and urge friends to do the same. It's a great way of sharing some of your can't-live-without-it products."* She looks up at me. "I think you can give that one a pass."

"I like that lipstick you wear," I tell her honestly. "The one that tastes like peppermint."

Her cheeks flush, and she licks her lips. "Burt's Bees. It's a tinted lip balm."

"Scavenger hunt completed." I grin. "I feel better already."

I'd feel better if I were kissing her, tasting that minty coolness as her tongue grazes mine.

But Blanka keeps her focus on the computer. I draw a finger down the trackpad, moving to the next section of the article. *"Get to know yourself intimately,"* she reads. "Oh."

I peer at the screen, pretty sure she's messing with me. "*Self-soothing is an art form,*" I read. "It sure is."

She laughs and keeps reading. "*Your body is your temple, and it deserves a treat. Give your body ten minutes of mindful attention.*"

"Or longer," I add. "Sometimes it's better to take your time."

Her giggle and the pink flush in her cheeks has me desperate to touch her.

"Gaze upon your naked form," she says.

"What?"

She points to the screen. "That's the next one. *The next time you're nude, take a moment to stand naked before the mirror and repeat the following—'I'm a beautiful sunflower, fragile and proud, mighty and soft.'*" She looks at me and snorts. "I would pay one million dollars to see you do that."

I set the laptop on the chair and hop to my feet. "Let's go."

"I'm kidding, you idiot." She waves away the hand I've extended to help her up. "I don't have a million dollars anyway."

Now is not the time to admit there are many millions in the trust fund my father left me, or that I'd give all of it away for five minutes naked in a room with Blanka.

I heave an overly dramatic sigh and return to my seat. "You're really killing my self-care plans."

She laughs and pushes her ponytail off her shoulder "Tell you what," she says. "As soon as the doctor clears you for rowing, I'll take you out canoeing on Elk Lake."

"Elk Lake." I haven't been there yet, but the idea of being out on the water again sounds magical. "That's one of the high Cascade Lakes?"

"Yes." She frowns. "Wait, can you get an actual doctor's note saying you're cleared for paddling? And for the possibility of submersion if the boat tips."

"You planning to push me in?"

"Maybe." She smiles and skims a hand over my abdomen, making goosebumps march up my arms. "You're still healing, and canoes are notoriously tipsy. It takes very little movement to send the whole thing flipping."

"That's true of most things."

We're not talking about canoes. I'm not, anyway.

But as I look into her eyes, I start to wonder if it might be worth it. Just flipping ass over teakettle into the great, deep, unknown.

"It's a deal," I tell her, still not talking about canoes.

CHAPTER 8

BLANKA

a week later, my father calls. I'm sitting on a bench outside my office at the US Geological Survey's satellite lab watching clouds on my lunch break. The fluffy white shapes tangle themselves on distant mountaintops, and I'm so deep in a fantasy of cloud watching with Jonathan that I answer the phone without looking.

"Your mother and I are issuing our farewells."

He says the words without preamble as I sit blinking in the bright sun.

"You're getting a divorce?" Belatedly, I realize I don't sound even a little shocked.

"Of course not," he snaps. "We're saying goodbye to the relief organization here in Nairobi. I've headed things up long enough, and it's time to hand the reins to someone else."

"Oh." This is actually more shocking than the prospect of my parents splitting up. "What will you do now?"

"I've got some irons in the fire." His use of the cagey idiom sends me back to that first conversation with Jonathan. Back to *penny for your thoughts* and *give your two cents* and the smell of

Jon's aftershave as he leaned close to conspire with me about getting Izzy to the doctor.

I nearly miss the next thing my dad says. "We'll be traveling, too. We've actually booked a trip to come see you."

"B—both of you?" Only once since I've been in America have they visited together. I was seventeen and an exchange student at the time, so this I'm not expecting. "At the same time, you're both coming?"

"Yes, Blanka." His patience is strained around the edges like a too-tight sweater. "We thought we could spend time with you. We're not getting any younger, you know."

"Of course, Papa." It's only then that I realize our whole conversation has been in English. When did we stop speaking Ukrainian with one another? I honestly can't remember.

"I'm excited to see you." My voice cracks a little, and I'm not sure why. "You and Mama both."

"I have to go now." I hear voices in the background, something about a new shipment of donations. "Perhaps when we visit, we can meet the young man you're dating."

And here we go. "Why would you think I'm dating anyone?"

My father sighs. "I just assumed by now you'd be—"

"Send me your flight information," I tell him. "I can come get you at the airport."

He's not accustomed to being cut off, so he doesn't respond right away. "Take care, Blanka."

"I love you, Papa."

But he's already hung up, so I'm not sure he hears me. It's just as well. We're not an *I love you* sort of family. We never have been, but I wanted to try the words on for size. To know what they felt like coming out of my mouth.

Releasing a long breath, I glance at my watch. I need to get back inside, to stop gazing at clouds or worrying about my dad or thinking obsessive thoughts about Jonathan Bracelyn.

But as I get to my feet, I know that's easier said than done. I've got a one-o'clock appointment with his family, a tour of the USGS facility. As I come through the side entrance, Jon's mom, stepdad, and sister Gretchen are walking through the doors at the other end of the hallway. His mother beams when she sees me.

"Thank you so much for doing this." Wendy pulls me in for a tight hug, reminding me of Jon's words about her face cream. I breathe her in, enveloped by a soft cushion of maternal comfort. "Jonathan's been running himself ragged trying to entertain us, so it's good to give him a break."

I'm relieved she noticed. That I'm not the only one concerned about his overly selfless nature. "I love showing off the facility." I smile at Gretchen, who's tall and broad-shouldered and unselfconsciously beautiful. "Congratulations on all the professorship offers. Sounds like you're in high demand."

"Thank you." A curtain of golden hair drifts over her forehead, and she pushes it back. "I haven't made a decision yet, but I love Bend so far."

"Good to see you again, Blanka." Chuck's handshake is warm and firm, and I'm delighted he remembers my name. "We sure appreciate the tour."

"Come on," I tell them. "I'll show you around and answer any questions you have about our work here."

I lead them through the Volcanology lab where Lily works. I keep stealing looks at Wendy and Chuck, remembering what Jonathan told me earlier.

"I'm worried they're not spending enough time together," he said on the phone last night. "That they're having problems in their marriage."

"What does your mom say when you ask her about it?" I know they're the kind of family that talks about these things. That discusses feelings instead of sweeping them under the carpet.

"She's worried about Chuck being distant," he told me. "Not

wanting to do things with her. But she's not sure what's behind it."

They don't seem distant as I lead them through the corridors of the facility. Then again, I'm hardly an expert on what a normal marriage looks like. When Chuck takes Wendy's hand as we pass from the south hall to the north lab, she smiles at him like he invented dark chocolate.

I can't remember my parents holding hands. Not ever.

Gretchen stops to study a map on the wall, and we all pause with her. So far on this tour, she's engaged with everyone from my boss to the janitor, and I find myself liking her immensely. What would it be like to have a sister?

When she catches me watching her, Gretchen smiles. "It's really sweet of you to do this for us," she says. "I can see why Jon loves you so much."

My breath catches in my throat as the word *love* zings through my brain like an electric shock. I know it's just a figure of speech, but I can't help how my heart responds.

"He's a great guy," I tell her. "Always looking out for everyone."

Everyone but himself.

I don't say that part out loud. Gretchen smiles and we continue our tour. When we reach my office with its wall-sized hydrological map of the United States, Chuck steps up to study it. Blue threads of rivers traverse the states like veins, and he traces a finger over one of them. "Maybe now that I'm retired, I'll buy a motorcycle," he says. "Set out to see rivers and lakes in all fifty states."

Wendy's face clouds, but she steps up beside her husband and laces her fingers through his. "Would I be in a sidecar or on my own bike?"

He looks startled, like he hadn't considered that. But the smile that replaces his shock is warm and genuine. "Neither," he says, wrapping an arm around her. "You'd be right there on the bike behind me, holding on tight with the wind in your hair and your legs wrapped around me like when we were—"

"Stop right there." Gretchen laughs as she shoots me a conspiratorial look. *Parents—what are you going to do?*

I smile back like I'm in on the joke. Like I have any idea what it's like to have a mother and father so ridiculously in love.

I also make a mental note to tell Jonathan about this. Maybe I'll help alleviate his concern. Maybe if he's not worried about everyone else all the time, he'll focus more on himself.

By the time I finish up the tour, I've got just enough time to swing by the drugstore before running home. Then it's off to Ponderosa Resort for the big event. For the exam we've scheduled for The-Cat-Who-Is-Not-Called-Jessica-Because-That-Would-Mean-She's-Staying.

Jade agreed to swing by and do a checkup so Jessica won't be stressed by getting stuffed into a cramped cat carrier and driven to a clinic. From the look on Jon's face when he greets me at the door, the cat's not the only one stressed.

"She's acting lethargic," he says by way of greeting. "I'm worried about her. I should have found a way to get her to the vet sooner."

"Relax." I pat his chest, which probably doesn't relax him a bit, and definitely makes my blood pressure soar. "You've known her a few weeks," I point out. "Are you really so in tune with her moods that you can identify lethargy and depression?"

His smile is equal parts bemusement and self-deprecation. "Welcome to the world of crippling empathy."

He's just captured his own personality in seven words, and I wonder if he knows this. I also wonder if I should take my hand off his chest. Just two or three more seconds. Or four.

"You should have those words tattooed on your forehead," I suggest.

He laughs, easing some of the worry lines in his forehead. Sliding his arms around my waist, he pulls me against him for a hug. "Thanks for being here." He says the words into my hair, and I could swear I catch him breathing in.

"Did you just smell me?"

He laughs and lets me go. "Yeah, sorry. You smell like lupines."

"It's my shampoo," I tell him. "White lupine is supposed to stimulate the scalp."

And there I go with the Google trivia. Blame it on the way he's looking at me, the way my heart shudders at the heat in his eyes.

"I love it." His smile is almost boyish. "Definitely one of those uplifting smells."

"Oh, speaking of that—" I draw back to hold up the drugstore bag. "I got you something."

"What is it?"

I thrust the bag into his hands. "A gift. I thought it might help with self-care."

The wonder in his eyes makes my heart twist. "A present?" As he opens the bag and pulls out the contents, his glee morphs into bewilderment. "Is this some sort of self-care massage lotion or—*oh.*"

Realization dawns as his eyes meet mine again. "My mom's face cream."

I nod in confirmation, relieved he seems to like it. I realized on the drive here that my offerings to him have included cough drops, Ukrainian dumplings, and face cream. Not exactly romantic.

You've sworn off romance, remember?

Right. I keep forgetting.

Jon's got the lid off the face cream and is smelling the top of the jar. The happiness on his face makes my heart twist. "This is it exactly," he says.

"I asked her about it today," I say as he puts the lid back on the container and sets it aside. "I thought it might help create a soothing bedtime environment."

"You have no idea what this means to me." This time, his hug nearly crushes the breath out of me. His body is warm and solid against mine, and I sink into it with pleasure coursing through me. "This is the nicest thing anyone's done for me in ages."

"That can't be true." Jon's the kindest person I know with gobs of loving family around him.

But as I say those words, I start to wonder. Is he so busy doing everything for others that no one thinks to do anything for him? I already know he's lousy at looking out for himself, but maybe there's more to it than that.

He pulls back, releasing me from the hug. I'm conscious of the loss as he picks up the face cream again and studies the label. "I can't believe you thought to do that."

"I can't believe you never did."

But I can. It would honestly never occur to Jon Bracelyn to do something for himself.

"I hope it's helpful," I tell him. "Soothing."

"It's perfect." He studies my face, brow creasing again. "Are you okay?"

"Of course, why?"

I can't still look disappointed he isn't hugging me anymore. But as Jon's eyes sweep my face, I know he's reading something else in my expression. "You seem a little off."

"I'm good, really." But my brain snags on thoughts of my parents' visit, and a little zap of nerves jolts through me.

He misses nothing. "Did you get bad news today? Or is something wrong with—"

"My father," I blurt, stunned to hear the words coming out of my mouth. "He's coming to visit. My father and mother both, actually."

"Oh," he says, watching my face. "They're both coming. Here. To Bend."

I nod, not sure why I feel a prick of tears behind my eyelids.

"Our last visit didn't go great, but maybe it'll be different with my mom here."

He nods like he understands, though I'm not sure he could. "Is there anything I can do to make it easier?"

I laugh, unable to contain it. "You could convince him I'm not an utter disappointment as a daughter." I'm surprised by how much the words sting coming out. By the fact that I've just said them to a man so skilled at burrowing beneath my armor. "Barring that, you could pull a fire alarm anytime the conversation gets uncomfortable."

"Why do I suspect we'd see an awful lot of the fire department?" He's watching my face like he sees what's behind my lame jokes, and the empathy in his eyes makes my breath hitch.

"It'll be fine," I assure him, smoothing my hair from my face. "Father stuff. It's just awkward, you know?"

He does know, though he doesn't agree with words. Just pulls me in for the warmest, tightest hug I've ever felt. It's exactly what I needed, and I feel the tension melting from my shoulders as I lean into him. I take a deep breath I didn't know I was holding, committing his bright, seawater scent to memory.

"Hey, guys." Jade King's voice echoes behind us, and we pull apart to see her and Amber coming up the walkway behind us. "Sorry we're late. Two of the reindeer decided to get their antlers stuck together."

Amber tosses her dark ponytail over one shoulder. "You haven't lived until you've pried apart two angry 300-pound ladies."

Jon looks perplexed, and I open my mouth to report on an article I read about reindeer being one of the only deer species in which females have antlers. But there's suddenly no need. Soothing my emotional discomfort with random trivia isn't necessary because Jon hugged the discomfort right out of me.

Go figure.

"Thank you for coming," I tell Jade, squeezing her in a warm hug before doing the same with Amber.

Amber and I are closer in age, and she misses nothing as she hugs me tight and whispers in my ear. "You smell like aftershave or cologne or something," she murmurs. "What were you up to before we got here?"

Heat floods my cheeks as Amber draws back and feigns innocence. Jon's looking at us funny, so I turn my attention to Jade. She's surveying the cabin with a dreamy look on her face.

"Wow, this is a blast from the past." The big stone fireplace, the cedar walls that seem to glow, the caramel leather sofas centered on a red wool rug. "This was Brandon's place before he moved out to the ranch. Lots of memories here."

"Naked memories," Amber teases, dodging her sister's elbow almost before Jade swings it. "It is a pretty sweet place."

Jade smiles, and the color in her cheeks tells me Amber's not too far off. "So where's the patient?" she asks. "Were you able to get our feline friend contained?"

"Back bedroom," Jonathan says. "She's been in there gorging herself on canned chicken and tuna."

"Will she allow you to handle her yet?" Jade asks.

"Not really," he admits. "But I set up a table in case you want it for the exam."

I shoot him a look, hoping he hasn't been moving furniture. As far as I know, he hasn't been cleared to lift anything heavy. I haven't had a chance yet to ask about his last appointment.

"Let's take a look." Jade starts toward the room, well-acquainted with the layout of the house.

It occurs to me that this cluster of Bracelyn cabins has seen more action in two years than most humans see in a lifetime.

"Ah, there you are." Jade's nudging the door open, speaking softly to the cat. "Hey, sweetheart. I'm here to check you out."

There's a soft "brrrrow" as the four of us file into the room. Jon's careful to shut the door behind him, trapping Jessica inside. She's hunkered under an end table with her bottom fang poking out and one eye closed, looking like a disgruntled pirate. Ignoring us, she focuses on cleaning one oversized mitten paw.

"She likes chicken," Jon offers. "If you want to use that to lure her out from under the table."

"Nah, I'll just get down there with her." Jade drops to a crouch on the carpet, and the rest of us follow suit.

Jessica eyes us one by one, trying to figure out what game we're playing. "It's okay, girl," I soothe. "This nice lady is just going to check you out."

"She's not that nice," Amber says. "But she's a damn good veterinarian."

Jade's ignoring us all, intent on inspecting the ragged-looking feline. "Facial scarring appears well-healed," she muses. "Same with the tail. The ear looks more recent, though."

"Ear?" I peer over Jade's shoulder. "I thought the tipped ear means she's spayed."

"Typically, yes." Jade moves closer as Amber closes her hands around the cat's plump body. I wait for the growl, for Jessica to take a swipe.

It doesn't happen.

"This isn't a surgically-altered ear," Jade continues. "Might be the result of a fight. See how it's a little ragged right through here?"

Now that she's pointing it out, I do. "Poor girl." How did I miss that?

"You should have seen the other guy," Amber coos, stroking a hand down Jessica's back. "I'll bet you kicked his ass, sweetie."

Jade's still frowning as I glance at Jonathan. "Sorry," I whisper. "I could have sworn she was fixed."

"Not your fault," he says, reaching over to squeeze my hand. "I didn't even know she was female."

Jade's still palpating the cat, still frowning as she works her way down. "Has she been acting more affectionate lately? Eating more?"

"Maybe a little." Jonathan's brow furrows. "She's been meowing at me a lot, sort of a weird yowl thing."

"Pacing around?" Jade asks. "Napping a lot?"

Jon scratches his head. "I think so."

Jade sits back on her heels, stethoscope looped around her neck. "Well, guys. You've got a very pregnant cat on your hands."

"Pregnant?" Jon blinks, then looks at me. "I'm going to be a—cat dad?"

I'd laugh if the look on his face weren't equal parts horror and wonder. "Um, this is a surprise."

It probably shouldn't be. I should have known a feral cat wouldn't be this chubby. "It's the ear tip that threw me," I admit, feeling dumb.

"Would have fooled me, too," Amber says, probably just trying to be nice. "As fluffy as she is—"

"And hefty," Jade adds, glancing at Jessica. "She looks like she's been eating well."

"She has." Jon glances at me, then back at Jade. "So, uh—how far along is she?"

Jade strokes a palm over the cat's middle. Jessica's leaning into Amber's hands and purring like her life depends on it. "She's about sixty days. Maybe more."

"Which means what, exactly?" he asks. "I'm not familiar with the gestational period of a cat."

Jade sits back on her heels. "Average is sixty-five to sixty-nine days," she says. "In other words, get ready for kittens."

* * *

AN HOUR LATER, Jonathan and I are bundled in blankets on his front porch with a bottle of rosé between us. He's looking out at the clouds as he holds the glass, not sipping from it at all.

"I think she'll be comfortable in there, don't you?"

He sounds so unsure, and it's all I can do not to crawl into his lap and promise everything's going to be okay. "It's the nicest cat maternity ward I've ever seen," I tell him.

Lifting the glass to his lips, he raises one eyebrow as well. "You've seen a lot of cat maternity wards?"

"Just this one," I admit. "But I doubt many cat owners haul in a full-sized refrigerator box lined with an ocean of towels and blankets."

He smiles and runs a finger over the rim of his wineglass. "Don't forget the full-sized down comforter."

"Or the six-million pillows."

He laughs and sips his wine. Most of the maternity ward comes courtesy of Mark and Chelsea's remodel. Mark refused to allow Jon to lift any of it and even dropped off a spare litterbox from their rabbit, Long Long Peter. Before he left, Mark fixed me with a gruff, brown-eyed stare, rubbing one hand over his beard. "Take care of him."

"The cat?" Confused, I glanced back at the room where Jon was focused on coaxing Jessica into the box with scraps of chicken. "But she's—"

"Not the cat." Mark jabbed one massive finger in his brother's direction. "The dumbshit who makes it his job to look out for every living creature on the planet. You're the only one he lets take care of *him*."

He turned and lumbered out the door before I could reply. Before he could witness the shock on my face or the pathetic flash of wonder. Me? The only one?

I'm embarrassed by how good that made me feel. How amazing to think I might have something special to offer Jon Bracelyn.

"Jade seemed pretty sure Jessica was someone's pet at some point," Jonathan says now, pulling me back to our conversation on the porch. There's a sharp edge to his voice, and I glance over to see him glaring at the mountains. "Who would abandon a helpless animal like that?"

"People can be jerks," I acknowledge. "That was nice of Jade to offer to spay and neuter everyone when it's time."

"Yeah." He takes another sip of wine, and sighs. "Is it dumb that I don't want her to find them homes as barn cats?"

"Not dumb, no." There is literally nothing dumb about this man. "I mean, people need barn cats. They've got an important job to do."

"But the lifespan's probably not too long," he says, shaking his head. "I can't believe the Humane Society is that overcrowded."

"It goes in cycles," I tell him. "Amber said this was a really heavy kitten year."

Jon sets his wineglass on the arm of the chair. "There must have been something romantic happening in Catlandia two months ago."

I laugh and take a sip from my glass. "Creamer in champagne flutes?"

Jon grins. "Sexy music, courtesy of Alexa?"

I shouldn't be surprised he's found a way to make Jessica's pregnancy a reason to worry about every other homeless pet in Central Oregon. "Even if she has the babies today, you're at least six weeks from having to make any decisions about their future. You've got time to figure out the barn cat thing."

Jon says nothing, and I wonder if he hears my unspoken question. My curiosity about how long he might stick around. He's given no indication he's considering it, and I know it shouldn't matter. The last thing I need is a bigger risk of falling for him.

"Someone should do a fundraiser," he says. "To help the Humane Society."

I glance over, pretty sure I know who "someone" is. I can already see the wheels turning, see him assuming responsibility for all the region's displaced animals.

"What about making a donation?" That has to be simpler,

though maybe money's an issue for him. I have no idea if he got the same inheritance as his siblings. Even if he did, he's the kind of guy who would have given it all away. That's Jonathan Bracelyn in a nutshell.

"Already donated." He slips his phone out of his pocket and holds it up a little sheepishly.

My eyes skim the first couple lines, a generic "thank you for your donation" message time-stamped less than ten minutes ago. "So that's what you were doing when Amber was showing me honeymoon pictures?"

His shrug causes his thumb to slip just a little, revealing the dollar amount he'd discretely tried to hide. *Holy crap.*

I glance back at his face, which is perfectly nonchalant. "It's not enough."

"Um—"

"I don't mean the dollar amount." He shoves the phone back in his pocket, looking embarrassed. "You weren't supposed to see that."

"Consider it unseen." Like that's possible. Good Lord, that's enough to feed every cat in Deschutes County for a decade.

Jonathan fiddles with the stem of his wine glass. "I mean money isn't enough. That's what my father would do."

So that's what this is about. "Non-profits always need money."

"It's not enough," he repeats, more adamant this time. "This is an opportunity to give back in a more meaningful way. To connect with the community and educate people about pet overpopulation. To make a *real* difference, not just a financial one."

"I see." And maybe I do, just a little. There's a note of longing in his voice, a hollowness in those green eyes. "So, it's personal."

"It always is." He takes a sip of wine and says nothing more.

"Fundraising's a lot of work," I offer gently.

"I know," he says. "I was here when Bree did that cop calendar. The eighties prom, remember?"

I do remember, though I didn't realize he was there. "How is it we never met until a couple months ago?" I ask.

He looks at me and shrugs. "I wasn't around much. The second we found out we inherited this property, Bree and James and Mark and Sean knew exactly what they wanted to do."

"The resort, you mean?"

"The resort," he confirms. "I thought it was a great idea. Still do. But I couldn't be a part of it."

"Why?"

"Too much to do," he says. "I couldn't just stay here in paradise building luxury cabins and deciding whether sage or buttercream is a better wall color for a spa. Not when people are suffering all over the world."

There's a heaviness in his voice that makes my chest ache. I admire the hell out of him for his conviction. For the fact that he's such a good man. Not just a good man. Maybe the best man I know.

I shouldn't ask the question. I know I shouldn't, but I do.

"Do you ever see yourself settling down?" I ask. "Telling yourself you've done enough, and now you can focus on making your own corner of the world better."

He looks at me for a long, long time. I hear my heartbeat pounding in my ears and wish I could rescind the question. Just yank the words out of the air and stuff them back in my mouth.

"It's not a requirement," I blurt, heart pounding against my own nervous tension. "Studies show the marriage rate among our generation is expected to drop to around seventy percent, which is nearly twenty percent lower than previous generations."

God, there I go again. Let no awkward silence remain unfilled, that's my motto. Jon's still looking at me, and I wonder what he was going to say. What I might have just ruined with my fact spouting.

"Is that actually a good thing?" he asks.

And now I'm off and rolling. I can't help it, can't find another way to fill the emotional whirlpool swirling in the center of my chest.

"Statistically speaking, married men are healthier than unmarried men, with a death rate that's forty-six percent lower." I look down into my wine glass, knowing I should shut up. I should forget the data and the truth I've seen in my own parents' union.

But I don't stop. I can't. "On the other hand, married women in America have shorter life expectancies than single women," I continue. "Married women are also statistically more likely to suffer from depression and less likely to advance in their careers."

I hate myself for going there almost as much as I hate the silence that follows. The fact that I've just brought this conversation to a screeching halt. Would a shrink say I'm doing it on purpose? That I'm sabotaging any chance I might have had at getting somewhere with Jon?

I'm still looking at my wineglass when he speaks. "You know what I love about you?"

I look up, astonished by the admiration in his voice. I'm too startled to answer, so he continues without my response.

"I love how fucking smart you are," he says. "How curious you are about the world around you, and how that translates to filling your mind with buckets of new knowledge."

All the breath leaves my body. Never in a million years has any man found this trait to be endearing. Annoying, maybe. Irritating. In a way, it's how I've kept my distance, kept my armor up all these years.

I open my mouth to speak, but I don't know what to say.

"Thank you," I finally manage, conscious of how shaky my voice sounds.

"No, thank you." He grins and sips his wine. "You're amazing. You're the best thing about being stuck here recovering."

I order myself to focus on the word *stuck*. To remind myself he's not here long, that he's destined to go eventually.

But my heart sinks its teeth into those other words.

What I love about you.

You're amazing.

You're the best thing.

How long have I wished I could hear those words from someone? Anyone, but especially a man like Jonathan.

I'm still struck dumb by his words, but he doesn't seem to mind. Just keeps the conversation flowing while I sit wordless with my head spinning.

"Do you ever wonder if your parents are happy?" His voice is achingly soft, and something in it helps me find my words again.

"My father is." I chew my lip, considering the question. "He's always happy when he's serving the greater good."

"And your mother?"

I hesitate, not wanting to betray her. Not wanting to share the tears she's kept hidden, even from me. "I think my mother reached a point where she forgot her own happiness matters," I tell him. "She's content enough, being part of my father's missions. Setting aside her passions for the chance to make the world a better place."

Jon turns his wineglass slowly on the arm of the chair, considering my words. "Maybe it's the same with my mom and step-dad," he says. "I always thought they were deliriously happy. They love each other like crazy. You've seen them, they can't keep their hands off each other."

I laugh, charmed by his weirdly romantic simile. "My parents are nothing like that. Not even close. Your parents make mine look like a pair of cohabitating Stormtroopers."

Still, I've noticed the tension Jon's mentioned. The fissure between Wendy and Chuck. It's subtle, nothing at all like the wide, icy gap that settled between my parents years ago. It's more like Wendy's speaking French and Chuck's speaking Italian and neither can thumb quickly enough through their foreign language dictionary.

I keep my mouth shut, not wanting to worry him further, but Jon frowns anyway. "Do you think they're having problems? My mom and Chuck, I mean."

I hesitate, not sure what the right answer is. "There's tension, sure," I tell him. "Don't all marriages have it?"

"Not theirs. Not that I've noticed, anyway." He sighs and shakes his head. "I don't know. Maybe I missed it. Maybe things always seemed so perfect between them because it was so different from what my mother had with my father."

"How old were you when they split up?"

"Six or seven." He stares straight ahead at the mountains, but the tips of his fingers brush mine. "It was ugly. He left James's mom for my mom, which she's not proud of. It wasn't long before he started fooling around with Bree's mom. This was before Bree was conceived, obviously."

I'm trying to follow along, not sure where Sean and Mark and Izzy fit into the timeline. The fact that every one of them had a different mother tells me plenty about Cort Bracelyn.

"You know you're nothing like him, right?" I say the words softly, not sure how they'll be received. "I realize I never knew your father, but the way you've described him—the way *everyone* has described him—you couldn't be more opposite."

I hold my breath, worried I've said the wrong thing. That I've just denigrated his dead father.

As he turns to look at me, a slow, tender smile spreads over his face. "Thank you," he says. "You have no idea how much that means to me."

But I do. He's determined not to replicate his father's selfishness, just like I'm determined not to repeat my mother's self-sacrifice. We're not so different, Jon Bracelyn and me.

I nod, not sure what else to say. I lift my wineglass instead, conscious of the melody of cricket song kicking up from the field behind us. The rosé is silky and warm, laced with hints of strawberry and spice. "You're cleared for wine now, I take it."

I probably should have asked earlier, but we were caught up in Jon's impending cat fatherhood. In the dizziness of that hug, which is still lingering now, hours later.

"It would have been okay weeks ago, since I wasn't on pain meds long," he says. "A little bit's fine in moderation. Oh! I almost forgot."

He sets down his glass and slips his phone out of his pocket. I can't tell what he's toggling to until he finds the audio recording app. He flashes a grin and hits the button. "I made this for you."

There's a short burst of static, followed by a female voice. "Hello, this is Dr. Leslie Warren with the Legacy transplant team," she says. "This message is for Blanka Pavlo. Blanka, this is my official clearance of Mr. Jonathan Bracelyn to participate in the next tier of physical activity. This includes hiking, jogging, moderate gym workouts, and very light paddling."

There's a mumble of voices, followed by laughter. "*Canoe* paddling," the doctor continues. "Not BDSM. Jon asked me to clarify."

I laugh, covering my mouth with my hands as the recording continues.

"He's still not cleared to do any abdominal exercises or heavy lifting, so don't allow him to assist in carrying any watercraft." From her tone, I can tell she knows Jon well enough to recognize this warning is essential. "If you have any questions about this medical clearance, you can reach me on my private number."

She rattles that off while Jonathan sits grinning in his chair, sipping from his wineglass.

"Very nice," I tell him. "Very thorough, too. You're not going to fight me on carrying the boat, are you?"

"You've already assured me you're a master of handling your own canoe." He grimaces. "That wasn't supposed to sound dirty."

"Noted."

"For the record," he says, grin spreading slow and easy across his face, "it does kinda turn me on. The thought of you being this badass Amazonian hefting a damn canoe overhead."

"Also noted." The smile is contagious, and I can't help loving the way he's looking at me. Like he's picturing me doing that heavy lifting in a bikini or maybe without a stitch of clothing. Not a sexy picture in my mind, but the heat in his eyes suggests he feels otherwise.

"So you're clear to go canoeing."

"Yes, ma'am."

"And hiking."

"Affirmative."

His green eyes hold mine, electricity crackling between us. I know there's no future between us. Long-term relationships are off the table for me, and Lord knows how long Jon will stick around.

But is it wrong to want him for just a little while?

I lick my lips and watch his eyes flash. "What about sexual activity?"

His smile curves slow and sexy as he slips out his phone again. "I wasn't going to say anything, but since you asked."

He picks up his phone, taps the screen a couple times, then meets my eyes again. The heat there sends a delicious shiver down my arms.

"Oh—yes." It's the doctor's voice again, tinged with humor this time. "If you feel up to it, you're cleared for sexual activity. Nothing too vigorous for now—we don't want you overexerting yourself before you're ready. But you're cleared to resume regular sexual relations."

I hear him thanking the doctor in the recording, but I can't hear anything else through the buzzing in my ears. He stares at me, and I stare back with fire rushing through me.

"I didn't want to be presumptuous," he says, grinning. "But I thought there was a chance you might ask."

I nod slowly, aware that my body has just gone from zero to

nuclear fusion in thirty seconds. I'm grinning like a kid on Christmas morning, but there's nothing kidlike about the desire coursing through me.

How does he do this? Just one smile, one tiny flicker in his eyes, and a dam inside me bursts, filling my insides with liquid heat.

I don't know, but there's nothing I want more than to get him inside. To touch him and stroke him and—

"Come on." I set my wineglass on the porch and stand up, reaching down to offer him my hand. "Let's continue this conversation inside."

CHAPTER 9

JONATHAN

I stumble into the house on Blanka's heels, aware that something big is happening.

For the record, my lack of coordination has nothing to do with wine and everything to do with how much I want her, how desperately I'm hoping this is really headed where I think it is.

My mind spins with ways to flood her with pleasure. To that spot on the underside of her left breast that made her speak in tongues. I'm swimming in ideas, in a million ways to leave her writhing and gasping and calling out my name.

Blanka pauses just inside the doorway and points to my bed. Thank God I remembered to make it this morning. "Lie down. Please."

"Okay." Not like I'm going to object to that.

I ease onto the bed, carefully guarding the surgical site. It barely hurts at all, but I'm still conscious of it. Still testing it the way you slide a tongue over a sore tooth.

Blue eyes flash with heat as Blanka surveys my body. I can't help noticing her eyes linger at the fly of my jeans. "Take off your shirt."

"Yes, ma'am." I've never been bossed around in bed, but it's pretty hot. "Is this whole thing going to be you issuing commands? Because with that sexy accent and—er, what are you doing?"

She holds up a necktie she's grabbed off the top of my dresser. "Is this yours?"

"No, it's James's," I tell her. "I borrowed it a couple days ago when I gave a presentation to the Rotary Club."

I managed to raise over a thousand dollars in donations for pediatric nephrology services in Central Oregon, a pet project of mine since the surgery.

Blanka looks at me a moment, then drops the tie. She picks up a second one and frowns. "Why do you have two identical ties?"

"Look closely." Why the hell are we talking about neckties? I thought we were going to—okay, never mind. Whatever it takes to get her in the mood. "See how it's almost the same pattern as the other one? But if you study the pattern—"

"Oh." Blanka peers closer at the second tie. "Are these tiny penises?"

"Bingo." I grin, willing her to join me on the bed. "I'm giving that one to James to see if he notices the swap."

Which I know sounds juvenile, but I live to mess with my tight-ass big brother.

Blanka puts the ties down and shakes her head. "You're not making this easy."

"Making what easy?" I pat the bed beside me. "I already ditched the shirt. All I need is for you to join me so I can get busy stripping off your—"

"No." She shakes her head. "This is not about busy. Or work."

I cock my head, watching her stroll to the other side of my room. "I wasn't suggesting we run spreadsheets."

But hey, whatever floats her boat. I just need my hands on her, preferably soon. "Come on. I promise I'll make you forget all about neckties and Rotary Club and work of any kind."

And maybe forget her own name, if I do my job right. I'm dying to see Blanka come undone.

She shakes her head, picking a discarded sock out of a laundry basket before making a face and setting it down. "That's not how we're going to do this."

"Do what?" Okay, now I'm confused.

And yeah, even more turned on as I watch her stride to the other side of the room and bend down to grab something off the floor. God, that ass. And the way her breasts shift under that pink T-shirt as she straightens up holding—

"Balloons?" She quirks an eyebrow, studying the pack of extra-long pastel latex. "Why do you have these?"

"Would you believe they're condoms for someone with a two-foot long, quarter-inch wide penis? Which is *not* me, in case you're worried."

Blanka rolls her eyes and tosses the pack on the bed. "You just sealed your fate, smarty-shorts."

Her Blanka-esque twist on *smarty-pants* is too adorable to correct, so I don't. Instead, I watch her drop to her knees and crawl up the bed toward me. My mouth goes dry as she draws closer, moving until she's right over me. Her hair skims my bare chest, making me shiver. I reach for her, but she sits back and picks up the balloons.

"Why do you have these?" She shakes her head. "Never mind, let me guess."

"You're not buying the condom thing?"

She ignores me. Well, ignores my words as she shakes two balloons out of the package and tosses the rest aside.

Her gaze rakes my bare torso, pupils flaring. She's almost close enough to touch. One small ab crunch, and I can sit up and catch her hips in my hands, pulling her down on top of me.

I swear she reads my mind, because she plants one hand in the center of my chest to hold me down. "No, you don't."

"What?"

Her palm curves over my pec, stroking the curve of muscle. I'm not sure she meant for this to turn into prolonged touching, but she takes her time running her fingertips over my bare skin, up and over one pec and back again. She licks her bottom lip, then seems to shake herself out of a trance.

"You heard the doctor," she says. "No abdominal work. You were going to do a sit-up."

"I was going to strip your clothes off with my teeth and put my hands all over you." Might as well be honest.

"That sounds vigorous." There's a teasing note in her voice, but her expression is anything but jovial. "Nothing too vigorous, remember?"

"I'm beginning to regret playing you that message."

She smiles and holds up the two balloons she liberated from the pack. "Let me take a guess what these are for."

"This should be good." I'm curious, actually.

She rests her hand on my chest again, palm stroking slow circles over my breastbone. It feels amazing, which is a testament to how turned on I am. The heel of her hand grazes my nipple, and I shiver. When did that become an erogenous zone?

"My guess," she says, reminding me we're having a conversation. "My guess is that you've been blowing up balloon animals for those pediatric patients you mentioned. True or false?"

"Is this an interrogation?"

She doesn't give in to the smile tugging the corners of her mouth. "Answer the question."

"True," I admit. "Libby and I have been volunteering at the Ronald McDonald House."

"Which is *not* taking it easy," she says. "And also probably an over-exertion of your lungs and abdominal muscles and—"

"Would it make it better if I tell you I used a hand pump?"

I'm not saying I did. Fine, the truth is that we visited three times this week, and I totally felt it in my abs and airway after blowing up all those balloons. The pump was Mark's idea.

I don't tell Blanka any of this, but somehow, she knows. Her palm slides down my chest, moving between the healed incisions. Her touch is gentle, but sexy as hell with her eyes holding mine. I swear I could come in three seconds if she moved her fingers a few inches lower.

When she draws her hand back, it's all I can do not to groan in frustration. "You're killing me here."

"I'm trying *not* to kill you," she says. "Or not to let you harm yourself."

"I can promise you I'm undamaged and fully functional."

Her stern composure cracks, and she smiles as she drags a palm over the front of my jeans. "I can see that."

"God, Blanka." The words slip through gritted teeth, and I reach for her again.

Again, she moves back, and my fingertips skim her knee. Lifting the first balloon to her lips, she blows into the end. Once, just a quick puff of breath. Then she ties it off and does the same to the second one, leaving her with two slightly puffy noodles a half inch in diameter.

"This is officially the weirdest form of foreplay I've ever experienced." But also hot. Maybe it's the way she's holding eye contact while blowing those damn balloons.

"There's a plan here," she says.

"Naked water balloon fight?" I'm game. "Balloon darts?" Hell, she could ask me to hold the target over my junk, and I'd oblige as long as she kept looking at me the way she is now.

"Here's the thing." Blanka leans forward and grabs hold of my left hand. "You are very, very bad at taking things easy."

"Didn't you just accuse me of *not* making things easy?"

She grabs my right hand, pulling it tight against the left. "You don't know how to relax."

"I didn't know we were coming in here to nap." I stare at my wrists as she twists one softly inflated balloon around the left, then the right.

"Oh, we're definitely not." She finishes binding my wrists together and grabs the second balloon. I could easily break the hold, but why?

Fascinated—and yeah, still turned on—I watch as she twists the second balloon into a perfect double-half-hitch to bind my wrists to the headboard. Her breasts brush the side of my face, and I close my eyes and breathe her in.

When she sits back, I'm still lightheaded. "You are the sort of guy who'll be hellbent on pleasuring me six ways to Sunday," she says.

"And that's wrong because—?"

"It's not wrong." She leans over to adjust the knot at my wrists, loosening it just a little. It's plenty comfortable already, but I welcome the graze of her breasts against my cheek a second time.

I turn so my lips brush her nipple through her T-shirt and bra, and Blanka makes a soft sound in the back of her throat. I expect her to press into me. To allow me to pleasure her, to indulge her in the sort of gratification she deserves.

Instead, she sits back and looks at me. "Not wrong," she repeats. "But also, not what the doctor ordered."

I tilt my head to check my balloon-bound wrists, strangely aroused by her handiwork. "I don't remember anything in the post-surgery paperwork about bondage with limp balloon animals."

Blanka ignores me and tugs her T-shirt over her head.

"Holy shit."

Her bra is a wisp of lavender lace, nipples clearly visible and begging to be touched. My hands ache to reach for her, which I'd do if I weren't trussed up like a Thanksgiving turkey. A turkey bound with balloons.

She flashes that gorgeous, unselfconscious smile with the perfect gap between her teeth. Eyes locked with mine, she reaches behind her to unhook the bra. As the straps slide down her arms, her breasts spill out. My mouth goes dry as Blanka skims her fingertips over her nipples and smiles.

"Christ," I choke out. "Anyone ever tell you that you have the world's most perfect breasts?"

"Yes." She tosses the bra aside and leans down, skimming those soft globes of perfection across my chest. "Thank you."

"Guh," I manage as the tickle of her hair sparks every nerve in my body to life.

"Here's the thing," she says, breathing the words soft against my ear as she kisses her way along my neck. "I want you to be selfish. I want you to lie back and focus on your own pleasure. Not mine, not anyone else's but your own. Think you can do that?"

"I—uh—I can try." To be honest, I've never done it before. "I'm not positive I can."

"That's why you're tied up," she whispers, flicking her tongue over my earlobe. "You're going to learn to be selfish. To take care of you."

I close my eyes, dissolving into her touch. Into the dizzying pleasure of her breath against my skin. "Kinda tough to take care of myself with my hands tied behind my head."

"Very funny."

I flex my fingers, enjoying the unfamiliar tug of the restraints around my wrists. "I suppose I could get you off with my feet."

"I'll pass on that." She laughs and sits back again, doing her best to keep up the stern Ukrainian headmistress act. "Here's how this is going to go down." She pauses, blue eyes flashing. "I am."

I stare at her, wondering what I missed. The sight of those perfect, bare breasts is making my brain short-circuit. "What?"

"*I'm* going down," she says. "On you. And you're going to lie back and enjoy it. Do you have a problem with that?"

I should, I know I should, but I can't recall why. Something about being a considerate, selfless lover, which I swear I've done my whole adult life.

But the fire in Blanka's eyes has me wondering what the other side looks like. What it might be like to focus purely on my own pleasure. What kind of selfish dick would that make me?

"Uh—" my voice comes out in a croak as I give a halfhearted yank on my bound wrists. "That seems a little unfair to you. I'm just supposed to lie here and let you—uh—"

"Yes." She licks her lips, making my brain spin again. "That's exactly what you're supposed to do. For a few minutes at least, I want you to be selfish. I want you to learn how good that can feel. I want you to think of only yourself."

But all I can think of is Blanka. The flush in her cheeks, the scent of her skin, the spill of her hair over those perfect breasts. Christ, she's beautiful.

I know I should argue. Should insist on pleasuring her, too.

But part of me wants what she just described. Selfish pleasure, purely for the sake of pleasure. I've never done that before, not at the hands of someone else. Is it wrong to want that, just this once?

"Ung," I manage.

She smiles and strokes her hands over my chest again, her touch light and electric. "So, I have your consent?"

I nod, even though I'm not sure I ought to. I should insist on getting her off. I should promise mutual pleasure and multiple orgasms. I should at least—

"Yes," I croak. "Yes, please."

The smile she gives me is priceless. Satisfaction mixed with enough heat to make my brain boil. "Excellent."

She leans forward and kisses me, bare breasts brushing my chest. The kiss is slow and soft and full of promise, igniting a flame in the center of my belly. I kiss back, unable to twine my fingers in her hair or pull her against me. There's a fissure of frustration in my chest, but it's snuffed out by an unfamiliar sensation.

It's the feathery light breath of letting go. Of letting someone else be in charge.

Christ, is this what it's like?

"Blanka," I groan against her mouth. "You're good at that."

She laughs and draws back. "Kissing?"

"That mouth." I shake my head, not sure I'm making sense. "It's fucking magical."

"Thank you." Still smiling, she kisses her way down my throat, taking her time. Her hair trails along my collarbones as she lays a path of warmth across my sternum, my pecs. Her nipples are soft pebbles tickling my belly, tracing lovely, curved waves around my torso.

I groan and close my eyes as her tongue grazes my nipple. She uses her teeth, and I arch up, unaccustomed to the sensation. I've never thought about that part of me being an erogenous zone. On women, sure, but this feeling, this electricity—

"Christ, that feels good." I tug at the restraints again, grateful they hold. Grateful for whatever she's doing down there with her tongue and the soft scrape of teeth. "Don't stop."

She laughs and moves to the other side of my chest, giving its twin the same treatment. Her breath ruffles hot against my sternum.

"Did you know men's and women's nipples have a similar nerve supply?" she murmurs against my chest.

I shake my head, then shiver as she blows lightly on one of mine. "Uh-uh."

"The nerves in male nipples lie closer together, but those in the female breast are spread out more widely." She strokes her tongue over mine, and I shiver again. "But male nipples are much more sensitive than most people give them credit for."

I stifle another groan as she drags her teeth over me. How did I never know this before? "Thanks for the education."

And for everything else she's doing. She goes back to kissing me, moving lower down my torso. When she reaches the first incision site, she brushes a feather-light kiss near the edge of it. "Does this hurt?"

I shake my head. "Not at all."

It feels fantastic, honestly. Every inch of my skin is electrified, buzzing with sensation. The way she's kissing me feels like an act of worship. Like she's memorizing every scar, every freckle, every hair follicle.

Her mouth drifts lower, and the anticipation buzzing in my core morphs into a full-on swarm of killer bees. I suck in a breath as her lips graze the patch of hair right above my jeans.

"Jonathan," she murmurs. "You feel so good."

She has no idea. I've never felt this insanely good in my life. I know it's wrong; I know I should be fighting harder to get my hands on her.

But when her fingers find the button on my jeans, I forget all about that. I forget everything but how fucking good it feels to have her hands on me. I watch as she unzips my fly, working my jeans down over my hips.

She meets my eyes and grins. "This should be fun."

I try to say something witty, but my throat stops working as she kisses me through my boxer briefs. A strangled hiss forces its way from my mouth as she rubs her lips over my erection, teasing me through the cotton.

"Shall we get these off you?"

I nod because that seems like the right answer, and also because my voice isn't working. Breasts glide over my thighs as she pulls down my jeans and boxers, stopping every few inches to plant a kiss in some random spot. Thigh, kneecap, shin—her mouth lighting tiny fires everywhere she touches.

When she starts to work my shoes off, I struggle to sit up. "Lie back." She pushes my chest, making sure it happens. "If I need help, I'll ask."

This seems so wrong. "I'm not used to being helpless."

"You're not helpless," she says, stripping off the last of my clothing and returning to dot a million tiny kisses over my hips and abdomen. "You're powerless."

"That's not reassuring." But it is. My insides go gooey as her breasts skim my cock. Everything inside me is humming, just a big, sloshy sea of sensation.

I could get used to this.

"Feels good, doesn't it?" Her tongue grazes my belly button, and I shiver. "It's nice sometimes to let go of control."

I nod because I want her to keep kissing my hipbone like that, and also because she's right. This loss of control, it's something I've never imagined. Something I never knew I needed.

"Christ." Her breasts brush my thighs as she slips into the space between my legs. Her warm breath fans across my cock, and I close my eyes. The instant her lips touch me, I nearly fly off the bed.

"Sensitive guy," she murmurs, laughing a little. "I could have guessed."

"Oh, Jesus—Blanka." I grit my teeth as she takes me all the way into her mouth.

Constellations burst behind my eyelids as her tongue curls around me. The gentle suction, the way her fingers clench the base of me, it's too much. Mouth, palm, breath, teeth—I can't tell where one sensation begins and the other ends.

I give up trying to categorize anything and just melt into an ocean of pleasure.

"You're so fucking good at that," I grind out. "Did you write a thesis on giving the perfect BJ?"

She laughs, sending a fresh wave of vibrations moving up my body. "Maybe I should. Want to be my guinea pig?"

"Keep doing that, and I'll be any animal you want me to."

"Hedgehog?" She murmurs the word around me, letting the syllables vibrate up my shaft. "Platypus?"

Her giggle sends a ripple of pleasure through my cock, or maybe that's what she's doing with her tongue. How the hell did a recitation of zoo animals become sexy?

"Anteater," I choke out, conjuring the first animal I can think of with suction expertise. "Plecostomus."

She laughs and a warm, swirling current moves through me. She sucks me in deep again, moaning around me. "Parastratiosphecomyia."

"What the hell is that?" I choke out.

"The longest insect name I could think of," she says. "You seem to like the vibration of syllables."

Like doesn't begin to describe how insane I am with pleasure. How close she's bringing me to the edge with the tremor of her words and the softness of her mouth.

She sucks me in deeper, then releases me. "Tasselled wobbegong." That one she delivers with her lips pressed against the underside of my shaft, a gentle buzz of breath. "A species of carpet shark, if you were wondering."

"I wasn't." I'm too close to coming my brains out, too close to the edge to turn back now. "Blanka."

I should tell her to stop. That's the right thing to do; I know it is. "Blanka."

That's the only word I can manage.

"Let go," she says. "Do it, Jon."

That's the last thing I remember. Then my brain explodes. It's a bright burst behind my eyelids, a rush of pleasure so intense I call out.

"Holy Christ."

The waves slam into me, one after another after another, knocking me back against the bed. My hands ball into fists at the headboard as a whirlpool of pleasure pulls me under. I'm drowning in sensation, gasping for breath.

So help me God, I never want to come up.

As the last wave ebbs, Blanka slows down. She draws back

softly, and with one gentle kiss on my hipbone, sits back on her heels.

That smile. My God, I'll remember it for the rest of my life.

"Admit it," she says, wiping the back of her hand over her mouth

Jesus.

"Admit what?" At this point I'd confess to killing Gandhi.

"Admit that being selfish feels pretty damn good."

I nod, hoping that's concession enough. I'm not sure I can manage a complete sentence. My heart's threatening to blast through my ribcage, and my body's buzzing like a can of warm Coke tossed down the stairs.

Still smiling, Blanka leans up to unfasten the balloons. I beat her to it with one hard yank. That's all it takes, and I'm free. It was as easy as that.

But not really. There's something inside me bound tight. A new tether, fragile as a spider's web, tying me to the woman beside me.

"Come here." This time, I don't give her a choice. I pull her against me, burrowing my face in her hair. "I want to hold you."

She relaxes into me, curling against my side as she tucks herself into the space under my arm. She's careful not to bump the incisions, unbearably gentle as she settles her head onto my chest.

Her hand comes up to touch the medallion hanging from a cord around my neck. Fingertips graze the warm metal, and I shiver.

"What is this?" she asks softly. "I've been meaning to ask about it."

I take my time answering. I don't want to ruin this moment, this connection between us. "A gift from my father," I say. "He gave it to me when I was seven."

I don't specify which father. There's no need, and I can tell by the way she tenses in my arms that she knows I mean Cort Bracelyn.

"He must not have been all bad," she murmurs softly. "Not if he helped create you."

I close my eyes tightly, breathing in and out as Blanka lets go of the medallion and strokes her hand over my chest. Right now, in this moment, I almost forget I'm stretched taut between two worlds. Between the family that raised me, the one where I most want to belong, and the father whose shadow I can never quite shake.

Blanka's palm makes slow circles over my breastbone, and I feel myself relax. Feel the slow, gentle ebbing of tension, the softness of the woman who only sees the best in me.

Admit it.

Her earlier words echo in my head, but I'm not thinking about blowjobs or balloon animals or that multi-syllabic insect she named.

I'm thinking the one thing I'm not ready to admit. Not out loud, not even to myself.

I'm falling in love with Blanka.

No amount of persuasion can convince Blanka to stay the night. Not even when I point out that she might miss the miracle of kitten childbirth.

"I need to start cleaning for my parents' visit," she insists as she kisses me goodbye at the door. "I'll see you this weekend for our canoe trip, right?"

"Yes." I know it's lame, but I hate the thought of going even that long without seeing her. "Want me to let you know if I see kittens emerging from the business end of the cat?"

"Yes, please," she says, brushing back a flyaway strand of hair.

"I know Jade said she shouldn't need assistance with the birth, but I feel like we ought to be nearby just in case."

"Agreed." I'm not above using my cat to earn more time with Blanka. Wait. "Not my cat."

Blanka tilts her head. "What?"

"Nothing. Just—never mind."

She rolls her eyes as she goes up on tiptoe to kiss me again. "You're a good man, Jonathan Bracelyn, but you're a strange one."

"I'll have that printed on business cards."

I can't take my eyes off her as she walks to her car, gets in, and heads off down the driveway. I'm still staring when I hear a sharp, whistled catcall from next door.

Turning toward it, I spot Gretchen and Izzy sitting in Adirondack chairs in front of the cabin that used to be Bree's. Iz is wrapped burrito-style in a blue and green blanket, while Gretchen sits spooning ice cream out of a vessel the size of a mixing bowl.

"Nice one, bro," Gretchen calls around a mouthful of what I'm assuming is chocolate chip mint. She ate it by the gallon when we were growing up. "I wondered how long it'd take you two to get together."

I amble toward them, not sure how to respond. "We're not together."

Gretchen rolls her eyes at me while Izzy pats an empty chair beside her.

"Join us," Izzy says, eyes full of apology. "I wanted to thank Blanka for the books, but it seemed like an inopportune time to interrupt."

Gretchen snorts and scoops up more ice cream. "You mean when his tongue was in her mouth? Yeah, bad time for conversation."

Izzy laughs and rolls her eyes at Gretchen. "You're the absolute worst."

"I love this," I tell them as my attention swivels back and forth between sisters.

Gretchen eyes me like I've lost my marbles. "That we're abusing each other?"

"Yes, actually." I ease into the chair next to Izzy, then reach out to take the ice cream bowl out of Gretchen's hands.

"Hey—" she protests, but hands me her spoon.

"I love that my sisters—who have zero blood relation to one another—have become friends." I shovel ice cream into my mouth, savoring the minty coolness. "And I love that Izzy's gotten over feeling like a burden all the time. And I love that you're both here."

"Jeez, what a sap." Gretchen watches me shovel up another mountain of ice cream before waving at me to give it back. I steal one last spoonful before she can take it, swallowing a little too fast.

"Ow," I complain around the freezie brain headache.

"Serves you right," Gretchen says as she reclaims her bowl and spoon. "I like it here. I can't believe you're not sticking around."

"What would that even look like?" It's the first time I've tossed the idea out loud, and both sisters blink.

"Well," Gretchen says slowly, "You'd choose to remain at the resort with your family instead of racing off to some war-torn region of the world to save lost souls. And you'd stay here and look for lost souls instead."

There's no way it's that simple.

But that doesn't stop me from picturing it in my head, wondering if there's enough charity work here to keep me occupied. It isn't the charity work I'm imagining. It's Blanka with her hair fluttering in the breeze and that beautiful, gap-toothed smile.

"I'm thinking of staying," Izzy says shyly. "After I'm cleared to travel, I mean. I might choose to stay, at least part of the time."

"Iz, that's amazing!" I pull her in for a hug, delighted by the news. "It'd be great to see you all the time."

Gretchen cocks her head. "You just said you're not staying, didn't you?"

"So? I visit a lot."

More in the last year than I ever did when my dad was around. There's something that keeps pulling me back here, giving me excuses to return for family meetings and weddings and random holidays.

Izzy looks thoughtful. "Blanka does seem pretty independent."

"Which is key if you're talking about a potential long-distance relationship," Gretchen puts in.

"We're not in a relationship," I insist. "Blanka's adamant about not wanting that."

My sisters exchange a look I can't quite read.

"What?" I ask.

"Nothing," Izzy says. "I'm sure you're right. You know her better than we do."

I refrain from saying anything about how well I've gotten to know her just recently. Kissing and telling is *not* my thing.

"I admire her, actually," Gretchen says. "When she gave us the tour of USGS, she was telling us about all these trips she's taken. Said she loves traveling by herself."

"That's so brave." Izzy smiles and swipes a finger over the rim of Gretchen's ice cream bowl, stealing a lick of chocolate chip mint. Is this the same woman who almost died at a wedding because she didn't want to trouble anyone? "And she lives by herself," Izzy adds. "Said she prefers it that way."

"See?" I don't know why I think this proves my point. "The last thing she wants is a relationship. Some guy hanging around, breathing down her neck, following her everywhere."

Gretchen gives me a look. "If that's how you think relationships work, we need to talk."

"Sounds more like stalking," Izzy agrees.

I grab the bowl back from Gretchen and reach a hand in to grab a golf ball-sized hunk of ice cream. Shoving it in my mouth, I make the obnoxious smacky sounds that used to bug the crap out of her when we were kids.

"Disgusting," she says, yanking the bowl back as she whacks me on the head with her spoon.

Then she goes back to eating with it, her expression one of fond frustration. "You know we're all proud of you, right?"

"What?" I'm suddenly self-conscious, not sure where she's going with this. "Yeah, sure, I know."

Gretchen sighs like I'm being dense. "Mom and Chuck and all the rest of us—we'd be proud of you no matter what you did for a living."

"Of course." I'm agreeing because it's easiest, but deep down, I know it's not that simple. Gretchen's their daughter—Mom and Chuck's. I was there when she took her first steps. I saw the pride in their eyes the first time she brought home a science fair trophy.

It's different for me. We act like it's not, but deep down, *I'm* different. I'm Cort Bracelyn's son, no matter how we pretend otherwise. I've always known I need to work harder, need to earn my place in the family.

I finger the medallion at my chest and order myself to remember that. To never lose sight of the fact that I've got something to prove. To my parents, my siblings. To myself.

Even if it means eventually letting go of Blanka.

CHAPTER 10

"God, this feels good."

Jon's voice behind me has my brain ambling back to his bedroom a few days ago, and I'm grateful he can't see my face.

"You're not overexerting yourself, right?" I glance over my shoulder to see his mile-wide grin on full display.

"No way," he says. "Being out on the water is the purest form of self-care. This is like a bubble bath and a hot fudge sundae and an orgasm all rolled into one."

"Sounds messy," I point out, smiling as I dip my paddle in the water and look out over the mountains on the horizon.

We're both paddling, but his spot in the stern means he's doing more of the steering. It's the awkward thing about canoeing as a date. You spend the whole time facing forward instead of looking at one another. One person's stuck staring at the other's back instead of gazing romantically into each other's eyes.

Then again, romance isn't the point. We've already established there's a time limit on our fling. Today is about getting Jon to relax, not about getting into each other's pants.

"Look, an osprey." I point to the sky where the slender-bodied hawk is swooping low over the water. As we watch, he dive-bombs the glassy surface and comes up splashing.

Jon slips his paddle out of the water to watch. "Why do I suspect you know everything there is to know about ospreys?"

I smile, flattered he sounds proud instead of annoyed. "Not everything."

"Do they mate for life?"

I hesitate. "Yes. Usually." I'm facing forward again, grateful he can't see the heat creeping into my cheeks. "They're monogamous and generally return to the same mate year after year."

"You mean they separate for migration?"

I nod and dip my paddle in the water as the osprey swoops low again, water flickering in the sun like crystals on its wings. "They can migrate more than three-thousand kilometers in a season. But the males in established pairs always return to the breeding ground before the females do."

"No kidding. To prepare the nest or something?"

"Exactly." I don't know why this feels so intimate. Why I'm fretting that my words sound like some way-too-obvious hint. "After eggs are laid, they work together to fight off intruders and defend the nest."

We both watch as the osprey plummets again, his body an arrow aimed straight down at the lake. Wings flapping, he surfaces again.

"He got something," Jon says.

Sure enough, there's a flashing silver fish clutched in the osprey's talons. The fish wriggles, but it's no match for the bird's fierce grip.

"Bad day to be a trout," Jonathan observes.

"Good day to be an osprey."

We watch as the bird disappears into the trees, eager to devour his dinner in peace. Jon's quiet behind me, and I assume he's still watching the sky for birds. I see bald eagles here a lot, and once a great horned owl.

"Blanka?"

I glance over my shoulder. The serious look on his face has me pivoting completely on the seat. "What is it? What's wrong?"

"I feel like I should apologize for what happened in my bedroom the other day," he says. "For the fact that it was all about me and I didn't uh—pleasure you at all."

I sigh and dip my paddle in the water. "Jonathan, the whole point—"

"Wait, let me finish." He smiles, green eyes sparkling like the water around us. "I said I feel like I should apologize, but the truth is, I don't want to. That was fucking phenomenal, and I don't regret it. Not one bit."

Heat blooms in the center of my chest. I fight the urge to pat myself on the back. "You don't have to answer this if you don't want to," I tell him. "But I get the sense you're not used to giving up control in the bedroom."

His chest flexes as he strokes his paddle along the left side of the boat to turn us. "I didn't catch the question part of that," he says. "But if you're asking whether I've been tied up before, the answer's no. And definitely not with balloons."

The heat that started in my chest spreads in a warm rush down my arms to the tips of my fingers. "I wasn't trying to pry—"

"Pry away," he says. "Want to know if that was the best blowjob of my life? The answer is yes. Wait, no, the answer is oh-my-fucking-God, *yes*."

I feel myself blushing to the roots of my hair, but I'm not embarrassed. It's honestly a relief to speak this frankly about a sexual encounter. Besides, what woman doesn't want to hear she's got skills that make a man glow like Jon is right now?

"I liked it," I tell him honestly. "If you're thinking it was some sort of chore or duty or that I spent the whole time making my grocery list in the back of my mind, that's a resounding no."

"The grocery list hadn't occurred to me," he says. "But I'm glad." He's quiet a moment, paddle resting across his knees as we drift along the surface of the lake. "Maybe it's a control thing."

Are we still talking about blowjobs? "What's a control thing?"

"The reason I'm so hell-bent on helping," he says. "Maybe it's less about being kind and selfless and more about being a control freak."

I frown, resting my own paddle across my knees. "Has it occurred to you that maybe you're just a good guy?"

He shrugs and glances out over the water. "It's never that simple. If you think about it, wanting to help people is a selfish thing."

Now he's really lost me. "What are you talking about?"

"When it comes right down to it, isn't my volunteer work just a way to feel good about myself? It's selfish at the core."

I sigh, tamping back my irritation. "Is there a reason you're determined to see the worst in yourself all the time?"

He shrugs. "Maybe because I'm waiting to turn into my father."

There's a vulnerability in his eyes that steals my breath away. I know I should turn around and pay attention to where the canoe is headed, but I can't look away from him. "I never knew your father, obviously," I tell him. "But from where I stand, you've got more in common with *my* father."

He idolizes my dad, so this should be a good thing. I brace myself for the hero worship, for the smile in his eyes.

But Jon just looks at me. "Why do I get the feeling that's not a good thing?"

The intensity in his gaze makes me look away. I turn and dip my paddle in the water, conscious of the fact that we're drifting closer to shore. "My father's a two-time Nobel Prize winner. He was honored in *Time* magazine as one of the world's most influential people."

"And yet his visit has you tenser than a cat in a rocking chair factory."

I bite my lip, not sure whether to smile or be startled by his perception. "Maybe that's what happened to Jessica's tail."

He laughs, but it's a stilted laugh. Not his normal full-bellied laughter. "Could be."

"Have you ever noticed how many English idioms center around cats?" I ask. "There's 'raining cats and dogs' and 'cat got your tongue' and—"

"Have you ever noticed that you default to language analysis or spouting data when you're nervous or emotional?"

I have noticed, though I didn't think anyone else had. I pivot on my seat again, unable to stop looking at him for more than a few seconds. That's how strong this connection is between us. "You're right. I'm nervous about my dad's visit."

"It's more than that," he says. "Want to know what I think?"

Always. More than anything in the world, I want to know what goes on in that beautiful mind of his. "I'm not sure."

"I think in a weird way, we have different versions of the same issue."

I turn fully on the seat, no longer focused on where we're headed. "How do you mean?"

"I mean I'm petrified of becoming my father," he says slowly. "And you're petrified of dating yours."

Damn. His words suck the breath from my lungs, and it takes me a few heartbeats to find my voice again. "So, where does that leave us?"

"With some seriously fucked up daddy issues." He laughs, somehow able to find the humor in something that's not all that funny. "But I get it," he continues. "This is why we can't get involved. Why this can't go beyond a fling."

He's saying exactly what I've said all along. Just parroting my words back to me, agreeing with everything I've asked for up to this point.

So why does it sting so much? Why does the pit of my stomach feel like I've swallowed a lead ball?

"Whoa, heads up!"

Jon jams his paddle into the water as I spin on my seat to face forward. Too late, I realize we're on a collision course with a peninsula of land jutting into the lake. Worse, there's a big group of people clustered around two battered green picnic tables. They're laughing and eating and not looking much like they want a pair of party crashers.

I stab the water again, working with Jon to back us up. From the corner of my eye, I see a white-haired gentleman lurch up from the table and teeter toward the water's edge. He lifts one shaky wrist to point at us.

"Angela!" He's clutching a chicken drumstick in one hand, and he shakes it like a conductor's baton. "You made it. Everybody, Angela's here."

I look behind me for another arrival, but nope. It's just Jon and me.

Jonathan shrugs, then waves to the group. "Howdy, folks," he says. "Sorry, we'll get out of your h—"

"I knew you'd be here, Angela." The old guy is still waving his drumstick around, and now he looks misty-eyed. "They kept saying you couldn't be here, but you wouldn't miss my eighty-fifth birthday."

I'm staring at him trying to decide how to respond when a second man gets up from the picnic table and takes the old guy's arm. "Pops, we've been over this," he says. "Mom died in 1998. Remember? You were on that cruise to Alaska when she—"

"Mom, welcome!" A sandy-haired woman in khaki shorts bolts from the table and runs toward Jon and me. She's got the same blue eyes as the old man, but hers are frantic and wide as she sprints to the lake's edge. Her red T-shirt bears a smear of mustard on one shoulder, and she charges into the water without kicking off her sandals. As Jon and I stare, she wades knee deep into the lake and grabs the front of our canoe.

"I will give you a hundred dollars to play along." Her voice is both a whisper and a shout as she looks into my eyes and grips our bow so hard her knuckles go white. "My father has advanced dementia, and this is probably his last birthday. He thinks you're my mother, and there is absolutely no harm in playing along. *Please.*"

The tears shimmering in her eyes tug the corners of my heart, but it's the determined jut of her jaw that gets me moving. I scramble out of the boat, casting a quick look back at Jon. "What are the odds I'd be asked twice in a month to play someone's wife for medical reasons?"

He blinks. "What?"

I'm already turning back to the woman, peering behind her to the old man standing on the shore. His arms dangle helplessly at his sides, one hand still gripping the forgotten chicken leg. The younger guy—his son, I'm assuming—is giving some kind of pep talk I can't make out, but I catch the word "dead."

The old man's lip trembles, but he's shaking his head. "Angela," he says. "I know it's her."

I hold my hand out to the woman in the water, and she lets go of our boat to shake it. "Blanka," I tell her. "But you can call me Angela."

Relief floods her face as she pulls me in for a hug. "I'm Cindy."

"What's his name and how long have we been married?"

She releases me and glances back at her father, frown lines creasing her forehead. "Archibald," she says. "But my mom called him Archie." She bites her lip. "He might think this is 2019, or 1985 or 1943, so there's really no telling how long he believes you've been married."

Clearing her throat, she calls back to her father, who's still on the shore with a hopeful expression. "Hang on, Dad," she calls. "Mom just needs to grab some things out of the boat."

"I've got it," Jonathan says, already clambering out of the canoe and tucking his paddle under the seat. "Go. I can handle this."

I shake my head, knowing damn well the canoe weighs more than he's supposed to lift, even with the stern still in the water. Shoving my own paddle under the yoke, I snag the handle at the front of the boat and drag it ashore before he can make a grab for it.

Cindy sloshes along beside us like she's afraid we might change our minds and paddle away. "Thank you so much," she whispers, swiping the back of her hand over her eyes. "Let me just grab my purse, and I'll get you some cash."

"No need," I assure her as I beach the canoe. I glance back at Jon, aware that this isn't how we'd planned for Self-Care Sunday to unfold. "Are you okay with this?" I ask him. "We can paddle afterward."

"Are you kidding me? It's great." The admiration in his eyes is ten times more intense than what I saw there in his bedroom the other day. He's more awed by kindness to confused old men than he is by fellatio, which says something about his character.

I turn back to Cindy and catch her arm. "Wait. Anyone else whose name I should know?"

She nods toward the guy clutching her father's arm. "My brother the realist is Damon, and my husband in the blue T-shirt is Brady."

A bearded guy in blue waves from the picnic table, looking mildly puzzled. But he's already grabbing two more paper plates from a stack, ready to play along even if he's not sure what's happening. As we trudge ashore, several relatives call out their greetings.

"Angela. Um, good to see you again."

"Hey, Ang. I like your hair like that."

Adjusting my ponytail, I nod in greeting and head right for Archie. He's watching me with hopeful eyes, and I stretch out my hand with the broadest smile I've got. "Archie." I take his gnarled fingers in mine. "It's so good to see you again."

His smile is like a light blinking on in a dark attic. Rheumy blue eyes glitter as he pulls me to him for a bony hug. "I knew you'd come," he says. "Over here. I saved you a spot right next to me."

"I'd love that."

We link hands and head for the picnic table as Jon and Cindy's voices murmur behind us. I can't make out the words, but I love the note of awe I hear in Jon's voice. The way he's watching me like I'm his favorite woman on earth.

I hate how much I love it. How completely it fills the empty space in my chest.

Archie leads me toward the picnic table and makes like he's going to pull out my chair. Only there's no chair, so we do this awkward dance trying to get back behind the bench.

"Thank you," I tell him when we're seated side by side with a befuddled array of relatives. "What a beautiful day, isn't it?"

"It's my birthday," Archie announces proudly. "Eighty-five."

"I know." I put an arm around his bony shoulders and offer a little side hug. "Happy birthday, honey."

The endearment flows naturally, and I cross my fingers it's the right one. That Archie and Angie weren't the kind of couple opposed to pet names the way my parents are.

But Archie just beams and takes a bite out of his drumstick. "No one's spanked me yet."

"Oh." I'm not sure what to say, but Cindy takes the cue as she settles into a spot beside her husband.

"We'll save the birthday spankings for another time, Dad," she says. "Have some more potato salad."

Archie deems this a fair substitution, because he holds up his plate before turning back to me. "Do you remember when we first met?"

I nod, hoping someone will throw me a lifeline. "I do. What do you remember?"

"We were at a lake just like this one. It was springtime, and you were the most beautiful thing I'd ever seen."

Fondness clogs my throat, but Damon the Downer offers his own mumbled account from across the table. "It was the ocean. And autumn. And—"

"Shush." Cindy hands me a paper plate piled with my own servings of chicken and potato salad, then passes one to Jonathan. "What else do you remember about that day, Dad?"

"It was hot as hell, I'll tell you." He turns and gives me a bashful look. "'Scuse me, I know you don't like it when I swear."

"Not a problem." I take a bite of my chicken, warming to the idea that this genial octogenarian and I are a happily wedded couple. "I remember you looked so handsome."

He grins again, and this time there's mischief in it. "You said you liked a man in uniform," he says. "That's why you let me kiss you on the first date."

My God, I might die from the sweetness. I glance across the table at Jonathan, who's doing his best to blend in with the family. He's gripping a smiling sliver of watermelon and throws me a wink as Archie keeps talking.

"We danced all night, didn't we?" Archie's face is clouded in the bliss of memories, his food forgotten for now. "You remember the song?"

"Of course I do." I rest a hand on his arm. "Hum it for me?"

"We'll hum together." He launches into a tuneless rendition of something I can't identify. I do my best to keep up, going low and high when Archie does. The melody is familiar, but I have no idea what it is.

"'We Will Make Love' by Russ Hamilton," Jonathan supplies, throwing me another wink. "My grandmother loved that song."

"So did Mom." Cindy sniffs, then seems to catch herself as her gaze lands on me. "Didn't you love that song?"

"I sure did," I tell her. "Still do."

I take a bite of my chicken. It's crispy and full of flavor, home-made instead of store-bought. I could get used to being part of this family.

Archie's still nodding along with the silent music as he studies Jonathan across the table. I'm trying to come up with some explanation for Jon's presence here when Archie does it for me.

"You were none too pleased I met her first that night." His conspiratorial tone gets Jonathan nodding in agreement.

"No, sir," he says. "But I'm glad you got her."

"Wouldn't have happened at all if you weren't there to save my life." Archie takes a bite of drumstick, and his dentures wobble in his mouth. "Pushing me out of the line of fire the way you did."

"Best move I ever made." Jon doesn't miss a beat as he takes another bite of watermelon. "Yours was a life worth saving."

Archie grins, seemingly unaware that his top dentures are sagging on one side. "We sure had us a time with that—what's the word again?"

"Military ball?" Jonathan tries.

"Nah, the French word."

"Fete?" Jonathan tries. He glances at Cindy, who gives a small shrug.

Archie shakes his head and the top dentures droop lower. "Nah, the other French word."

"Soiree," I offer, shifting easily into the familiar language. "J'adore danser avec toi."

I pray that's right—that Archie and I really did love dancing together.

But he shakes his head and frowns. "Nah, that's not it." He runs his tongue over his teeth, shoving the top row of dentures back into place. "Hang on, it'll come to me."

Determined, I give it another shot. "Le festival? Le petite réception?"

Archie's blue eyes flash, and he snaps his fingers. "Ménage á trois." He bangs a hand on the table, jostling his drumstick off the plate as he throws an arm around me and tips his chin at Jonathan. "Man, the three of us had one helluva time. There was Angie, spread out like a—"

"More chicken anyone?" Cindy bolts up and grabs the Tupperware container in the center of the table. "We've got breasts, thighs…" She trails off, perhaps realizing another dish might be less suggestive. "Or watermelon?"

Damon the Downer jerks a thumb in the direction of the three teenagers gawking from the other end of the table. "Why don't you go play in the water or something?"

Grumbling a little, the kids scamper off while Cindy busies herself loading Archie's plate with a slice of chocolate cake. "Here you go, Dad," she says. "It's Mom's special recipe."

"Oh yeah?" He grins at me and gives a nudge with his elbow. "Is it that one you always made with real flour instead of that almond crap because you said Cindy's faking the gluten allergy?"

I grimace and shoot Cindy an apologetic look. "Archie," I chide patting his knobby back. "You're such a kidder."

"Life of the party," Jonathan puts in, hiding his laughter behind a drumstick. "You always had the best jokes."

"Yeah," Archie agrees, smiling at the shared memory as he stabs into his slice of cake. "Like how we told Damon I'm his dad, but really we don't have the foggiest who slipped one past the goalie. I mean we were all so drunk—"

"Okay, moving on." Cindy shoots an uncomfortable look at Damon, and I can't help noticing he's the lone brown-eyed family member at this table full of blue-eyed blondes. Yikes.

"This chicken sure is good, Cindy," I say, floundering for some safe topic of conversation. "You're a terrific cook."

"Thanks," She glances at her husband. "I had the good sense to marry a guy who cooks like a dream, since I can't boil water to save my life."

"You got that right." Archie laughs and sucks the dentures back into place with a big glob of chocolate against his gums. "That three grand we paid him to go out with you was money well spent."

Cindy's brow furrows, but Brady jumps to the rescue before she can follow up that line of conversation. "Tell us about your favorite birthday, Archie," he says, steering the conversation back onto neutral turf. "Maybe from when you were a kid."

Archie mulls that over, chewing his chocolate cake with deep reverence. "That year Cindy turned six. You remember that, sweetheart?"

Cindy nods as tears flood her eyes again. "You guys got me that bicycle I'd been begging for."

Archie pats her hand and stabs another piece of cake. "Taught you to ride it at the end of the driveway."

Smiling again, Cindy gives a soft little hiccup sob. "You were determined I'd have it down by the end of the day."

"We did it, too, didn't we?" Archie's beaming like a proud papa, and I can't help feeling my own twinge of pride. *This.* This is why we're playing along.

"I didn't even need the training wheels by the next day," Cindy says. "You were a good teacher."

Archie shakes his head a little sadly. "I felt so damn bad when you fell off that time," he says. "Knocked out both your front teeth."

A tear slips down Cindy's face, but she's laughing, too. "I got two silver dollars under my pillow for that. It was my first visit from the tooth fairy."

Archie leans conspiratorially over his cake and holds a finger to his lips. "Don't tell, but I was always the tooth fairy. You kids thought it was Mom, but it was me every time."

Even Damon looks touched by this bit of news. "Really? You wrote all those notes?"

"Every single one," Archie confirms, leaning back on the

bench. I put a hand between his shoulder blades to steady him, and he turns to me with a smile. The dentures sag to the left again, so I keep my eyes on his. "You helped with the poems sometimes, but the notes were all mine."

Circling my palm over his back, I flounder for something to contribute. "You were the master of tooth fairy penmanship."

He laughs and takes a swig from a can of Pepsi. "I was, wasn't I?"

Jonathan's smiling, too, caught up in the same nostalgia as the rest of us. "My dad was always the tooth fairy, too."

I catch his eye and know instantly he means Chuck. The man he wants to be instead of the one he fears becoming. His green eyes hold mine, and I'm seized by the urge to share my own stories of lost teeth and childhood memories. In Ukraine, there's no tooth fairy. Just a tradition of tucking the lost tooth in a square of tissue and hiding it in the darkest corner of the house.

"Viz'my miy staryy zub i prynesy meni novoho," my mother taught me to whisper, just like her mother taught her. "Take my old tooth and bring me a new one."

My father, brooding, called out from across the room. "You're teaching her to be selfish. Some kids don't have food or shelter or—"

"Some don't have love," my mother countered, tightening her hold on my shoulder. "And that's worse."

Beside me, Archie heaves a satisfied smile of nostalgia and pats my hand.

"So that's why I've got a box of teeth under my bed," he continues, still stuck on his own tooth fairy tale. "Not 'cuz it's some kind of sick fetish or anything."

Cindy blanches and dabs her mouth with a napkin. "We'd never think that, Dad."

"Or that box of ladies' underthings, size extra-large when Angie here's a size small," he continues. "Some things a man

155

keeps under his bed are his own private business, and even when he's dead and gone—"

"Who wants another soda?" Damon stands up, his dream-killer demeanor looking a lot more sensible now.

Cindy stares at her empty soda can, at a loss for what to do next. Her husband leans down and pries open a cooler, fishing into the icy depths. "Here." He sets a can of beer in front of her with a touching reverence.

"Thank you." She pops the top and chugs half of it without coming up for breath.

I glance over at Jonathan to see him watching me with an expression I can't quite read. "Family," he says, giving me a look I can't quite read. "Gotta love it."

Cindy shakes her head and grips the blue and white can. "God help us," she says before knocking back the rest of her beer.

* * *

"THAT WAS NUTS." Jonathan grins, one hand balanced on the steering wheel while the other covers my bare knee through the artfully frayed hole in my jeans. "I seriously had no idea what Archie was going to say next."

"I guess every family has secrets," I muse, remembering Cindy's pained expression as she ushered us to our canoe and thanked us for playing along.

"It's possible my brother had a point," she whispered, glancing back to where Archie and Damon waved goodbye from the shore. "Maybe it's smarter to keep Dad anchored in reality."

In the car beside me, Jonathan clears his throat. "I suppose that's true enough."

"What's true?" I do a mental rewind through the conversation, then remember where we left off. "Oh, you mean family secrets?"

"Lord knows my family has their fair share of them," he says. "It's amazing any of us turned out even halfway normal."

"You think you're normal?" His squeeze on my knee has me laughing and wriggling away, but who am I kidding? I don't want him to stop touching me. His hand feels good there, like it belongs. Like we belong, even though I know that can't be true.

Daddy issues.

What he said is true for both of us, and it's the reason we can never work out. I know it. He knows it. We both know it.

Right?

I cross my legs and end up sandwiching his fingertips between my thighs. I expect him to pull away, but he squeezes tighter. He's still got one hand on the wheel as he turns toward Ponderosa Resort, and I'm suddenly grateful I left my car there this morning. That he's not taking me home just yet.

"Poor Archie," Jonathan says. "I can't imagine losing your mind like that."

"He actually seemed in good spirits, all things considered," I point out. "It's his family bearing the brunt of things."

"True."

I shift again, my body following the urge to drift closer to him even though the rest of me knows it's a bad idea. "What is it with guys who aren't in their right mind wanting to talk about their sex lives?" I ask. "Something to do with the subconscious, I assume."

Jon quirks one eyebrow but keeps both eyes fixed on the road. "You've been around a lot of dirty-talking dementia patients?"

I look out the window as we move past the golf course, past the main lodge and onto the road leading to the family cabins. "Dementia, anesthesia, same thing." When he doesn't respond, I turn back to find him wearing an utterly blank expression. "The conversation in the hospital?" I prompt.

He takes his eyes off the road, brow furrowing as he studies me. "What do you mean?"

It occurs to me we've never had a conversation about this.

That maybe he recalls nothing of that ten-minute exchange at the hospital.

"You were delirious when you came out of surgery," I tell him. "Your mom said I should just play along. That you get loopy sometimes with anesthesia."

"My mom," he repeats, trying to jog his own memory. "What did I say?"

"Well," I begin, not sure how much to tell him. "You thought we were married. That we had two children."

He frowns out at the road, and I can practically hear the wheels turning in his head. "Sinbad?" He glances over at me, one eyebrow lifting hopefully. "And Eloise, right?"

"You remember." I'm not sure if I'm relieved or nervous.

He laughs and shakes his head. "Not really. I'm getting little flashes of stuff, but it's fuzzy."

"You told the nurse that you grow prizewinning zinnias," I tell him. "And that I bake the world's best cinnamon-raisin bread."

"No kidding?"

"For the record, I've never baked cinnamon-raisin bread," I admit. "I've never even tried it. I went home and googled to find out what it is."

He laughs again, green eyes catching the sunlight as he pulls into the parking spot in front of his cabin. "And let me guess." He kills the engine and turns to face me. "I talked about our sex life."

"You did," I confirm as heat trickles into my cheeks. "In front of your mother."

"God." He shakes his head, hand still on my knee. "It's coming back to me now. I said we had a fantastic sex life?"

"In a manner of speaking."

Our sex life—it's like—out-of-this-world phenomenal.

Jon grins, and I can tell it's all coming back to him. "And I asked how soon we could have sex."

"Yes."

His eyes lock with mine, fingertips tracing an invisible

pattern on the bare circle of flesh at my knee. "I'm still wondering that."

My heart kicks into a gallop, and I take a steadying breath. It's more than the intensity of his gaze turning my insides to lava. It's more than the suggestion of sex, though that's turning other parts of me to liquid.

It's the fantasy, the life I know we won't have together.

But maybe we can have something. Just one small piece, only for a little while.

"Now," I say softly. "How's now for you?"

"Now's good." His smile spreads slow and sexy, like butter on hot toast. Cinnamon-raisin. I'm melting, I'm dissolving into a buttery puddle, but I don't want to stop.

"Let's go," I say, and reach for the door handle.

CHAPTER 11

JONATHAN

This time, I'm the one leading the way down the hall to my bedroom. This time, I know exactly what's going to happen.

I think, anyway.

"Blanka." I turn in the doorway of my room to cup her face in my hands, kissing her softly before drawing back. "I want you so damn much."

She smiles and drags her fingers through my hair, going up on tiptoe to kiss me again. "I want you, too."

Her other hand cups my ass, and she presses herself against my fly, leaving little doubt she means it.

"How long?" I ask.

She blinks, probably assuming I mean my dick.

"How long have you wanted this and not gone for it?" I clarify, leaning down to kiss the soft hollow of her throat. "Denial of self-care, as it were."

Laughing, she tips her head back to grant me better access. Her throat, her shoulders, the soft trail of skin leading between her breasts. I devour it all while she considers the question.

"Since career day at the school." Her voice hitches as my

tongue skims the top of one breast, and her fingers clench in my hair. "Since the first time we met."

A surge of energy pulses through me. So it wasn't just me. I wasn't the only one who felt it, who recognized the lightning zaps of connection the first time we laid eyes on each other.

"Me, too," I murmur against her cleavage. "Or maybe longer."

Even before we met, I knew someone like her was out there somewhere. I felt it, even if I had no evidence. I believed in her the way a child believes in the tooth fairy, and isn't that what love is?

This isn't love, I remind myself as I edge us both toward the bed. *Not love, just lust.*

My head might hear the words rattling between my ears, but the rest of me isn't buying it. Not with Blanka pressed warm and soft against me, tumbling onto the bed with her hair spread like silk on the pillow. Kissing her deep, I come up for air and thread my fingers through hers.

"No balloons this time," I whisper against her throat. "I want this to be a two-way street."

She nods, flesh moving under my lips as I roll her onto her back. Releasing her hands, I unbutton the blue chambray shirt until I reach the tails knotted at her waist. I unwrap her like a birthday gift, watching as the fabric falls open to reveal the softness of her breasts under a cotton tank the color of cream. There's an edge of lace over her breasts, and I take my time dotting kisses across the span of it.

"Jonathan." She pulls me back up and draws my mouth to hers, as hungry as I am for hot, wet kisses that seem to last for days.

I could do this forever, the kissing, the touching, the soft echo of her sighs filling the room. She's first to break away this time, lips moving to explore the stubble at my jawline. Her fingers skim my chest as she kisses her way along my temple, her tongue flicking the pulse throbbing there. Hands move

161

down to grab the hem of my shirt, and I roll to help her tug it off.

"You are so sexy," she murmurs, planting a trail of kisses down my chest, across my abdomen, lower still.

"Wait." I draw her back up until her mouth is level with mine. I can't resist kissing her again and almost forget what I meant to say.

"Let me taste you," I murmur as I draw back. "Please, I want my mouth on you this time."

She laughs, which is hardly the response I expected. "Pull my arm," she says.

"What?"

Frowning, she appears to replay the words in her mind. "Pull my finger?"

"Um—"

"No—*twist!*" She laughs so hard she almost falls off the bed. "Twist my arm."

She's still laughing as I kiss my way down her center, pausing long enough to unbutton her jeans and draw them down her legs, along with her panties.

But as my tongue grazes her slippery seam, laughter spikes into a sharp cry of pleasure. "Oh, God."

I circle my tongue around the sensitive nub of nerves as she cries out again and arches under me. Anchoring one arm under her hips, I angle her up to meet my lips. Jesus, she's sweet. So sweet and soft and unbelievably wet. The sounds she's making in the back of her throat are turning me on like nothing I've felt before, and I reach down to unhook my jeans and give myself some relief.

Blanka laughs again, but it dissolves into another moan. "Need some help?"

"I've got everything in hand," I assure her, stroking my gratefully freed cock before returning my hand to its proper place between her legs.

Slipping two fingers inside her, I suck her clit into my mouth. *"Ty moe povitria."*

Her words don't stop me. Nothing could stop me, not even the uncertainty of what they mean. I keep devouring her, letting her voice flow over me. There's no urgency to know anything, no need to have it all spelled out. It's enough to feel her moving beneath me, to hear her breath quickening and my own name tangled among the unrecognizable syllables falling from her lips.

Her slick walls clench around my fingers, and she bunches the sheets in a white-knuckled grip. She's close.

"God, yes," I groan around her as she cries out and arches into the stroking of my tongue.

"Jon!" She cries out my name again and again as I move inside her, fingers, tongue, a dozen other parts of me that aren't touching her at all.

She's gasping as she comes back down, and I expect her to lie still and catch her breath.

But Blanka grabs me by the shoulders and drags me up her body. "I need you." She's wild-eyed and beautiful and the sexiest woman I've seen in my life. "Make love to me, please."

It's a phrase I've never used. *Having sex*, sure. *Hooking up* or *knocking boots* or even *fucking*.

But making love, that's not something I've thought about. Not until now, with Blanka breathless and bright-eyed and looking at me like she sees inside my soul and likes it.

"God, you're gorgeous." I can't look away as I fumble in the nightstand for a condom. I come up with a screwdriver and a pack of matches before Blanka sits up laughing and grabs the foil packet from the drawer.

"Let me," she says, and proceeds to roll it on.

It's my turn to groan as I slip between her thighs and push slowly inside. Her eyes go wide as I ease into her, sliding as deep as I can until I can't distinguish where my body ends and hers begins.

Making love.

My God, is that what this is?

Her thighs clench around me, breath hitching as she murmurs words I can't understand but know on some primal level. I'm murmuring back, lips against her throat, brain bursting with bright spots of color like the field of zinnias beyond the pond.

I fight my way back through the fog, determined to see to her pleasure. To make sure I give as well as take. Pushing back to slip a hand between our bodies, I find hers already there, fingertips gliding over slick folds.

"God, I love that." I love that she's confident enough to touch herself, to take what she needs.

And I love the way her eyes go wide, the way she clenches around me as I drive in deep. Her hands fly to my hips, and she digs her nails in. "Jonathan. *Now.*"

We shatter together, coming apart at the same time. It's otherworldly, our breath in sync, hearts drumming to a beat I've known forever but never recognized. She cries out and arches tight against me but doesn't close her eyes. We're locked together by breath, by body, by something I can't name.

"Holy Christ," I pant as we come back down.

We're both breathing hard as I pull the covers around us. She murmurs something against my shoulder as I draw her against me. I don't think it's English, but I understand anyway.

I kiss the spot just above her ear and whisper the words I googled weeks ago, just after our bath. "Ja vas kohaju," I whisper.

She tenses in my arms. "What did you say?"

"Ja vas kohaju," I repeat, hoping I read the pronunciation key correctly. Hoping Google didn't steer me wrong. It's hard to find phonetic pronunciations, and the Ukrainian alphabet is a mystery.

Blanka says nothing. Just lies there breathing. My urge to crack the tension with humor overwhelms me. "Okay, so right now I'm really hoping I haven't just asked if I can borrow ketchup."

She laughs, a welcome sound. And since I'm still hard inside her, I feel the clench of her body around me. "No, but—" she licks her lips, looking into my eyes. "You learned to say 'I love you' in Ukrainian?"

I nod, not sure whether I'm happier I got it right or that she hasn't sprinted screaming from the room. "I love you," I repeat in English, just to make sure we're clear. "I know we're not supposed to, and there are all kinds of reasons we shouldn't go there, but I can't help it. I'm crazy about you."

The smile spreads slowly over her face, like she can't quite believe what she's hearing. I don't expect her to say it back. It's enough to have her lying here with me, heart thudding against mine as we hold each other tight.

"I love you, too," she murmurs. "Ja vas kohaju."

"Your accent's a lot better than mine."

She laughs again, and this time I slip out of her body. "Thanks," she says as I reach down as discreetly as I can to get rid of the condom. "I've been practicing."

So have I. Everything I've done in life has been leading me to this moment, right here, right now, with Blanka.

I just never knew it.

As I kiss her again, I say a silent prayer I'll find a way to hold onto it. That I don't screw this up somehow.

* * *

SOMETIME IN THE NIGHT, I wake to the weirdest sound I've ever heard. At first, I think something's wrong with Blanka, and I bolt upright in bed.

But she's fast asleep beside me, one fist curled against her cheek and her hair fanned softly across the pillow.

The sounds are definitely coming from down the hall.

Throwing off the covers, I fumble in the darkness for a pair of sweatpants. Blanka comes to as I'm pulling on a T-shirt, and she rolls with the sheets clutched to her breasts.

"What is it?" Her voice is sleep-husky, which sounds a lot like sex-husky. It takes superhuman strength not to crawl back in bed and make love to her again. Superhuman strength and another guttural yowl from down the hall.

"I think it's Jessica," I tell her. "Something's wrong."

That's all the explanation she needs. Blanka leaps out of bed, not bothering to locate her own clothes. She grabs my robe off the back of the door and pulls it around herself as we hurry down the hall to the closed office door.

"That sound," Blanka whispers. "It's like a horse choking on an apple."

"You're familiar with the sound of a horse choking on an apple?"

"I volunteered at an equine rehab center in grade school," she says as I reach for the doorknob. "I also watched YouTube videos of cats delivering babies, and it sounds the same."

We push through the door together, and my eyes adjust slowly to the dimness. Over in the corner is the glowing green nightlight I plugged in last week, and beside it is Jessica. She's sprawled at the edge of her refrigerator box maternity ward looking like an angry, beached walrus.

"Brrrrow," she growls as her sides heave. "*Brrrrrrrrrrow.*"

"That one had more syllables than normal." Blanka drops to her knees beside the box. "She might be close."

"How do you—oh my God."

I blink as a wet, furry potato emerges from Jessica's back end. The potato wiggles, freeing four tiny paws and a gray golf ball head with the smallest ears I've ever seen.

"Your first kitten," Blanka coos. "Congratulations."

"Thank you." I'm surprised by the tightness in my chest.

"Not you, Jessica."

Jessica's not thrilled as her sides heave again. She muscles through another contraction, then curls in on herself to clean the little fur blob.

"Oh!" Blanka draws her hands to her mouth and bounces back on her heels. "Have you ever seen anything so precious?"

Precious is not the word I'd use to describe the gooey, alien-like hairball wriggling on the pile of clean towels, but I nod anyway. "Precious," I repeat for lack of a better word.

"Look!" Blanka points to a second fur potato moving around on the gray towel beside Jessica. "There's another kitten. She must have had one before we got here."

"Brrrrow," says Jessica, signaling us there's a third one coming.

We watch in wonder as the miracle of birth unfolds in all its technicolor glory. All its messy, slimy, *oh-my-God-what-is-that* glory.

Blanka leans in and strokes Jessica's side, palm soothing the ripple of muscle moving down her abdomen. "Jade mentioned that might help with contractions."

"You're doing good," I tell them both, wishing I'd watched the YouTube videos or maybe studied up on Lamaze. "Breathe or push or—whatever you're supposed to be doing."

"Brrrrow," Jessica grumbles, and gives another mighty heave.

"Four," Blanka whispers triumphantly, giving a silent clap. Her eyes sparkle in the green glow of the nightlight as Jessica leans down to tend her newest crotch fruit.

We wait in silence for more kittens to appear, or for Jessica's head to spin around. It's the first time I've witnessed feline birth, and it's not unlike an exorcism.

But also magical. When I glance at Blanka again, my heart does a little shiver of wonder.

"Pretty cool," I admit, sliding around her and kissing the side of her head.

"That was amazing." Blanka breathes the words like a prayer. "Good job, mama."

The cat ignores her, intent on cleaning the tiny, alien creatures clawing at her side. There's a gray one, two tiger stiped kittens, and one in mottled shades of orangey-tan. Their eyes scrunch tightly closed as they make their way to the dinner nozzles jutting from their mother's side.

A soft, low purr fills the space around us, and it takes me a moment to recognize it as Jessica and not my heart rumbling its contentment.

This.

This is what I want.

This right here, Blanka curled against me in the warm little room that smells like cedar shavings and wet fur. The patter of rain against the skylight, the softness of Blanka's hair tickling my chin.

I've spent a lifetime doing meaningful work, but none of it has felt as meaningful as this moment, this magic, right here. I could be happy with this.

In that moment, I totally believe it.

CHAPTER 12

BLANKA

*J*on and I name the kittens together that night, laughing like kids at a slumber party. We're radiant with the intimacy of what we've witnessed and the glow of what came before that.

And what came an hour later. And twice more before I left at dawn the next morning, just as the sun was creeping up over the juniper-lined horizon.

"So, we're in agreement," Jon says as we kiss goodbye for the hundredth time. "Sinbad, Eloise, Raisin, and Zinnia."

"You know Eloise might turn out to be a boy," I point out, pulling my car keys from the pocket of my fleece jacket. "Or Sinbad. What makes you think he's male?"

Jonathan just shrugs. "We'll figure it out." He plants one more kiss on the side of my head. "I don't just mean the kittens."

Something flutters in my belly. "What else?"

"Us." He laces his fingers through mine. "I know it's complicated, and it's way too soon to start making plans. And I know you hate the idea of traditional relationships for all kinds of totally valid reasons. But—"

"Okay."

He blinks, then smiles slowly. "What?"

"I'm sorry, I should let you finish."

He laughs and shakes his head. "I'm pretty sure you'd complete my thoughts better than I could."

"No, go ahead." God, I'm an idiot. Why didn't I let the poor man finish? "Please."

Still grinning, he squeezes my hands. "I want to be with you. Whether that means putting down roots here or some other solution we work out between us. Bottom line, I'm not letting you go."

I stand frozen in that moment, heart thudding in my ears as my brain replays those words again and again. *I'm not letting you go.* They're exactly what I've wished for. Deep down, despite all my protests to the contrary, this is what I've wanted. To be claimed. To matter this much to another human.

Never before have I laid that desire out for myself or anyone else, but there it is, naked on the sun-dappled lawn.

Jon's face twists in an exaggerated grimace, and it occurs to me I haven't said anything out loud for a long time. "Did I sound like a stalker?" he asks. "I didn't mean—"

"No, it's great." I laugh and squeeze his fingers. "I want that, too."

"Thank God." He kisses me again, soft and sweet and tasting of relief. "I love you so much."

"I love you, too."

His grin lights up the whole porch. "So, we're on the same page. "

"Sounds like it."

"I'm glad." Releasing my hands, he takes a step back. "Okay, so now I really will let you go, but only so you can get home. Can I see you again tonight?"

I can't hold back the foolish grin spreading over my face. "I think we can make that work."

All of it, not just the date. Right then, I'm convinced we'll make it all work somehow. It's thrilling and terrifying and all the things I never expected to feel for anyone.

This is love. Not my parents' brand of it. It's the kind I've read about in romance novels. The kind I've caught glimpses of between Jon's parents.

I never thought I'd have it for myself. Now that I do, I can't stop smiling.

The thrill of it keeps me going as my parents' visit draws nearer. I clean like a mad woman, scouring my house from top to bottom. I put fresh sheets on the guest bed and bake a batch of my mother's favorite medianyky honey cookies.

The morning my parents arrive, I'm racing through the grocery store like a finalist in a speed shopping competition. I'm in sweatpants with my hair in a frizzy bun, and I'm throwing things in my cart at random when my phone rings. I slip it out of my purse, and a smile dissolves the tension in my jaw. It's Jon's name on the readout.

"Hey there." I grab a bag of kale, then put it back, remembering the time my dad chided me for buying pre-cut veggies in plastic instead of organic stuff from a farmers' market.

"Hey yourself," Jon says on the other end of the line. "Miss you already."

I laugh and wheel my cart around the corner, thrilled to have a guy missing me mere hours after we last saw each other. Even more thrilled that guy is Jonathan.

I toss a carton of eggs in my cart, wincing when I remember tossing isn't the right move with eggs. "I miss you, too."

Peeling open the cardboard carton, I'm relieved to see all twelve shells intact. I swear I'd buy them anyway. I know better than to be wasteful with food.

"What are you up to this evening?" Jon asks in his usual jovial tone.

"Er, picking my parents up at the airport?" Surely he hasn't forgotten.

"I know that, but did you have plans with them? Dinner, I mean."

"I was going to make Chicken Kiev, but I got a late start and now I'm wondering if they'll kill me if I take them out for burgers or something."

That's American, right? I can claim it's an attempt to show them traditional American food, rather than a sign I'm lazy and unwelcoming. I peer at the label on a package of gluten-free pancake mix. Another smile tugs the edges of my mouth as I remember lunch with Archie and his family.

Was that just two weeks ago? It feels like a lifetime since Jon and I became a couple. We've spent nearly every night together, making dinners and watching the kittens and snuggling on the sofa having sex.

Making love.

It really does feel like that.

"Don't bother."

Jon's voice jars me back to the phone call, and it takes me a moment to figure out what he's talking about. "Don't bother with burgers, you mean?"

"Right," he says. "My brother, Sean, has this friend in town from culinary school. She's visiting from the South somewhere."

"I think Amber mentioned it."

"Right, so they're testing out this gastronomic fusion thing. Some kind of mashup between Sean's Pacific Northwest stuff and her spin on Southern food."

"Sounds amazing." I can't actually imagine what that would be like, but my stomach growls anyway. I'm a sucker for culinary shows, especially the ones that geek out on the science behind the recipes.

"You're invited," Jon says. "You and your parents. They want to test it out before they launch the guest chef series, so Sean asked us to round up some guinea pigs."

"Er, they're not actually serving guinea pig, right?" I'm pretty sure that's a delicacy in Peru, but probably not the South he means.

He laughs, a sound that travels through the phone line and spears the center of my chest. "No rodents of any kind," he assures me. "Athena—that's the other chef—she's Michelin star famous, too. Even has her own cooking show."

"Athena Reynolds?" I ask. "From Misfit Kitchen?"

"You've heard of her?"

"I love her show." Damn, now I'm really excited.

And my dad will love her take on sustainable farming practices. That's a big thing with Sean, too, the whole farm-to-table movement and knowing where food comes from.

"We'll be there," I tell him. "Thank you. What time?"

"The dinner starts at seven, but there's a cocktail hour before," he says. "Show up any time between six and six-thirty. Are you okay with this?"

"Am I okay with having two famous chefs relieve me of the burden of preparing dinner for my parents? Let me think about that."

He laughs, but there's a nervous edge to it. "Having me meet your parents, I mean," he says. "I know it's kind of soon, but—"

"I love you," I blurt, amazed at how easily those words come to me now. "And they'll love you, too. It's going to be great."

There's a long pause, then a low whistle from Jon's end of the line. "Damn," he says, drawing the word out dramatically. "How did I get so lucky?"

"You picked me up at your sister's wedding," I point out, smiling at the mom coming down the aisle with an overflowing cart. She's got a toddler in the basket and an infant strapped in a carrier against her chest. Her husband walks up and drops a kiss on her cheek before setting a gallon of milk in the cart and rumpling the toddler's hair.

I want that.

Where on earth did *that* come from? Six weeks ago, I was

staunchly in the never-ever camp of matrimony. Now I'm ogling happy families like they're my personal porn?

But I can't ignore the twist in my chest, the fact that my brain is loping down a path of wonder. What would it be like to have that? The doting husband, the kids, the happy marriage. I've never allowed myself to consider it.

"So I'll see you around six," Jon says in my ear. "And Blanka?"

"Yes?"

"I love you, too."

I'm still glowing from those words as I drive home and unpack the groceries. The glow carries me all the way to the airport where I park the car and race to the entrance, a bouquet of fall flowers clutched in one hand.

If I've timed this right, I'll catch my parents as they come off the plane. Relief washes through me as I catch sight of them shuffling through the revolving doors. There's my father striding forward with his battered carry-on, his face tan and authoritative. My mom is two paces behind him, tired but relaxed.

Her face lights up when she sees me. "Blanka! Moya prekrasna divchynka!"

Even now, at nearly thirty years old, I'm her beautiful baby girl.

My mom and I crash together in a hug that's warm and smells like roses, and I'm reminded again of the face cream. Of the memories that draw us back to childhood. No matter how old you are, a mother's hug always feels like home.

"Blanka." My father clears his throat behind us, and I break away from my mom and turn to face him. "Good to see you again."

"You, too." I consider hugging him, but he makes no move to embrace me. I settle for stretching out a hand to shake his, but he mistakes it as a grab for his suitcase.

"I can get my own bag," he says, Ukrainian accent thicker than I remembered. "I hope you didn't buy those at a store."

"What? Oh, the flowers?" I look down at the bouquet in my hands. "I didn't, actually. I picked them at the resort where we're having dinner tonight."

"We're having dinner at a resort?" My mother's face turns up in a smile, the wattage cranking higher as I hand her the bouquet. "Oh, thank you, dear. They're beautiful."

"I'm glad you like them," I tell her. "We can put them in a vase when we get to my house."

"Hmm," my father says as the three of us fall into step together. "You're still in that place that's big enough to provide shelter for four families?"

My home is barely twelve-hundred square feet and perfectly modest, but I nod and smile and lead them to the door. "It's a good investment."

We chatter easily enough on the drive to my house, alternating between English and Ukrainian. My mother and I do most of the talking, but my dad chimes in occasionally about wrapping up the orphanage project in Nairobi and what's next on the horizon.

"We're starting a new program in Dovlano," he says proudly as I hit my blinker to take the Empire exit off the parkway. "That's a tiny nation in Southern Europe. The wealthiest of the wealthy and the poorest of the poor, all in one minuscule landmass."

"Isabella's home country," I say with a start.

"What?" my father asks. Apparently not caring very much about the answer, he continues with his announcement. "We haven't launched the project publicly yet. You're one of the first to know."

"Dovlano," I say out loud, glancing at my mother. She's staring straight ahead, her blank face giving no indication how she feels about another major move. "That's a long ways away."

My father frowns. "Your English is atrocious. What kind of slang is that? *Long ways away*? This is what happens when you live in America too long."

I sigh and turn the car onto the narrow street that leads to my little rambler. "No need to get bent into shape," I mutter.

Wait. That wasn't right. "Out of."

My father frowns. "What?"

"Never mind."

For some reason, screwing up an idiom reminds me of Jonathan. Of the fact that he finds my mistakes charming instead of irritating. I can't wait to see him again. Can't wait for my parents to meet him, to know I've found a guy who's smart and accomplished and—

"What's this about dinner at a resort?" my father asks as I unlock my front door and usher them inside. "You know I don't approve of spending absurd sums on gourmet dining when there are starving people in—"

"It's free," I interrupt, pretty sure that's true. Jon didn't specify, but isn't that what it means when someone invites you to dinner? "I'm friends with the family that owns the place, and actually—" I take a deep breath, preparing to say the words I've been practicing all day. "—Actually, my boyfriend is one of the owners."

Boyfriend. It's the first time I've said the word out loud, and I listen as it pings around my little living room, bouncing off the secondhand sofa and landing in the center of the wool rug from Morocco.

My mom clasps her hands over her chest and beams, glancing at my father. Even my dad looks taken aback, though there's skepticism in his eyes.

"You're dating the owner of a luxury resort?"

"His family owns the resort," I tell him, having rehearsed these words carefully. "Jonathan's a silent partner. He's spent the last few years captaining a ship for Sea-Watch, and before that—"

"Sea-Watch?" My father gapes, impressed for the first time in years. "The humanitarian group that rescues refugees in the central Mediterranean?"

"That's the one," I tell him, trying hard not to sound boastful.

"He's on medical leave right now because he donated a kidney to his sister."

"My goodness." My mother claps her hands like I've just recited a cure for cancer. "He sounds like an amazing young man. I can't wait to meet him."

"And you will." I glance at my watch. "In less than an hour, so if you'd like to freshen up, the guest bath is all yours. The towels are clean."

For once, my father doesn't say anything about the impact of textile production on the environment or how more than thirty-five percent of the world lacks clean water and basic sanitation. Just grabs his suitcase and wheels it down the hall, murmuring to my mother in Ukrainian.

Is it wrong to gloat just a little? To feel proud he's impressed by something I've done, even if it's just landing a man who ticks most of the boxes for his approval.

Everyone's in good spirits as we drive out to the resort. The Ponderosa Luxury Ranch Resort sign in curlicue copper and iron makes my mom gasp in wonder, and my dad points out the herd of mule deer munching grass in the pasture. The sun's plummeting fast toward the mountains, and my mother pauses behind the car after we park and whips out her camera.

"I want to take a picture," she says. "To remember it by."

My father looks at his watch. "We should hurry if we want to—"

"Both of you, over there," my mother orders in a rare show of assertiveness. "I want to capture this moment."

My father sighs but drapes an arm around my shoulders as we turn our backs toward the mountains and my mom clicks away with her iPhone. "There," she says, tucking the phone back in her purse. "You two look so much alike."

I glance at my father, taking in his strong jaw, his cool blue eyes, the intense look of determination on his face. My mother's told us countless times we resemble one another, but I never see it.

"Let's go," I tell them. "We don't want to be late."

We've almost reached the front of the lodge when Bree steps out the front doors and smiles. "Blanka." She pulls me into a hug that feels like balancing a basketball between us. "I'm so glad you could make it."

"It's good to see you," I say, hugging carefully so I don't squish the baby. "How many weeks to go?"

"Three weeks, six days, and too many hours, but who's counting?" She winces and puts a hand on her belly. "Okay, I'm counting. Every minute and hour and—oh, sorry, where are my manners?" She stretches out a hand to my mother. "Bree Bracelyn-Dugan, I'm the VP of Marketing at Ponderosa Resort. You must be Blanka's parents?"

"Pleasure to meet you." My father offers her a stiff handshake. "Thomas Kushnir Kramer. Thank you for having us to dinner."

I wait for him to introduce my mother, but he's already turned to survey the sun sinking behind the Cascade Range. It's impressive from this angle, the snow-capped peaks jutting into whipped cream fluff of pink and orange. I give him a pass and introduce her myself. "Bree, this is my mother, Galyna Pavlo."

"Pleasure to meet you." Bree shakes my mother's hand before waving us inside. "You can head in if you like. There's already a good crowd, and Jon's saving you a table with the best view. We've got a gorgeous sunset tonight."

"Thank you." I rest a hand between my mother's shoulder blades, guiding her in the direction of Juniper Fine Dining. A sign at the entry announces the menu for the six-course Pacific Northwest and Southern Fusion Experience hosted by Sean Bracelyn and Athena Reynolds.

"Athena has a show called Misfit Kitchen," I tell my mother, hopeful she's seen it. "And Sean is Jonathan's brother."

My mother nods, pleasure spreading over her face. "And Jonathan is your man."

"Yes." It's all I can do to tamp down the pride in my voice. "Yes, he is."

"Blanka!"

I look up to see Jon striding toward us, trademark smile on full display. He's wearing a tie, and I blink twice to make sure it's not the one with the tiny penises. Face heating with the memory, I slip into his arms as he pulls me close for a hug.

"I'm so glad you made it." With a tight squeeze, he lets me go, then turns to my parents. "It's an honor to meet you."

It takes me a moment to realize it's my mother he's addressing first. He's clasping her hand in his, shaking it firmly while holding eye contact.

I didn't realize it was possible to love him more.

"I've heard so much about you," he says. "Blanka's showed me some of your art. I love that painting you did of the mother and child in front of the Charles Bridge in Prague."

"Why thank you." My mother straightens, visibly startled. I'm not sure if it's from Jon's recognition of the landmark, or the fact that I've shared her art with him. Either way, pride lights her eyes. "I painted that nearly twenty years ago. I've always wished I could find that mother to give her a copy."

"Did you paint it from a photograph or make up the whole scene?" Jon's holding eye contact, genuinely interested in the answer.

My mother blooms under his attention. Few people bother asking her about herself this way. "I took a photo the day I visited, but most of the detail was here." She touches her forehead, smiling a little.

"It's an incredible painting," Jon says. "The way you captured the light—it's almost ethereal."

I'm not positive my mother knows that word in English, so I translate quickly. "Ah," she says, beaming. "Yes, thank you."

Jonathan smiles. "It's an honor to meet you, Mrs. Pavlo."

"Please, call me Galyna."

"Galyna," he says. "That means calm, doesn't it?"

My mother blinks. "You speak Ukrainian?"

"Only a few words." His face flushes just a little as he throws me a wink. "I've had extra time on my hands lately, so I'm taking an online language course."

My mother and I do a simultaneous swoon, perhaps for different reasons.

As my boyfriend—*boyfriend!*—turns to my father, I can't miss the flash of hero worship in Jon's eyes. Who could blame him? My father has that effect on people, but especially a guy whose life's work has been all about helping people.

"Mr. Kushnir Kramer," he says. "Congratulations on your nomination for the Robert F. Kennedy Human Rights Award. I've followed your work for years, and it's an honor to meet you."

"You as well, son." He pumps Jon's hand, assessing him the way men do with each other. "I understand you've been working for Sea-Watch."

"Yes, sir," he says. "It's a terrific organization, and I'm proud of the time I spent with them."

Jon's use of past tense isn't lost on my father. "You've left the organization for good?" He tilts his head, and I can't tell what the right answer is in his mind.

Jonathan slips an arm around my waist, and a sense of rightness floods my system. *This.* This is the exact right answer in my mind. "I'm taking some time to assess what comes next," he says. "If I've learned anything, it's that the best opportunities appear when you least expect them."

There goes my mother swooning again, though my father seems to miss it. He misses the flush in my cheeks as well, though I feel like I'm burning up. Maybe that's Jon's arm around me, his presence simultaneously comforting and arousing. I should definitely not be getting turned on in front of my parents.

Fortunately, we're saved by Jonathan's mother.

"Hey, you two—sorry we're late."

Wendy's voice makes me turn toward the door as she and Chuck arrive hand in hand. Their proximity to one another, the casual ease of how they move together, is a marked contrast to my own parents' connection. Or lack thereof. There's five feet of space between my mom and my dad, a common enough arrangement that I've wondered how I was conceived at all.

"You're not late," Jonathan assures them, sliding his arm from around me to properly greet his parents. "We just got here ourselves."

Chuck scrubs a hand over his forehead, frowning a little. "I lost track of time. Got busy helping Gretchen plan her route for driving out to Denver next week."

"We're here," Wendy says brightly, but there's an off-note in her voice. A strain in her expression that she's trying hard to hide.

"Hey, Wendy." I pull her in for a quick hug, conscious of how tense her shoulders are.

She hugs me in return while Jon makes introductions. As I draw back, I watch Chuck for signs something's wrong. He looks the same as always, so maybe the tension is all in my head.

"So lovely to meet you." Wendy hugs my startled-looking mother, who rarely hugs anyone besides me. "We just adore Blanka," Wendy's saying. "You must be so proud of everything she's accomplished. Her work at the USGS—"

"Yes, she's very well-educated," my father interrupts with a glance at Jonathan. "But it's nice to see her becoming more well-rounded."

There's a long, awkward silence. Even Wendy seems unsure what to say.

But Jon slides his arm around me again, and his quick hip squeeze feels like a signal. "I've always found Blanka to be perfectly rounded," he says. "It's one of the things I love about her."

Love. He really just said it in front of my parents. His parents, too, which feels like a huge step.

My father clears his throat. "And how long have the two of you known each other?"

We're spared from answering when a middle-aged woman grabs Jonathan by the arm. "Dear Lord, you must be Cort's son."

And just like that, the light leaves Jonathan's smile. The smile stays locked in place, but there's a sudden dimness in his eyes. "I —um—yes."

The woman's still gripping his arm, oblivious to the impact her words are having on Jon. "I own a restaurant in town, and your father used to come in all the time," she says. "It's uncanny how much you look like him. It's nice to see you're here keeping his legacy alive."

"Right. Um. Yes." Jon's gone positively gray.

I'm ready to jump in and rescue him when the chime of an old-fashioned dinner bell punches through the curtain of awkwardness.

The woman wanders away as all eyes swivel toward the kitchen entrance where Sean stands in chef whites beside a beautiful woman with brown hair and gray eyes.

"Good evening, everyone," Sean says. "Thanks to all of you for coming tonight. For those who haven't met her yet, this is Chef Athena Reynolds of the Misfit Inn in Tennessee. Some of you might recognize her from her show Misfit Kitchen."

Athena smiles and surveys the crowd. "Thanks for having me, y'all. It's sure beautiful out here. I'll have to bring my boyfriend next time."

Sean grins and gives her a wink. "Makes a great place to get engaged," he points out. "Or have a honeymoon."

Athena's cheeks pinken, but her smile shows how much she likes that idea. "Let's not put the cart before the horse."

Sean and Athena riff back and forth about the menu, and twice I have to lean over and translate culinary phrases for my mother. A smartly dressed waitress moves past with a tray of icy cocktails made with Douglas Fir liqueur and some kind of fancy Southern bourbon. Each glass bears a garnish of juniper berries and mint leaves anchored on a tiny copper spear.

"This is delicious." Jonathan's mother sips her drink as we're led to a long, live-edge table in the corner. "I can't wait to see what else is on the menu."

Chuck glances at his watch. "How many courses did they say this is?"

Wendy's smile falters. "Six, why?"

He shrugs and pulls out her chair. "I was hoping to get some work done on that cradle for Bree's baby. Mark offered his woodshop tonight."

"Tonight?" Wendy frowns. "We agreed this would be date night. You said we'd hike up to that point to watch the stars."

"Right, right." Chuck plants a kiss at the edge of her hairline as he takes his seat beside Wendy. "Some other time."

Wendy opens her mouth, then closes it quick. I can tell she's wondering the same thing I am—some other time for the hike or the woodworking? —but she doesn't push.

Still, I can't be the only one to notice the flash of pain in her eyes. It's the sort of thing Jon would usually catch, but he's deep in conversation with my father.

"We're wrapping things up over the next couple weeks with the orphanage," my father's saying.

Jon frowns. "The orphanage isn't going away, is it?'

"No, definitely not." My father sips his drink and makes a face. He sets the glass down at the head of the table, claiming the spot for himself. "Just handing it over to local organizers so we can turn our efforts toward new endeavors. It's important to empower local communities, you know."

"Absolutely." Jon squeezes my hand once before releasing it to pull out my chair. He drops a kiss on my temple as I sit down, and I feel myself glowing again. As he takes the seat between my father and me, he slips a hand over my bare knee and gives another squeeze.

Love you, he mouths silently.

Love you, too.

He turns to address the rest of the table. "Does anyone mind if we save a spot for my niece? She wants to join us later."

"Of course," Wendy says, unfolding her napkin onto her lap. "This is Mark's girl?"

"Libby, yes." Jon shakes out his own napkin and smiles at my mother. "My brother and her mom got married a few months ago."

"How old is she?" my mother asks.

"Seven," Jon says. "I've loved getting to know her while I've been home."

Home.

There's that word again. It's not the first time I've heard him say that about Ponderosa, but I'm catching it more often now. I know it's presumptuous, but I can't help thinking of myself as part of that package. *Home,* whatever that means to Jonathan.

I glance around our table, cataloging everyone's seat choices. My father's at the head, of course, with Jonathan to his right. Across from Jon to my father's left is the empty spot reserved for Libby. Next to that is Chuck, who's got his arm around Wendy. My mom sits stiffly next to Wendy, diagonally across from me. She's ramrod straight in her chair, not smiling, but not looking uncomfortable, either. She's just...there. The furniture in my father's life, and a twist of sadness grabs my guts.

I watch her until she looks up, then give her a small smile. "I'm glad you're here, Mom."

"Yes, thank you." Her smile is tiny, but warm. "So am I."

I glance toward my father, holding court at the other end of the table. Does anyone else notice the distance between my parents? Not just physical, but everything. I wonder if there was a point long ago when the two of them burned with passion. If they ever felt the same way Jon and I do now.

Feeling my eyes on him, Jonathan catches my eye and reaches under the table to touch my knee again.

"Here, Uncle Jonathan." Libby bustles over and thrusts a basket into Jon's hands. "It's kinda like Indian fry bread—"

"From India or Native American?" my father interjects.

I open my mouth to point out a seven-year-old isn't going to know that, but Libby doesn't miss a beat.

"Native American," Libby says, lifting her chin. "The Northern Paiutes, the Wasco, and the Warm Springs tribes are part of the Confederated Tribes of Warm Springs, and their land is that way." She points north, and I half expect her to break out a map of the nearby reservation. "They make fry bread like this, and Chef Athena is serving it with bourbon bacon butter because she's from the South and in the South they put bourbon and bacon on everything."

I'm tempted to applaud both the child and the Bend Public School System, but I settle for giving her a discreet low-five.

"Sounds delicious." Jon takes the basket and winks. "They're putting you to work tonight, huh?"

Libby nods and shoves her hands in the pockets of her apron. "Mom says if I want another pet rabbit, I have to earn it. Uncle Sean said I could bus tables."

"Your mom's smart," he says. "You always appreciate the things you have to work for."

Libby looks dubious. "Mom and Mark want a baby and they're working at it all the time. Always in the bedroom with the door closed and—"

"Aaaand I'm guessing they don't want you sharing that with dinner guests." Jon's mouth twitches, and I can tell he's holding back laughter. "Did I just hear Sean calling you?"

"What?" Libby frowns. "Where?"

185

"The kitchen," he says. "Your services are needed."

Libby sighs and heads off toward the kitchen while everyone at the table fights to keep a straight face.

Even my father seems charmed, which is new for him. "You're good with children," he observes, directing his words at Jonathan. "You've worked with kids?"

Jonathan takes a sip of his cocktail. "I grew up with seven younger sisters."

Wendy sends him a doting smile. "You were always a huge help with the girls." She turns to my parents, sensing a need to fill them in. "Chuck was in the Coast Guard and traveled a lot. I don't know what I would have done without Jonathan sometimes."

My mom looks up from spreading butter on her bread. "That must have been difficult for you, having your father—your stepfather—" she hesitates, stumbling over the configuration of branches in the Bracelyn family tree. "—having the man of the house gone all the time."

Jon and Chuck exchange a look I can't quite read. "Separation's never easy," Jonathan says mildly. "We always understood Chuck was doing important work."

"Shared values were something we talked about a lot when the kids were young," Chuck adds. "Being part of something bigger, making sacrifices for the greater good."

There are nods around the table, and I see approval in my father's face. It's an expression I've seen so seldom that I have to look away. My gaze lands on Jonathan, who gives my knee another squeeze.

"Thanks for inviting us," I murmur.

"I'm glad everyone could come."

Sean steps to the front of the room again to explain the first course. It's an artichoke and corn fritter, and my stomach rumbles as servers march from the kitchen with platters piled high

"These are gluten free," our waitress says as she sets down the serving plate. "So is the honey and hatch chili dipping sauce."

"Gluten free," Jon murmurs as he holds out the plate so I can take one. "Cindy would be pleased."

I laugh and spoon a little of the sauce onto my plate. "Only if they're really gluten free and not fake gluten free like Angela and Archie might make."

His hand brushes mine as I take the plate, and a pulse of heat moves down my arm. I love that we have shared jokes. I love the physical closeness. I love him, and I can't believe how lucky I am.

"So, Jonathan." My father inspects his fritter before picking up his fork. "What's next for you in terms of work?"

As Jon finishes chewing, all eyes swivel to him. I get the sense everyone's interested in the answer. "I haven't decided yet," he says carefully. "For the moment, I'm enjoying spending time with Blanka."

"Right, but a man's gotta have a purpose," he says. "Something that lets him make the world a better place."

"True enough," Chuck murmurs as he lifts his wineglass. "We've always been proud of Jon in that regard. He's grown up to be a helluva good man."

Jon seems to glow beneath the light of Chuck's praise, but Wendy shoots Chuck a look I can't quite read. "You think tending to his health isn't enough of a purpose? Being around family and loved ones and—"

"I looked you up," my father says, interrupting with this nonsensical bit of information directed at Jonathan. "While Galyna was getting ready for dinner. Aside from your work with Sea-Watch, you've done volunteer missions all over the globe. Water conservation, children's charities, education initiatives. And the Coast Guard, too—like your father. Following in a parent's footsteps is admirable."

My dad shoots a pointed look at me, which I ignore. I'm too busy noticing the dynamic between Jon and Chuck. The way Jon sits up a little straighter, reveling in the comparison to his stepfather instead of Cort Bracelyn.

"I've been lucky to have the freedom to do those things," Jon says. "The freedom to make a difference."

Money. I know in this context that *freedom* means *money*, though he's too classy to say that. I suppose that's one thing he can credit to Cort Bracelyn. In the weeks I've spent with Jon, I've realized money's no object. He's frugal when spending on himself but gives generously to every charity under the sun. His late father's money makes that possible.

Chuck nods to Jonathan. "Nothing gives a man a better sense of purpose than helping others."

Beside him, Wendy fiddles with the garnish on the edge of her drink. I can't help noticing the way my mother watches her. How the two of them resemble each other in a way. On the surface, they have nothing in common. One is fair-haired and tiny; one tall and robust like me. One has a happy marriage filled with children and laughter, while the other has a lifetime of martyrdom and a lone daughter living six-thousand miles from her home country.

But it's the lines around their eyes, the stoic composure. Both mothers are a portrait of self-sacrifice and duty. It's a painting my mother could capture with her eyes closed.

"You've developed quite the resumé, son," my father continues.

Jon swivels his gaze back to my father. "I never gave much thought to my resumé," he says mildly. "The choices I've made, they're because it's the right thing to do."

"Excellent." My father says it like Jon's a game show contestant giving the right answer.

"That's my boy." Chuck sticks his palm out for a complicated hand slap ritual that makes Jon glow again. "From the time he was little, he never cared about money. His first lemonade stand, he gave all the cash to the local food bank."

My father nods, ready to adopt Jon on the spot. "Sounds like you and his mother raised him right," he says to Chuck. "I understand you're a decorated member of the military?"

Chuck waves him off, not one for the limelight. "Sure, but that's not the sort of thing you do for the glory. You've gotta be in it for the right reasons or it's just another job."

My father lifts his drink, though I can't tell if he's toasting Jon or Chuck or himself. "So nice to meet a family that understands the meaning of service."

Jonathan shifts his gaze to mine, and the smile he gives me holds a hint of unease. I recall what he said that day on the lake.

Isn't my volunteer work just a way to feel good about myself? It's selfish at the core.

I reach for his hand and lace my fingers through his. Does this feel awkward to him, too? Maybe it's too soon to bring our families together. We've barely discussed the idea of dating, and now we're dining with the in-laws.

In-laws.

I roll the word around in my mind, testing its weight. For the first time in my life, I'm not horrified by the idea of joining my family with someone else's. I catch Wendy's eye and smile, delighted when she smiles back.

I'd definitely be getting the better end of the deal.

"These fritters are outstanding," Wendy says, offering the plate to my mother. "I'm going to fill up before we get to the main course."

My mom nods and cuts one with the side of her fork. "Did you try the sauce? It is the perfect amount of spicy and sweet."

There's some more banter about the meal, and everyone cleans their plate before the next course arrives. My mom and Wendy dive headfirst into the peach and baby kale salad with warm bacon dressing, chatting like old friends about recipes and travel.

I glance at the men, picking up scraps of their conversation.

Several times I hear the word *duty,* and I can't help noticing Jon's rapt attention on my father.

Wendy leans across the table and smiles at me. "They're getting along swimmingly."

I take a sip of my water. "I always knew my father and Jon had a lot in common."

"I meant Chuck and your dad." She spears a juicy slice of peach. "I suppose all three of them have a similar drive."

A chill trickles down my arms. "I suppose that's true."

She dabs her mouth with a napkin. "Men fueled by an acute sense of responsibility. By a need to be of service to others."

My mother smiles faintly. "I'm glad you found a good man," she says. "Your Jonathan is wonderful."

I smile as I lace bits of baby kale onto my fork. "He is, isn't he?"

Jon's voice gets louder, animated as he speaks with swelling passion. "It makes no sense that money should be what separates people from resources our planet has in such abundance," he says. "Water, food, basic education—doesn't everyone deserve access regardless of whether they're born in the poorest countries or the wealthiest?"

"Absolutely," my father says, ignoring his food as he gives Jon his full attention. "And it's our job as members of the species to help close the gap between the haves and have-nots."

I take a big gulp of water, desperate to wash back the sour panic moving up my throat. This is wonderful. I agree with everything they're saying. I should be thrilled they're getting along so well. And yet—

"Juniper-smoked baby back ribs." A waitress sets a platter of meat at the head of the table in front of my father, then adds a bright silver bowl mounded with something orange and buttery. "The acorn squash for this maple-infused mash was grown right here in Ponderosa Resort's on-site gardens."

"Beautiful," my mother says, eyeing both dishes. They're far out of reach for her. Even I can't get to them. Why are these tables so massive?

"The ribs look delicious." Jon's mother clears her throat, trying to get someone's attention. My father, Jonathan. The platters are right between them, waiting to be passed.

I touch Jonathan's arm. "Sweetheart."

The word feels funny coming out of my mouth, but nice. I've never used terms of endearment with a significant other. Neither did my parents.

Jon doesn't move. Doesn't react at all to my hand on his sleeve. He's deep in conversation with my dad, something about medical care in third world countries. I stretch my arm past him, trying to reach the platter of ribs.

My father glances over and frowns. "Don't be rude, Blanka."

Heat warms my cheeks as I draw my hand back. Jonathan turns to me with an apologetic smile. "Let me get that."

He hefts the platter and I grab the tongs from the edge of it, ready to serve both of us. "How many would you like?"

"Two, please."

I settle the ribs on his plate, then grab two for myself. He holds the platter out for my father, who takes his time choosing his own. After settling them on his plate, my dad takes the platter and sets it down in the empty spot beside him, the one Jonathan reserved for Libby.

"As I was saying," my dad continues. "The water rights in parts of southern Europe are—"

"Um, excuse me." Interrupting my father is a sin akin to belching at the table, and he jerks his gaze to me like I've done just that.

Instead of cowering, I sit up straighter. "They haven't been served yet." I gesture to my mother and Jon's mom. The two women exchange an uneasy look.

My father sighs. "Honestly, Blanka."

"I've got it." Chuck stands up and takes the platter, carrying it to the space between Wendy and my mother. "Here you go."

"Thank you, dear." Wendy helps herself, then gestures to my mom. "How many would you like?"

"Just one," she says. "And I'd really like to try that squash."

I turn to Jon, who's gone back to talking animatedly with my father.

"What's unbelievable is how many of these deaths are totally preventable," Jon's saying. "Fifty-eight million from kidney disease alone, with thirty-five million of those attributed to chronic disease."

My father's nodding along, thumping his fist on the table. "And it's totally treatable, given the right resources."

I touch Jonathan's arm. "Could we please get the—"

"Just a minute, Blanka." He doesn't look at me.

I draw my hand back, feeling slapped. My mother gives me a pitying look. "Your father has that effect on people."

I nod, ignoring the unease in my gut. "Jon's passionate about human rights."

"He always has been," Wendy says. "We can wait for the squash."

"Nonsense, I've got it." Chuck sets down the platter of ribs and hurries back to the head of the table. Scooping up the bowl of squash, he carries it back to Wendy and my mom.

"Thank you." My mother glances at me as Wendy serves all three of us. "The food is certainly wonderful."

"It is." But this pressure building in the center of my chest isn't so much. I take a bite of squash, willing it to subside.

Jonathan still hasn't turned. His food sits untouched on his plate as he speaks passionately about equal access to medical care. He's in his element, and I can't fault him for that.

But I also can't stop the churning in my stomach. I pick up my fork and focus on the meal. The ribs are delicious, smoky and flavorful with just a hint of zing. Sean and Athena have outdone themselves.

Libby zips over and refills everyone's water glass, and my mother watches her with interest. As soon as she's gone, Wendy leans close. "Do you want children, dear?"

A hunk of meat gets stuck in my throat. I reach for my water glass while trying to force air into my lungs. Wendy scurries around the table and whacks me between the shoulder blades. She starts to wrap her arms around me, her inner nurse going for the Heimlich. I wave her off.

"I'm fine," I croak, flashing a weak smile for my concerned-looking mother. "I'm okay."

My mother glances at Jon, who hasn't noticed any of this. Catching Libby's eye, my mom signals for another water refill.

I chug half the glass in one gulp, hoping they've forgotten the question about children. I'd just as soon not talk about procreation or my plans to try it anytime soon.

No such luck.

"Children," Wendy says as my mother settles back in her chair. "Would you like them someday?"

"Yes," I say slowly. "I think so."

It's a dream I've only thought about in arbitrary ways. Yes to motherhood, without any concrete thought about how I'd get there. I've admired babies, but I never in a million years saw myself mapping out plans to start a family. To build a life with a husband and kids.

I glance at Jon, grateful he's still deep in conversation with my dad. I can barely say the words aloud to my mother, to Jon's mother.

"I do picture myself as a mother someday."

Both mothers beam, and I don't dare add the rest. The devoted, supportive husband. The happy family. The dream is raw and new, a featherless bird not ready to be shoved from the nest.

But I risk another glance at Jon and feel a faint flutter of hope. I know it's silly, but I can't help it. I pick up my water glass and use it to hide my smile.

"Children are just wonderful." Wendy lowers her voice to a conspiratorial murmur. "I hope it's not presumptuous of me to say you and Jon would make beautiful babies."

My mother nods. "He seems like he would be a good father," she adds. "He would provide well for you."

I mumble something unintelligible and shovel squash in my mouth. What would that be like? Jonathan, me, a child of our own. My brain reels with the possibility, with the picture of a happy, functional family. For something I never fully voiced as a life goal, it's suddenly all I can think about.

"Mmhmm," I manage as I swallow my food.

I concentrate on finishing my dinner, conscious of the buzz of conversation to my left. The men are so deep in their discussion, they've missed Sean and Athena's last couple announcements. At least everyone's getting along. No food fights or public drunkenness or squabbles about politics. It's mellow as far as meet-the-family scenarios go.

The clang of a spoon tapping a water glass draws our attention to the front of the restaurant.

Everyone except my father and Jon, who keep right on talking.

"Thanks again for joining us this evening," Sean says. "You'll find comment cards on the tables, and we'd love to get your feedback."

"Don't worry, we've still got dessert," Athena says. "Y'all are in for a real treat."

They go on to describe a scrumptious riff on pecan pie with locally grown hazelnuts standing in for their Southern cousins. There's a buttery filling and a side of vanilla-bourbon ice cream that sounds amazing.

Not that Jonathan hears any of it. He's nodding at something my dad's saying, ribs still untouched on his plate. "That does sound incredible," Jon's saying. "An amazing opportunity."

A plate of pie lands in front of me, and I wait until everyone else has been served before digging in.

"You'd be interested, then?" My father's voice jars me from my thoughts, and I turn to look at him.

Jonathan's nodding, water glass gripped in his hand. "It sounds like a great cause," he says. "How soon would you need me?"

Wait, what?

I turn toward Jonathan, not positive I heard right. He's still facing my father, still deep in conversation.

"I need to get someone on the ground in Dovlano right away," he says. "By the end of next month ideally."

"And the time commitment?" Jon sips his water, unaware I'm hanging on every word.

"Two years, to start. You'd be hands-on from the very beginning. As wealthy as Dovlano is as a nation, it has no major air service within its borders. Transportation in the poorest areas is particularly atrocious."

"Yes, my sister mentioned that," Jon says, nodding. "Most medical transports take place via water."

"So, you can see where you'd fit in."

"Of course."

So can I, obviously.

What I can't see is where *I'd* fit in. Jon and me, as a couple. How would that even work?

My father glances over and notices me watching. I don't know what he sees on my face, but he nods in my direction. "Blanka will be free to come visit, of course," he adds. "As long as it doesn't cause any interference with the mission."

Interference?

I blink, expecting Jon to say something. To tell my father he's not ready to race off on another international crusade for two years—*two years*! Or assure my father that I'm more to him than an interference.

When Jonathan covers my hand with his, I'm sure the words are coming.

"It all sounds great," he says. "I'd need to clear it with my doctor first."

I stare at him, not sure I've heard right. His doctor? That's the only person he'd need to clear it with before leaving the country for twenty-four months?

I take a sip of water, willing myself to stay calm as I address Jon in my most reasonable tone. "You're—leaving?" My voice cracks, brittle and sharp, and I order myself to take a few more breaths before speaking again. "Just like that?"

Jon squeezes my hand and smiles. "It would only be for a couple years," he says. "And you'd be able to visit."

I nod, unsure whether I'm more annoyed with him or with myself. What did I expect? "I see."

He must realize I'm not embracing this idea with enthusiasm. His smile dims, and he leans closer with his hand still covering mine. "It's a really good opportunity, Blanka."

"I understand." I don't, though. Not at all. I don't understand how he can go from "*I'm not letting you go*" to "*see you in a couple years*" in a snap of his fingers. Did I miss something?

Jon's deep in conversation with my dad again, the two of them hammering out the logistics. Flight schedules and budgets and the goals of the mission. Chuck chimes in with some Coast Guard tidbits about the type of vessel they'll be using in Dovlano, his pride in Jonathan shining through with every word. Their conversation becomes a dull buzz in my ears, and I shovel pie into my face to make the sound go away.

When I glance up, my mother is eyeing me with pity. Jon's mother, too. They're studying me, wordless, as I fight to hold back tears.

I need air.

I set my fork down with a clatter, fumbling in my brain for an excuse. "You know what?" The moms are the only ones who hear me, so I address my words to them in a wobbly voice that's not mine. "I just remembered I need to check the kittens."

My mom's eyes widen. "You have kittens?"

"Um, yes. Well, Jonathan does." I push in my chair as my napkin flutters to the floor. I bend down to pick it up, annoyed by the salty prick of tears behind my eyelids. "I'll only be a few minutes. I just need to be sure they're okay."

Or get myself together, which could take more than a few minutes. Twenty. Eighty. Maybe the rest of the night.

I need to stop my heart from splatting itself against my chest like a water balloon threatening to burst. I have to get my breathing under control, to smooth things back into place and readjust. This shouldn't be a surprise to me. I've always known the importance of service to Jonathan.

My mistake was thinking I might be important, too.

You're being selfish.

The little voice in my head has a point. At the same time, I'm the one who urged Jon to be selfish. To put on his air mask before helping others.

There's not enough air in this room.

I'm still standing by the table, frozen like a glob of spit on the sidewalk when Jon looks up. He frowns when he sees me out of my chair. "Are you okay?"

"I'm fine. Everything's fine." My face feels flushed, and I wonder if I should fake an illness. "I just—I need to check on Jessica. Remember what Jade said about massaging her nipples?"

My voice comes out too loud, doubly embarrassing since I'm lying through my teeth. I force a smile to show everything's okay. "I'm good," I assure him, placing a hand on his shoulder. "Everything's great."

But he's not looking at me anymore. He's already gone back to talking with my father, asking questions about sanitation and water quality in rural parts of Dovlano. Chuck reaches across the table to ruffle Jon's hair, fatherly pride glowing in his eyes.

I drop my hand from Jon's shoulder like I've been punched. I need to get out of here before everyone sees what a fool I've been. How stupid I was to think this could be different. That I could be the chosen one, the sort of woman a guy would give up his dreams for.

I would never ask that. *Never.*

But was it too much to hope he might choose me anyway?

Yes. *Yes,* it was.

I see that now, and at least it's not too late to save face. With as much of my mother's stoic dignity as I can muster, I turn and walk away.

I feel eyes following me, but I know they're not Jon's.

As I run for the exit, I count my footsteps to the doorway, ignoring the thunder of my own heart. I'm better off on my own. I've always known this, even if I forgot for a few weeks.

I just wish the reminder didn't hurt so much.

CHAPTER 13

I'm trying hard to pay attention to what Blanka's father is saying. He's making great points about the economy in Dovlano and the disparity between rich and poor. I feel the warmth of Chuck's pride shining across the table. I feel respect radiating from Blanka's father in big, pulsing heatwaves.

But more than anything, I feel Blanka's absence deep in my gut.

"Don't you agree, Jon?"

I jerk my attention back to Thomas and give a quick, decisive nod.

"Good." He smiles. "Excellent."

Crap, what did I agree to? Not just now, but in the last twenty minutes.

I'll admit it, I may have responded in haste when Thomas fucking Kushnir Kramer asked me to head up his new mission in Dovlano.

Dovlano, Isabella's home country where her mother is a Duchess and her father—the guy who raised her, just like Chuck raised me—is a goddamn Grand Duke. And this new mission, it's all about helping impoverished people in medical crisis, transporting them by boat to facilities that can help them. Is it any wonder I got swept away?

I glance at Chuck, who smiles at me across the table. "Proud of you, Sea Dog."

My gut clenches as I turn back to Blanka's father. This is what I've always wanted. Chuck's approval, a mission that lets me do good in the world while proving I'm not Cort Bracelyn. I should be thrilled. I should be elated.

I should be with Blanka.

Her father's still talking, and I wonder how long he'll keep going. At what point I'll get a word in edgewise.

"I'm delighted you'll be joining us," Thomas continues, taking a sip from his water glass. "Being on the ground twenty-four/seven at the command center is a vital part of having your finger on the pulse of operations."

"Right." I glance toward the door where Blanka disappeared. What the hell was she talking about with the cat nipples?

I turn back to her father and clear my throat. "I wonder if Blanka needs help with Jessica?"

Thomas grunts. "Blanka's fully capable of holding down the fort alone." He nods at his wife, and Galyna sits up straighter. "Just like her mother. She understands it's a team effort to make the world a better place. That there's always sacrifice involved."

I know that to be true. But I also know the flip side. "It's important to put on your own oxygen mask before assisting others."

Thomas stares at me like I've gone nuts. Maybe I have. "Is this about the cat?" he asks. "It's on some kind of medical oxygen? Because I'm sure Blanka can handle it. Cats are resilient like that. It'll be fine."

I don't even know what to do with that, and I'm not sure I can force words past the churning in my gut. Five minutes ago, I mistook it for the butterflies of new adventure. The prospect of sailing off to save some new corner of the world.

But these damn butterflies have grown fangs and are gnawing the inside of my stomach. Something's not right here.

I remind myself that Blanka is fiercely independent. That she values her time alone, that she's made it clear she doesn't need a man to complete her. Constant togetherness, the smothering blanket of a relationship—those are things she doesn't want.

But I can't shake the memory of that flash in her eyes, the flicker of hope that day on my front porch. The way she looked at me when I said those words to her.

I want to be with you.

I'm not letting you go.

What the hell am I doing going to Dovlano?

"Dovlano, huh?" Chuck's voice slides into my thoughts, bringing me back to the conversation. "That's right between Italy and Slovenia?"

"Correct," Thomas says, only half paying attention as he slides his phone out of his pocket. "A lovely nation, apart from its medical crisis."

Chuck nods and picks up his water glass. "I always wanted to visit that part of the world."

My mother dabs her mouth with a napkin. "You never mentioned that."

Chuck looks at her. "What's that?"

"Dovlano," she says. "Or Italy or Greece or any part of Europe at all. You never mentioned an interest in that part of the world."

Chuck glances at Blanka's father, like he's looking for the answer to a trick question. "I'm just now figuring it out, I guess," he says. "Retirement's opening up a whole new world."

Tension squares my mother's shoulders. She stares at Chuck, eyes glittering in candlelight.

"I've waited our whole married life to spend time with you." Her voice is low, soft enough I'm pretty sure Blanka's dad can't hear. "It's just funny," she says in a tone completely devoid of humor. "Because I've mentioned travel again and again since you retired. And you've never been interested."

Chuck's got a deer-in-the-headlights look about him, but his isn't the only face I'm watching. At the other end of the table, Blanka's mother sits with hands folded in front of her. She's watching me, not them, and her blue eyes bore into me with something I can't read.

It suddenly feels very hot in this room. Across from me, my mother's voice gets louder. "I thought we wanted the same things," she says. "To wake up together every morning. But you're out of bed at the crack of dawn teaching free classes at the Boys and Girls Club. And when I mention travel, you tell me *later*. Always later. When, Chuck? When is later?"

Chuck scrubs a hand over his chin, looking helpless. "I don't know. I want those things, too."

My mother looks more sad than angry. She's close to tears but holding it together like a boss. "We're entering our golden years. But lately it's like we're ships passing in the night." She clears her throat, looking down at her hands. "I don't want to be your afterthought."

I don't want to be your afterthought.

My mother's words echo in my brain, ping-ponging off my cerebral cortex and smacking me square between the eyes. Is that how I've made Blanka feel? I thought space was what she wanted. Independence, a chance to carry her own canoe.

Maybe I've read this wrong.

"Baby." Chuck's frowning, holding my mother's hand. "You were the one who always urged me to follow my dreams."

"I know that," she says softly. "But your dreams used to include me."

There's no anger in her voice. That's the worst part. Just resignation. She stands up and sets her napkin on her plate, offering a weak smile to the rest of it. "I'm going to help Blanka with the cat."

Chuck frowns after her, then turns to meet Galyna's knowing stare. "She was a nurse for years," he offers weakly. "Knows a lot about nipples."

His frown deepens as my mother vanishes around the corner. With a look of utter confusion, he turns back to me. "What the hell just happened?"

"I'm not positive." I glance at Blanka's father, wondering if he has the answers. The guy has two Nobel prizes.

And right now, he's glued to his phone. "Yeah, I found the guy to head up our nautical operations," he's saying to whoever's on the other end of the line. "It's going to be great."

What have I done?

My gaze shifts back to Blanka's mother. She's watching me with eyes the exact shade of Blanka's, bright and sharp. I realize I haven't seen her smile once this whole dinner. My throat clenches tight.

"Right, yes," Thomas says into the phone. "We should be able to get him over there within a few weeks. Yes, he'll be a perfect fit."

I'm not so sure.

Movement on the far side of the room catches my eye, and I look toward the hallway by the bathrooms. There stands Izzy, rosy-cheeked in a green sweater dress with her hair up in a fancy braid. She's staring at me across the crowd, green gaze bright and wide.

We lock eyes and she mouths one word.

Help.

I'm out of my seat in an instant, adrenaline pumping through me. Does she look paler? Oh, God, what are the signs of organ rejection?

By the time I reach her side, I'm sweating. I fight like hell to hold it together, needing to stay strong for her. "Izzy, what's wrong? Are you feeling—ouch, *ow!*—where are we going?"

"Come with me." She's got my arm in a vise grip, offering no room for argument as she drags me into one of the unisex restrooms. For a woman a foot shorter than me who may be rejecting a kidney, she's pretty damn strong.

Iz pushes the door shut behind us and flips the lock. Then she turns to face me. "You looked like you needed rescuing."

I sweep my gaze over her from head to toe, still trying to figure out what's wrong. "*You're* rescuing *me*? By asking for help and then pinching the crap out of my arm?"

She shrugs and folds her arms over her chest. "I knew the only way you'd accept help is if you thought you were coming to my aid."

It's a fair point, but I'm still not sure what's going on. I survey the urinal, the sink, the trash can brimming with damp paper towels. "You picked a weird place for an intervention."

"It's private, and this conversation requires privacy."

"What conversation are we having?"

She leans back against the door like a warden blocking an escape attempt. "I was sitting at the table next to yours," she says. "I heard everything."

"Everything," I repeat. "I take it we're not talking about whether hazelnuts and filberts are the same thing."

Iz doesn't smile. She doesn't even blink. "You're planning to leave Blanka."

The words stick in my chest like a thousand hot needles. "I wouldn't be leaving her." The words sound weak and watered down, and I barely believe them myself. "It's a temporary mission."

Izzy shakes her head. "Blanka loves you," she says. "She wants a future with you."

"I love her, too," I say automatically. "We've already discussed having a future together."

"Really?" My sister quirks an eyebrow. "Have you talked about what that future would actually *look* like? Or did you just assume, both of you—did you only *think* you knew what the other person wanted?"

I open my mouth to respond, then shut it again. She's right. All this talk about relationships and futures, we never made sure we were on the same page. That we were speaking the same language. Not English and Ukranian, but the language of love and relationships and what we both want. We talked in abstract terms, but never specifics. What got lost in translation?

"She wants the romance novel," Izzy says. "The happily ever after with the guy who sticks around and loves her more than anyone. A guy who puts her first, because he knows she'll do the same for him. A guy who needs her as much as she needs him."

"Of course I need her," I say, even though a slow, cold sinking in my gut tells me I might have failed to make that clear. "Relationships don't require constant proximity to one another."

Again with the eyebrow lift from Izzy. "I hope you're not basing that assumption on her parents," she says. "I've seen icefish with warmer relationships than those two."

I don't bother asking what icefish are, or if that's even a real animal. I can gather from context what she means. "My mother and stepfather had a great relationship."

I catch the past-tense slip before it's even out of my mouth. Judging by her expression, so does Izzy.

"The Duke and Duchess of Dovlano—my parents—have spent nearly every living moment together," she says. "From the time their marriage was arranged when they were four years old. They've been inseparable every moment."

I don't need to point out the obvious, but I do. "There might be a few moments unaccounted for in there."

"You're speaking of the moment in which your father—*our* biological father, Cort Bracelyn—managed to successfully impregnate my mother?"

Damn. I've never known Izzy to be so blunt. "You've grown a pair in the last couple months."

"Perhaps this is the trait I've received from you, my kidney donor?" The smile she gives me is quite unlike the refined, lady-like smile I've come to expect from her. "In that case, would you care to have your testicles back so you can go after Blanka as you should?"

Ouch. "I'm not sure I like the mean version of Izzy."

"Well, I do."

So do I. Very much. "Me, too." I take a shaky breath, needing to get back to the subject of Blanka. Of where I might have screwed things up. "Blanka's always said how she admires her mother's self-sufficiency. Her stoicism."

Her tolerance for being alone, which I'm not realizing may not have been what Blanka admired at all.

"That doesn't mean Blanka wants that life for herself," Izzy says. "Have you asked her?"

I shake my head slowly, rewinding through my brain's home videos for evidence to the contrary. "I don't think so."

Which is pretty damned dumb, now that I think of it.

Iz must read the shame on my face because she steps forward and puts a hand on my arm. "I never knew our father," she says. "But he does not sound like an especially good man."

I snort. "He once offered me one million in cash to join his yacht racing team instead of the Coast Guard."

"And your response?"

"I had some colorful suggestions for where he could put that money."

"Which means you are a good man," she says. "Not because of your service, but because of your principles. You might look like the man who sired you, but you are nothing like him. Isn't that obvious?"

It was to Blanka. And if this sister who's known me two months can see it, maybe it's true.

"I'm an idiot."

"You're not an idiot," she insists. "You're smart and kind and funny and generous, and you don't know when enough is enough when it comes to self-sacrifice. So I'm telling you now—it's enough. *You're* enough."

You're enough.

How many times did I wish I could hear my father say that to me?

How many times did Chuck actually say it?

Dozens. Hundreds.

I just wasn't listening. "My stepfather," I murmur. "He's a good man. And he raised me to be like him." Tried to, anyway.

Izzy levels me with a look so fierce my heart actually stops. "You are a good man without needing to throw yourself on the fire to prove it," she says. "Don't you see that?"

I'm starting to, maybe a little.

I owe that to Blanka. Christ, I owe so much to her.

"I need to find Blanka." I push off the wall, brain reeling with the need to make this right. To get us back on the same page and facing the same direction, which I realize is a seriously messed up metaphor. "I need to tell her how I feel."

To find out how *she* feels. Both of those things are vital. Without two sets of dreams laid out on the table, we can't begin to braid them together.

Izzy steps aside as I reach for the door handle. I yank it open and nearly collide with a woman waiting on the other side. I push past and watch her blanch as Izzy emerges behind me.

"It's okay," I call as I start for the dining room. "She's my sister."

Which probably makes it worse, but I don't have time to elaborate. I race though the dining room toward our table where Blanka's dad is still engrossed in his phone call.

"Right, yes," he's saying. "No, I can cut this trip short if I need to and get to Dovlano at once. My family will understand."

I'm not sure they will. Blanka's mother sits stoically at the other end of the table, hands folded in her lap. Chuck is deep in conversation with Libby, teaching her sailor's knots with a long piece of twine from one of the centerpieces. He used to do that with me, exhausted from work, when I'd beg him to teach me just one more knot.

He's a good man.

But being a good man isn't enough. Not if you're turning your back on the people you love most.

Galyna's face is a mask of perfect fortitude. I look behind her to see Iz returning to her seat at the next table.

"Izzy," I say. "Isabella."

She turns with a quizzical look. "Yes?"

"Do you have any of those paperbacks?" I ask. "The ones Blanka loaned you?"

Her brow furrows. "The romance novels?" She shoves a hand in her purse and comes up with a tattered paperback copy of a Rachel Grant novel. "I just finished this one."

"May I borrow it?"

Iz nods and hands it over without comment.

I turn back to Blanka's mother and hand her the book. "Here," I tell her. "This should keep you from getting bored."

It should also give her some ideas of the sort of happily-ever-after that's possible, but I don't mention that. Galyna stares at me a moment, then takes the book. The tiniest smile tugs the corners of her mouth. "Ty naykrashhyy muzhcyna."

I blink at her, dumbstruck. I know those words. I've googled those words, though the fact that I can't spell them made them impossible to find. "Did you just talk dirty to me?"

It's Galyna's turn to look confused. "What?" Her brow furrows. "I told you that you are the best man."

I swallow hard, watching her face. "What about *Ty moe povitria.*" I pray I'm saying it right. "I tried googling, but the alphabet's different and I can't figure it out phonetically—"

"*Ty moe povitria,*" she repeats, smiling. "You are my air."

God, I'm an idiot.

All along, this is what she's been telling me. I'm the one she's chosen. I'm the one who matters to her. She's been saying the words, even if she couldn't speak them in a language we both know.

Even if she couldn't admit them to herself.

I glance at Izzy, who's watching the exchange with a bemused expression. I open my mouth to ask for a pen, but the kidney telepathy is working in full force. Izzy whips a notepad out of her purse and hands it to Galyna with a pen tucked inside.

"Could you write that down for him?" Izzy asks. "Please?"

Galyna nods and flips the pad open. She scrawls the words in Ukranian, then phonetically in English.

"Thank you," I tell her. "I promise I will treat your daughter well. That I'll be the kind of man she deserves."

She nods approvingly. "Good."

Chuck's wrapping up his knot tying lesson with Libby and glances at me with a questioning look. "What's going on?"

I clear my throat. "Just getting some help pulling my head out of my—"

"Backside," Libby finishes for me. "You're not supposed to say ass."

"Thank you."

Chuck folds his hands on the table. "How'd you do that?"

I swallow hard, braced to say the hardest words I've ever uttered. "I can't do it anymore." I rake my hand through my hair, braced for his disappointment. "I can't spend my life running around saving the world when the person who matters most in *my* world is here."

Chuck stares at me. Just stares for a long, long time. "Christ, boy. You think you need my permission for that?"

I shake my head, forcing the words up past the lump in my throat. "I—I don't know. I want your respect. I want to be the kind of man you taught me to be."

"Son." He shakes his head, watching me sadly. "You already are. You're the best man I know. Shit, you're—"

"Shoot," Libby corrects, hands folded on the table. "Go on."

"Shoot," Chuck continues, smiling a little. "The fact that you figured all this out at your age when I'm over here with twice the years under my belt…" He trails off there, shaking his head. "That says something, Sea Dog. It takes a big man to change course when the wind's not blowing him the right direction anymore."

My chest swells with pride. And relief, to be honest. "So you're okay with this?"

"Okay?" Chuck stands up. "Hell, I'm coming with you."

"Heck," Libby puts in, helping herself to the unclaimed piece of pie in front of Blanka's father. "You're not supposed to say hell."

Chuck nods. "Thank you. Both of you. For helping me figure out what should have been obvious."

"You're welcome." Libby grabs Thomas's pie fork and digs in as Chuck and I turn and bolt for the door.

We get halfway across the dining room when I'm struck by an idea. I reroute to the kitchen, crossing my fingers Sean has what I need.

"I have to grab something," I tell Chuck.

"Will it fix things with Blanka and your mom?"

"I hope so."

"Good," Chuck says. "Grab one for me, too."

CHAPTER 14

BLANKA

$\mathcal{I}$ scoop a hand under Sinbad, gently cradling him against my chest for a few seconds before handing the fuzzy bundle to Jon's mother. "This is the first day we're allowed to handle them," I explain as Wendy coos over the tiny creature. "Our vet said it's best to wait and be sure their mother bonds with them."

"They're precious."

"They are." And they might be the closest thing I get to having babies anytime soon.

I glance at Jessica to be sure she's handling this okay. She doesn't appear to be on the brink of ripping our faces off, but it's tough to tell sometimes.

"Brrrrow." Jessica closes her eyes and rolls over, forcing the other kittens to release their fierce grip on her swollen mammaries.

"Looks like mom's ready for a break," I say.

"I can relate, girl." Wendy tucks Sinbad up against her chest, cupping him with her left hand while stroking her other down Jessica's sleek body. "I remember this stage well."

I bite my lip, avoiding Wendy's eyes as I reach down to scoop up another kitten. Raisin comes willingly, wriggly body curling into my hand.

"Was Jonathan a cute baby?" I ask.

I know the answer without asking, but I want to hear her say it.

"The cutest," Wendy says. "I'd never say that to the girls, but Jon was beautiful the instant he came out. The others took a few days to stop looking like rashy coneheads, but Jon sprang perfectly formed from the womb."

"Of course he did." It shouldn't surprise me that Jon was perfect from the start. He was probably planning fundraisers from his crib and organizing other babies to call their congressmen. "He really is a great guy."

Wendy doesn't respond right away. Just strokes a hand down Jessica's side, watching me in silence. "Does he know how you feel?"

I nod slowly. "Of course. We've said I love you, talked about a relationship."

"Right, but what kind of relationship?" She frowns, and I can see she's choosing her words carefully. "The kind of arrangement Chuck and I had isn't for everyone. Neither is your parents' marriage."

I snuggle the kitten under my chin, closing my eyes to sink into its velvety purr. "You and Chuck are perfect together," I say. "I can't imagine having something like that."

"We're far from perfect," she says. "And you *can* imagine it, sweetheart. I saw you imagining it over dinner. The first time I met you, I could see you mapping out a whole life together with my son. You may not have wanted to admit it, but it was plain as day on your face."

My breath catches in my throat. I can't meet Wendy's eyes, so I concentrate on smoothing back the fur behind Jessica's ear. "It was that obvious?"

"It was," Wendy confirms. I glance up to see her shifting the kitten to the other side of her chest, soothing him with soft, motherly strokes of her palm. "Maybe not to you. Not to Jon, either. But mothers see things their children miss."

I remember my mother's knowing look at the dinner table. Is that what she means?

"I never thought I wanted those things," I tell her. "I mean, yes, I admired babies. But I never really thought about wanting the husband and family and white picket fence."

"But now you want it."

I hesitate. It seems wrong to admit it to Wendy when I've barely admitted it to myself. And I certainly never told Jon.

"It's okay," she says, reading my thoughts. "You have time to figure it out."

"Maybe not," I admit. "Not if he's leaving the country."

"Ask him to stay."

"I can't do that." I bite my lip and stroke a finger under a kitten's downy chin. "I can't ask him to give up his dreams for me."

"But you can give him a chance to make the choice for himself," she says. "By letting him know what *your* dreams are."

Could it really be that simple?

As I think it through, I realize I've never tried to tell Jon what I want. Oh, sure, I've said what I *don't* want. The overbearing husband, the sort of marriage that holds me back instead of allowing me to flourish and thrive.

But have I ever made it clear what I *do* want?

I haven't. Because I've been too damned scared to admit it to myself.

"I'm afraid," I confess softly, closing my eyes so I don't see her pity. "What if I put it all out there, and he doesn't want the same thing?"

"Would it really hurt less than not trying?"

I laugh and open my eyes again, blinking hard so she won't

see the threat of tears. "How do mothers know the exact right thing to say?"

"It's in the manual," she says. "They hand it to you in the delivery room, along with a fifth of vodka and a pair of earplugs."

I laugh and set the kitten back in the box and start to reach for another one. Eloise, or maybe it's Zinnia.

That's when I hear footsteps on the front porch, then the bang of the front door.

"Honey, I'm home!"

I blink, turning to Wendy. "What on earth?"

But she's as surprised as I am. We place our kittens back in the box as footsteps thunder down the hall. I turn to the doorway as Jon marches in, a look of determination on his face. He's gripping a handful of bedraggled zinnias, dirt cascading off the roots like confetti. And in the other hand—

"Why are you carrying a loaf of bread?" I ask.

"It's cinnamon raisin." He thrusts it at me like an offering, and I take it because I'm not sure what else to do.

His green eyes are wild, and he's breathing like he just sprinted across the resort. "Blanka, the life I described that day in the hospital—the kids and the garden and the happy home where we fall asleep together every night and wake up together in the morning—that's what I want." His throat moves as he swallows. "I want that with you."

Tears flood my eyes, but I blink them back. "I thought you were going to Dovlano."

He shakes his head and drops to his knees on the floor beside me. "I got stars in my eyes when your dad started talking," he says. "The stuff about organ failure and the seagoing aspect—it all seemed like fate. But so does this."

He gestures with the zinnias, scattering dirt on the floor. I laugh and sweep a patch of it off my knee as a tear slips down my face. "I want the same thing," I tell him, looking down at the bread in my arms. "Even the cinnamon raisin."

"You don't have to bake bread or grow zinnias or do anything else that doesn't feel like the kind of arrangement you want." He takes the bread from my hands and sets it on the desk beside us, along with the zinnias. "You and me, we'll figure it out together. What we do and don't want. What we're willing to give up to be together, and what we're not willing to sacrifice. I love you, Blanka. The only thing that matters is that we're together."

I'm crying in earnest now, big, sloppy wet tears. Wendy fishes in her purse for a tissue and hands it to me, then gets up and steps discreetly to the door. From the corner of my eye, I see Chuck slip an arm around her and hand her a loaf of bread. Wendy takes it with a bemused look and snuggles closer. They don't say a word. They don't have to.

But Jon and me, we're still new at this. And forcing the words out is more important than I realized.

"I'm so sorry," I say to Jonathan. "I never told you what I wanted because I was scared to admit it. But I want the same thing you do—to be together no matter what." This next part is hard, but I make myself say it anyway. "I want to be chosen. I want to matter to someone."

"God, Blanka." He takes both my hands in his and squeezes, and I swear I see tears in his eyes. "You matter more than anything in the world to me. I will always choose you, no matter what. *Always.*"

Doubt creeps back in, despite my best intentions. "But your mission—"

"Doesn't matter if I'm not with you," he says. "Look, I know our parents made it through long separations, and that worked for them. And there's a part of me that will always be devoted to making the world a better place. But meeting you, that's when I realized how much better my own world could be. Maybe it's selfish, but I'm not giving that up. I'm not letting you go."

These are the exact words I've wanted to hear. For so long, even if I couldn't bear to voice that wish out loud. "I should have told you," I say. "From the very start, I should have said what I wanted."

"Marriage?"

I nod slowly, hoping that's not the wrong answer.

But it's the right answer for me, and it's time I started putting that out there. "Yes," I say softly. "Eventually, yes. I want that."

"Good," he says. "I'm already on my knees, so—"

"Wait, no." I laugh and put a hand on his chest. "Not yet, not here. We can take our time."

He grins and lifts my hand from his chest, planting a kiss across my knuckles. "What about children?"

I nod quicker this time, no longer caring if that's the right answer. If it's the safe answer. "At least two, maybe three."

"Excellent," he says. "I'll knock you up as soon as you say so."

Chuck clears his throat. "Uh, maybe you could wait 'til we're out the door?" He grins and turns toward his wife. "Let's go, baby. We should start packing."

Wendy blinks. "Where are we going?"

"Anywhere—Paris, Greece, Buenos Aires—anywhere you want to go, that's where I want to be, too."

Tears fill her eyes as he slips his arm around her and leads her from the room. Chuck pauses in the doorway, turning back to wink at Jon.

"You've got this, Sea Dog." Then he turns and walks out the door.

From the rumble of their voices fading down the hallway, I hear Chuck issuing apologies of his own. "…got so focused on feeling useful that I forgot my most important job is being your husband."

I can't hear what comes after that, but there's no need. I only have eyes for Jonathan.

He smiles and holds out his hand. "Smart guy, Chuck."

"He is." I slip my hand in his and let him pull me to my feet.

"Everything he just said—I can promise you I've downloaded

it into my brain bank. I'm never going to forget you're the most important thing. Not now, not thirty years from now, not a hundred. Not ever."

"Same," I tell him, gripping his fingers with mine. "I can't believe I almost lost you."

"Nah," he says, pulling me into his arms. "I'm like sea lice. Very hard to get rid of."

I laugh and step up on tiptoes to kiss him. "You're such a romantic."

"You're not with me for the romance."

"True," I acknowledge, kissing one corner of his mouth. "I'm with you for the bread and the balloon animal blowjobs."

He laughs and turns so my next kiss lands on the other corner of his mouth. "And the dish soap bubble baths."

Another kiss, this one right in the cleft of his chin. "And your ugly cat," I tell him. "She really steals the deal."

That one was on purpose, but he doesn't correct me. Doesn't even make a seal joke or offer to make a seal for me out of balloons. Just pulls me tight against him and claims my mouth with his. The kiss is soft at first, but we both lean into it. My breath catches as his tongue grazes mine, and his hands slide down to cup my backside. It's hot and possessive and everything inside me screams *this one.*

Forever. This one.

We're breathless when we draw back, and he looks deep into my eyes. "I love you, Blanka. You're what makes me happy. The rest is just noise."

"I love you," I tell him. "You float my boat. I feel like my ship's finally come in. We're in the same boat, right?"

He laughs and kisses me again. "You're getting good."

"You're already good," I tell him. "The best guy I know."

"*Ty naykrashhyy muzhcyna?*"

I stare at him, palm splayed on his chest. "How'd you figure it out?"

"Your mother," he says. "I even had her write it down for me." He fishes into his back pocket and pulls out a folded piece of paper. "I also learned this one— *Ty naykrashhyy zhinka.*"

Here come the tears again.

You are the best woman.

You are the best man.

"Maybe we bring out the best versions of each other," I tell him.

"There's no maybe about it," he says. "It's a fact."

As he bends to kiss me again, I know it to be true.

EPILOGUE

JONATHAN

"Should I get another blanket?"

Blanka smiles up at me, then snuggles closer. "I'm good. Snug as a bug in a rug. Which, for the record, dates back to a 1772 epitaph penned by Benjamin Franklin for a friend's dead squirrel."

I laugh and slip an arm around her. "I'm not going to touch that one."

I lean us both back against the bow railing so we're facing backward on the deck of our little pocket cruiser. It's the sort of sailboat my father would have grudgingly admired, a vintage 26-foot Balboa that's been completely rebuilt. I replaced the 1969 shag carpet with a high-grade marine carpet Bree helped me find, but the rest of the original features are intact. Even the teak dinette and the world map spanning the laminate tabletop.

It's the berth my old man would have really admired. New Tempur-Pedic mattress, plus a door that closes for privacy.

Not that we need it now. We're all alone out here on Cultus Lake, with a giant swath of stars overhead. "I thought it would be colder in November," Blanka muses.

"I'm plenty warm." I snuggle her closer, pretty sure I could be

219

naked on an iceberg in the Arctic and still feel toasty with this woman in my arms. "Won't be long before the snow comes."

It's the last weekend before they close the Cascade Lakes Highway for the season, so we're up here christening the new boat. Among other things.

Blanka picks up her wineglass and takes a small sip before setting it back in the suction-cup holder. "Is the signing still set for Monday?"

"That's the plan. Josh did all the forms on his end, so as soon as we sign our part, Dreamland Tours officially becomes part of Ponderosa Resort."

And I become its full-time manager. Crazy to imagine.

"Jonathan Bracelyn, boating entrepreneur." Blanka grins up at me again, starlight in her eyes. "Who'da thunk it?"

I laugh, imagining her father's response to this charming slaughter of the English language. "Not me," I admit. "But it feels right."

So does this. Being out here with her under the stars, the gentle lap of water rocking us into one another.

"Seriously, though, you'll do great," she says.

"I hope so." I squeeze her tightly, appreciating both her body heat and the fact that she supports my new endeavor. That my whole family does. "I definitely won't be running Dreamland as a money-making enterprise. We'll still do all the tourist stuff, but it's the other trips I'm excited about."

"I love that the school district approved everything," she says. "And so quickly."

"They were motivated." Not just by the huge donation, though I suppose that helped. Dad's money comes in handy sometimes.

"There are so many kids who've never had a chance to get out on the water," I continue. "Never paddled a kayak or watched shooting stars on a moonlight canoe trip. I'm happy we'll be able to give that to them."

Underprivileged kids will go whitewater rafting in the

summer. In the fall, they'll learn water safety and proper paddling strokes for canoes and kayaks. They'll see the beauty of aquatic landscapes and learn about wildlife and caring for equipment.

All the things Chuck taught me, with some of my father's lessons mixed in. It's the balance I've been searching for my whole life.

"I love that you're still able to chase your dreams from here."

"Nah, I've caught them." I kiss her temple, pulling her closer to me. "You know what's funny?"

"Neckties with tiny penises?"

I laugh and kiss her again. "That, too. But I was thinking about my father." Not his sense of humor, though he did have a good one. "I was thinking how he was kind of an asshole. He cheated on his wives, abandoned his kids—"

"That's funny?" Blanka's brow is furrowed, and I can tell I'm not making sense to her.

"Not that part, no," I admit. "But for all his asshole tendencies, he was a charitable guy. He donated to good causes. He took in my cousin, Brandon, after his mom left. He bailed Bree out of big trouble once. Even though his methods were usually messed up, his heart was in the right place."

Sometimes. Mostly it was in his pants, but that's not what I'm talking about.

"I guess what I'm saying is that there were good things about my father, too," I tell her. "And maybe I'm finally tapping into those. Not throwing the baby out with the bathwater, so to speak."

"That expression I know," she says. "And you're right—bathwater's a good place to find special things."

I laugh and kiss her again. "Way to carry that metaphor. Which reminds me—we're due for another self-care bath."

"I'll add it to the calendar." She settles back against my chest, the lupine scent of her filling my lungs. "I'm glad they're getting to travel," she says, shifting the conversation easily. "Your mom and Chuck, I mean."

"I can't believe it worked out like it did."

Except I can. It's so obvious Chuck was the best choice to head up the new medical mission in Dovlano. His skill and wisdom, not to mention decades of experience in the Coast Guard, are the perfect complement to my mother's nursing background. They're a great team. Always have been.

And with the two of them working together, they'll still have time to see and explore and enjoy retirement.

"They seem so happy," she says. "If their emails are any indication."

"They are." If anything, their post-retirement communication blip has made their marriage stronger. "Guess we're all getting your romance novel happily ever after."

Blanka's brow furrows. "Not everyone. There's still Izzy. And Gretchen. And—"

"And let's just focus on our happy ending for now." Preferably on that new mattress. I shift to stand up, helping Blanka to her feet. "Ready to head in?"

"Let's check the kittens," she says. "It's their maiden voyage, too."

"Good point." I pry the hatch open carefully, not wanting anyone to escape. As we move down the ladder, I spot Raisin and Sinbad curled in the fuzzy donut bed we brought for them. Eloise is perched on a kitchen cabinet, while Zinnia—always the mama's boy—is snuggled up to Jessica on a towel we left puddled on the table.

"Brrrrow," Jessica says, and narrows her eyes at me.

"I love you, too." I scratch behind her ragged ears, earning myself a rusty purr.

"They're so cute," Blanka says. "I'm so glad we decided to keep them all."

"Me, too." They're all spayed and neutered, and perfectly

happy with their massive cattery Mark helped build off the side of the cabin. The jury's still out on whether they like sailing, but right now, they seem content.

"These paws are built for boating," I tell Jessica, touching one of her massive polydactyl mitts. "And you've definitely earned a vacation."

"Brrrow," she says again, then swats at Sinbad for playing with her tail. The kitten scampers off, making little chirping sounds.

I laugh and stroke a hand down Jessica's back. "You done good."

"Your English is atrocious," Blanka says in the perfect impression of her father's voice. "What kind of slang is that?"

Still grinning, I grab her hand and tug her toward the berth. "My English might need work, but my French skills are on point. Want me to show you?"

Blanka giggles, surging ahead to leap onto the bed. "Ooh-la-la."

She falls back against the pillows, blonde hair making a curtain around her face. Eyes sparking with mischief, she pats the bed beside her. "Jetez vos pantalons!"

"What does that mean?"

She smacks the bed again, grinning. "Discard your pantaloons!"

"Oui." That's pretty much it for my French vocabulary. In words, anyway. I ease onto the bed beside her, anticipating the taste of her on my tongue.

"Ja," I add, throwing a little German into the mix. "Evet."

"Turkish?"

I nod, pushing her back onto the bed as my mouth finds the spot. That perfect, sensitive spot that works like magic every time.

"Sí," I breathe against her throat.

"Sim," she gasps, digging her fingers into my shoulder blades. "Tak. Ya."

I can't identify the languages, but I know the sentiment.

Yes.

A thousand languages, a million times over, *yes.*

Again and again for the rest of my life.

***

Itching to get your hands on more Ponderosa Resort rom-coms? Izzy and Bradley are heading your way in 2020 with *Dr. Hot Stuff* and you can pre-order that here:

https://books2read.com/u/3G2VKa

But before that story hits shelves, how about a sexy novella starting Jon's sister, Gretchen? That's *Snowbound Squeeze,* and keep reading for your exclusive excerpt...

YOUR EXCLUSIVE PEEK AT
SNOWBOUND SQUEEZE

GABLE

I don't know if I've ever been this tired. Bone deep, balls dragging the floor exhausted.

As I sag against my buddy's front door, he drops the key into my palm. I curl my fist around the metal lifeline and hold tight.

"Stay as long as you need to." James's voice is pitched low, and I hate the pity in his eyes.

Pity and whatever it's called when a dude has three sparkly red lipstick marks on his face.

"Thank you." I force the words past the tightness in my throat and try not to stare at the kiss print just above his jaw. Did Lily miss his mouth on purpose? "And—uh—no one else knows about this? Me being in Oregon."

James braces an arm against the cedar-planked wall of his cabin's foyer. He has questions, and I'm grateful he's not asking them. Grateful we're doing this here. That he's not luring me in for wine and friendly catch-up.

I'm not feeling friendly. Just tired. Tired and really fucking raw.

Also confused about the lipstick. Seriously, does he not know it's there?

"Lily knows," James says, and it takes me a second to remember what we're talking about. "I told her you were headed this way. She's been worried since we saw everything on the news."

"I'm fine." I don't know if I'm trying to convince him or me.

"The rest of resort management doesn't know you're here," he assures me. "And they definitely don't know about that."

He nods at the key, and I clutch it tighter. "Thanks."

I've met most of James's siblings and love the crap out of them, but right now, I need discretion. "Privacy's sort of key at the moment."

"You'll have that in spades at the cabin," he says. "To be honest, I think everyone forgot it exists. We inherited it together, but it's so far in the middle of nowhere that no one ever uses it."

Perfect.

James rubs a hand over his chin, narrowly missing a smear of lipstick. I debate mentioning it but decide not to. I won't be here long, and there's no sense embarrassing him. I'm sure he's eager to get back to whatever produced the lip prints in the first place.

A gust of wind hurls ice chips at the door behind me, and I glance out the window to my left. Trees sway in the darkness, their needles flickering with moonlight.

"The snow's not supposed to hit until tomorrow night," James says. "You should be fine."

"I will be."

I'm not sure we're talking about snow.

He studies my face for a moment. "I wasn't sure you were still coming."

"It took me a while to get out of town. LA traffic, you know?"

He nods, making the lipstick on his left temple flash in the light from the sconce beside the door. "Right. Still, I was worried."

James isn't the only one. It's my agent who finally persuaded me to get out of town. "Perhaps you should find someplace to lay low," he suggested on the phone last week. "Just stay out of the public eye until things quiet down."

My brother, Dean, was more direct. "Get the fuck out of Hollywood," he growled. "Hide out until we tell you to come back. Or fuck it, don't come back. God knows I'd love to get out of here."

So that's what I'm doing. Getting lost, at least for a little while.

The key feels warm in my palm, its metal ridges biting into the fleshy undersides of my fingers. I should get going.

"Thanks again," I say, taking a step back. "I'll get out of your—"

"Gable!" James's fiancée swoops in wearing a silky red kimono belted at the waist. Lily pulls me into a soft, fragrant hug, reminding me again that my college pal is one lucky son of a bitch. "We weren't sure you'd make it. How's your family?"

"Great." I channel as much enthusiasm as possible into that syllable, adding a smile for good measure. "Lana and Lauren say hi. They keep asking when you're coming back to visit."

"We're hoping they'll come see us this time." She smiles and glances at James. I see her register the lipstick on his face the same instant he pushes off the wall and launches into full-on CEO mode.

"I really think you'd be better off staying here." He's pacing like a courtroom lawyer, which he was once upon a time. "We've got a full-time security team at Ponderosa Resort."

Lily nods, choosing to ignore the lipstick in favor of ganging up on me. "He's right. The resort's full for Valentine's weekend, so we'd have lots of eyes and ears watching out for you."

This sounds as appealing as smashing my testicles in the cutlery drawer. "I appreciate the offer, but I'm really looking for some alone time."

The two exchange a look I can't read. That's possibly because the red smear beside James's mouth makes his polished façade look vaguely clownlike.

Lily lifts a hand to wipe it at the same moment James turns and sweeps a hand toward their living room. "We have a guest suite that's very private," he insists. "You could have meals brought in and would never have to interact with anyone."

Dropping her hand, Lily gives an infinitesimal shrug and regards me with a bemused smile. "We're very discreet."

The kindness in her eyes is almost enough to change my mind.

Almost. "This cabin will be perfect." I shove the key in my pocket before they can snatch it back. "No phones, no internet, no television."

No calls from my agent, no hate mail, no televised reminders of my great fuckup.

James sighs and yanks at his tie. Tries to anyway, but there isn't one. Whatever they were doing when I got here jettisoned his ever-present neckwear.

Lily sticks her hands in the pockets of her kimono and regards me with concern. "We sent someone out to the cabin to get it ready for you," she says. "It's clean, but it's really rustic. You know how to chop firewood and all that?"

"I've got some dynamite left over from that last action flick," I deadpan. "Figure I can use it to fell a couple trees."

Lily laughs, then whips a tissue out of her pocket and raises it in triumph. She edges toward James, poised to swipe.

And misses, because now he's pacing again. "Look, we're just worried about you." He rakes his fingers through his hair, smearing the lip print at his right temple. "Maybe if you talk to someone about—"

"I'm fine," I insist, more urgently this time. "Really, I promise. I just need to go somewhere no one recognizes me and no one's reminding me of what happened."

There's that look again, that silent exchange between two people who know each other well enough to have a full conversation with no words. I'd envy them if I weren't a jaded asshole intent on being alone.

Lily looks back at me and sighs. "At least promise you'll be careful. And that you'll go into town at least once to call and let us know you're okay."

"Promise." I put a hand on my heart the way James and I used to do when reciting the school pledge, and my heart twists at the memory. How did life get so messed up?

"Fine," James says. "Can we at least feed you dinner?"

"Not hungry." My stomach chooses that moment to rumble like a gravel crusher.

Lily arches one eyebrow. "Really?"

I reach behind me for the doorknob, determined to flee before they tie me to a dining room chair and force coq au vin down my throat. I wrench the door open, walking backwards in case they try to tackle me. "Fine, I'm starving. I haven't eaten since I left LA. I promise I'll eat on the way. I just want to get—"

"Whoa! Heads up, big guy."

The female voice registers half a second before I crash into the female body. The very soft, very warm female body.

I whirl around, stumbling as I turn to face—

"Holy shit." The words slip out before I consider this is not the way to greet a total stranger.

But this stranger is the most stunning woman I've ever seen. Hair the color of warm caramel is piled on her head in a swoopy, loopy bun. Eyes like blue sea glass spark with light from the porch, and there's a dusting of cinnamon freckles on her nose. She's wearing—clothes, I think. I can't look away from her face to check out the rest of her.

She laughs and flips a stray lock of hair off her face. "Okay, not the greeting I'm used to, but hello." Her smile is warm, and there's not a trace of makeup on her face. "Gretchen." She extends her hand to me. "Sorry to startle you. I just came over to borrow dill."

"Dill." I pat my pockets absurdly like I might have some tucked away. "I—um—"

"I'll get it." Lily hustles away. "What are you making?" she calls from the kitchen.

"My famous salmon chowder." Gretchen gives me that smile again, and my guts turn to chowder. "It's a family recipe."

I'm too dumbstruck to think of a response, so James comes to my rescue. "Gretchen is my brother Jonathan's sister."

"Your sister," I repeat, only catching some of his words. Seriously, I had no idea sweatpants could be so sexy. How have I never met this woman?

"Not *his* sister." Gretchen shoves her hands in the pockets of her blue hoodie, which matches her eyes almost perfectly. "The Bracelyn family tree is kind of a mess. Jon's the second oldest, but we have different dads. I'm not a Bracelyn at all."

Lily rushes back to us with a glass jar and presses it into Gretchen's hand. "Gretchen's been staying out here while she's at OSU Cascades. She's an adjunct professor and an absolutely brilliant researcher."

"A researcher." I look back at her, watching as her eyes scan my face. I brace for the flicker of recognition in her eyes. For what comes next. What *always* comes next.

Wait. Didn't I see you in an article about—

Aren't you the guy who—

Don't I know you from—

"Want some soup?"

I blink as Gretchen holds up the glass jar of dill. "This is the finishing touch. I made a ton of it and I heard you say you were starving."

I did say that.

But I also said I was leaving. Hitting the road, getting far, far away from here as soon as possible. I should definitely do that.

"I'd love some soup."

What the hell?

"Great." Gretchen grins. "I'm sorry, I didn't catch your name. And I'm hoping you're a friend of James and Lily and that I didn't just invite the vacuum cleaner salesman to dinner."

"Gabl—Gabe," I stammer.

God, that was dumb. Even with the abbreviated version of my name, she's going to recognize me. Put two and two together and figure it out.

Weren't you the one who—

"Gabe and I are friends from school," James supplies. "And Gretchen—reads a lot."

I'm trying to figure out what that has to do with anything when she laughs again. "That's his polite way of saying I don't get out much. Probably why I'm accosting strangers with dinner invitations. It's okay, you don't have to come in and sit there making awkward dinner conversation if you don't want. I can package up the chowder for you to take wherever you were going."

Where was I going?

Right. The cabin. The remote cabin in the woods more than an hour from here. I should be getting on the road.

"I'm not in a hurry," I hear myself saying. "I'd love to join you."

"Great." She quirks an eyebrow at James and Lily. "You'd tell me if he was a serial killer, right?"

My gut twists at her words. I'm grateful she's not looking at me. That she missed the wince, the flash of guilt I'm positive flickered in my eyes just now.

But James catches it. He's staring at me, icy gaze boring hard into mine. "Not a serial killer." He speaks the words to me, like he's willing me to believe them. "Not a murderer of any kind."

Gretchen cocks her head, eyeing him curiously. "You know, it's a little hard to take you seriously when your face is covered in lipstick."

"What?" James swipes a palm over his face, missing the biggest smear by half an inch. "Where?" He turns and frowns in the mirror by the door, then makes an exasperated noise. "Was someone going to tell me?"

Lily shrugs and turns with her tissue to mop her handiwork off his face. Gretchen regards me with a curious look. "Not a very good friend, Gabe. Letting your pal walk around with lip prints on his face?"

"I'm kind of an asshole." Might as well put it out there.

Gretchen smiles. "In that case, should I rescind my dinner offer?"

"No soup for you," I quip, doing my best imitation of the Soup Nazi from *Seinfeld.*

Gretchen blows a strand of hair off her forehead with a vaguely sheepish expression. "Okay, I'm guessing that's a movie reference."

"Television, actually." Wait, she's never heard of the Soup Nazi?

"I don't watch that, either."

"What?"

She shrugs, hands fisted in her hoodie pockets. "Movies, TV—any of it. I don't even own a television."

I've never heard of such a thing. "Are you Amish?"

She laughs and shakes her head. "I'm a research scientist. And a PhD candidate. And a professor. Not a lot of time in there to add TV junkie to the list."

Lily finishes swiping the lipstick off James's face and turns to join our conversation. "We're sort of hoping once she finishes her dissertation, she'll become one of us," she says. "Binge-watching *Grey's Anatomy* and *Stranger Things* over large quantities of wine."

"Dare to dream." Gretchen holds up the dill and takes a step back. "I'd better finish my chowder. Gabe—come on over when you're ready. It's the cabin next door. Jon and Blanka's place."

I know I should get on the road. I've got a ninety-minute drive ahead of me. This is my chance to back out. To be alone. To get in my car and drive far, far away.

But as I look at Gretchen, I know I'd walk on my lips across crushed ice to eat a bowl of cold oatmeal with her.

"I'll be right over."

***

Want to keep reading? Click to nab *Snowbound Squeeze* now!

Snowbound Squeeze

https://books2read.com/b/m2rayr

DON'T MISS OUT!

Want access to exclusive excerpts, behind-the-scenes stories about my books, cover reveals, and prize giveaways? Not only will you get all that by subscribing to my newsletter, but I'll even throw you a **FREE** short story featuring a swoon-worthy marriage proposal for Sean and Amber from *Chef Sugarlips.*

Get it right here.

http://tawnafenske.com/subscribe/

1

ACKNOWLEDGMENTS

Thank you to everyone who had a hand in educating me about kidney donation. What an amazing, terrifying, heartwarming world this was to learn about, and I owe all of you a debt of gratitude. I've taken a few liberties throughout, but I hope most of the details ring true.

Big thanks to Fenske's Frisky Posse for helping me kick ideas around and for being so badass with early reviews, proofreading, brainstorming, and moral support. Thanks especially to Jen Williams, Nicole Westmoreland, Adrienne Bird, and Regina Dowling for your eagle-eyed reading of the ARC, and your willingness to help me avoid looking too much like an illiterate moron.

Extra-huge thanks to Samaya T. Young for the balloon idea (and apologies to my kiddos, who were appalled to learn those fun things they'd been playing with were purchased for sex scene research).

Thank you to Skye Fitzgerald for creating the incredible documentary film *Lifeboat*, and for reminding me that everyone can do something to bring awareness to human tragedy—even with a romantic comedy novel. For readers who want to learn more about the very real crisis that captured my fictional ship captain's heart, visit www.lifeboatdocumentary.com, or watch the 30-minute film in its entirety at the following link:

https://www.newyorker.com/culture/culture-desk/the-screening-room-lifeboat

Endless gratitude to Michelle Wolfson, my agent of 11+ years and 30+ books. Thanks to you, the Ponderosa Resort series will be making its way to audiobook. Thanks also to Taryn Fagerness for expanding the Ponderosa world into foreign markets.

Huge thanks to my agency sistah and critique partner Linda Grimes, for endless last-minute read-throughs and amazing insights. Thanks zillions to Wonder Assistant Meah Meow for keeping my shit together both on the home front and in the author world.

Big hugs and sloppy smooches to Susan Bischoff and Laura-lynn Elliott of The Forge for the amazing editorial work. I couldn't do this without you! I'm also immensely grateful to Lori Jackson Design for the fantastic teaser graphics, banners, and bookmarks.

Love and gratitude to my family, Aaron "Russ" Fenske, Carlie Fenske, and baby Paxton, plus Dixie and David Fenske. Everything I know about warm, loving family dynamics I learned from you guys, and from Cedar and Violet, my amazing stepkids.

Most of all, thank you to my own romance novel hero, Craig Zagurski. You float my boat, hot stuff.

ABOUT THE AUTHOR

When Tawna Fenske finished her English lit degree at 22, she celebrated by filling a giant trash bag full of romance novels and dragging it everywhere until she'd read them all. Now she's a RITA Award finalist, *USA Today* bestselling author who writes humorous fiction, risqué romance, and heartwarming love stories with a quirky twist. *Publishers Weekly* has praised Tawna's offbeat romances with multiple starred reviews and noted, "There's something wonderfully relaxing about being immersed in a story filled with over-the-top characters in undeniably relatable situations. Heartache and humor go hand in hand."

Tawna lives in Bend, Oregon, with her husband, step-kids, and a menagerie of ill-behaved pets. She loves hiking, snowshoeing, standup paddleboarding, and inventing excuses to sip wine on her back porch. She can peel a banana with her toes and loses an average of twenty pairs of eyeglasses per year. To find out more about Tawna and her books, visit www.tawnafenske.com.

ALSO BY TAWNA FENSKE

The Ponderosa Resort Romantic Comedy Series

Studmuffin Santa

Chef Sugarlips

Sergeant Sexypants

Hottie Lumberjack

Stiff Suit

Mancandy Crush (novella)

Captain Dreamboat

Snowbound Squeeze (novella)

Dr. Hot Stuff (coming soon!)

The Juniper Ridge Romantic Comedy Series

Show Time

Let It Show (coming March 2021!)

Standalone Romantic Comedies

The Two-Date Rule

At the Heart of It

This Time Around

Now That It's You

Let it Breathe

About That Fling

Frisky Business

Believe It or Not

Making Waves

The Front and Center Series

Marine for Hire

Fiancée for Hire

Best Man for Hire

Protector for Hire

The First Impressions Series

The Fix Up

The Hang Up

The Hook Up

The List Series

The List

The Test

The Last

Standalone novellas and other wacky stuff

Going Up (novella)

Eat, Play, Lust (novella)

Made in the USA
Monee, IL
03 September 2020